QUIXOTE'S ISLAND

QUIXOTE'S ISLAND

A novel by

SALLY SMALL

QUIXOTE'S ISLAND

iUniverse books may be ordered through booksellers or by contacting:

iUniverse
1663 Liberty Drive
Bloomington, IN 47403
www.iuniverse.com
1-800-Authors (1-800-288-4677)

Because of the dynamic nature of the Internet, any web addresses or links contained in this book may have changed since publication and may no longer be valid. The views expressed in this work are solely those of the author and do not necessarily reflect the views of the publisher, and the publisher hereby disclaims any responsibility for them.

ISBN: 978-1-4917-9754-9 (sc)
ISBN: 978-1-4917-9755-6 (e)

Print information available on the last page.

iUniverse rev. date: 06/23/2016

For the great-great-great-grandchildren of Escolastica:
Jonah, Mia, Ana, Sophie and Hannah

ACKNOWLEDGMENTS

My thanks to the staff of the Bancroft Library who have patiently helped me for the last ten years as I sifted through the history of the period in search of Escolastica and her family. The staff at the State Historic Park at Monterey were also extremely helpful, leading me up to the attic and into their vault in search of scraps of dresses and jewelry. Rose Marie Beebe of the University of Santa Clara was most generous in editing my manuscript for historical flaws. John Muir Laws was equally helpful in weeding out non-native plants. John Lyons designed the beautiful cover and the layout. Shirley Hobart, my editor, was invaluable.

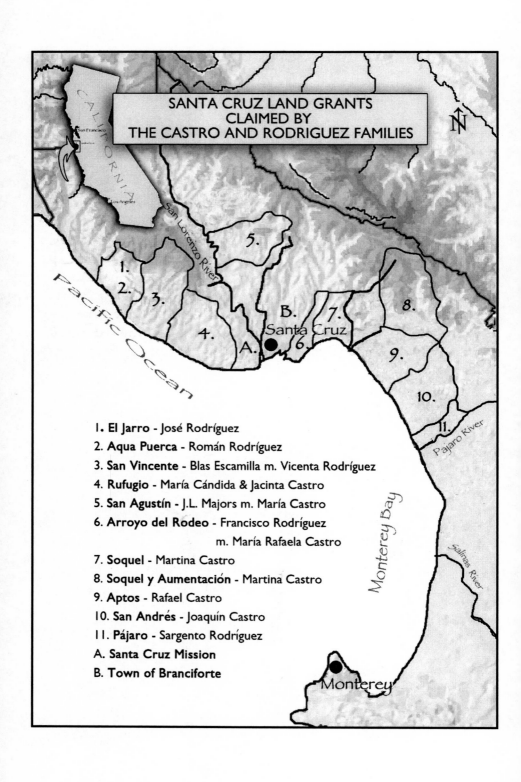

SANTA CRUZ LAND GRANTS
CLAIMED BY
THE CASTRO AND RODRIGUEZ FAMILIES

1. **El Jarro** - José Rodríguez
2. **Aqua Puerca** - Román Rodríguez
3. **San Vincente** - Blas Escamilla m. Vicenta Rodríguez
4. **Rufugio** - María Cándida & Jacinta Castro
5. **San Agustín** - J.L. Majors m. María Castro
6. **Arroyo del Rodeo** - Francisco Rodríguez
                                        m. María Rafaela Castro
7. **Soquel** - Martina Castro
8. **Soquel y Aumentación** - Martina Castro
9. **Aptos** - Rafael Castro
10. **San Andrés** - Joaquín Castro
11. **Pájaro** - Sargento Rodríguez
A. **Santa Cruz Mission**
B. **Town of Branciforte**

"Sometimes I think that Don Quixote has found his way into the core of our being. Either we inherited this quality or it is because we have read the novel with such pleasure. I can see the 'ingenious gentleman' right here." *Doña* Angustias de la Guerra Ord, January 6, 1846.

Quoted in an interview by Thomas Savage as translated by Rose Marie Beebe and Robert M. Senkewicz, *TESTIMONIOS* (Berkeley CA, Heyday Books, 2006)

All the passages quoted in this novel come from *Don Quijote*, by Miguel de Cervantes, Translated by Burton Raffel (W.W. Norton & Co., New York, 1996). This translation preserves the Spanish spelling of the hero's name, rather than the more familiar Quixote preferred in most English texts. I have used the English spelling except when quoting directly from Raffel.

Sally Small

[T]hose solemn historians … tell us things so briskly and briefly that we hardly know what's going on, since the best parts of the book, whether from carelessness or malice, have been left in the inkwell.

DON *QUIJOTE*, by Miguel de Cervantes, translated by Burton Raffel (New York: W.W. Norton and Company, 1996) Volume 1, Chapter 16, page 81

MONTEREY BAY
1834

They journeyed over land, these enchanted pilgrims, led by a legendary Spaniard, *Don* Juan Bautista de Anza, so her grandfather tells her. He was just a boy of 6, riding behind his mother and, when the Indios stole some of their horses, trudging through the hot sands on foot. The year was 1775. Their destination, their dream, was a gilded island that few had seen, where great bears and lions roamed, an island covered, some said, with orange poppies so thick the hills glowed gold.

Tica and her grandfather ride up El Camino Real, the coast road that is just a track, rutted in winter by *carretas* and elk herds, dusty in summer.

"And when you reached the Yuma, Grandfather, were you not afraid?"

Grandfather smiles and reins his mare back beside his granddaughter's horse.

"They lined the path on either side of us, the men on one side, the women on the other. They had never seen white women or white children. They reached out to touch our hair, our mothers' skirts. They marveled at our blue eyes, your Tía Martina's blonde curls. Mother was terrified, but they revered our *comandante*. He had met them on other expeditions. They dug watermelons out of the sand and cracked them open for us. Never have I feasted on such melon, after that long, thirsty desert. We loved the Yuma."

Tica has heard these stories many times, but she never tires of them. Grandfather has also read to her of an imaginary California and of its ruler, Queen Calafia, a strong-limbed, dark Amazon, the most beautiful of them all, robust, strong. Her armaments were all of gold and so was the harness of the wild beasts she rode. For in the whole island there was no metal but gold.*

These stories and the tales of Don Quixote her grandfather has read to her all merge into one grand legend, the first civilian expedition to California, the Golden Isle that the Spanish novelist Garci Rodríguez de Montalvo had dreamed into existence.*

Her great-grandparents fled Northern Spain to escape the wrath of their families. Her great-grandmother was French, María Martina de Botiller. Both families objected to the match. So her grandfather tells her as they ride north, descending the bluff now because Tica prefers the beach, loping now because Tica is always impatient to run.

She spurs her horse ahead of her grandfather's along the beach. The ocean rushes toward her breaking in unruly waves that splash in the sunlight, run in on the bright sand, chase the sandpipers, foam at her horse's feet. A day such as this she should pack away in her heart, folded and sprinkled with dried *tapash* of bay leaves, as her Kalinta nurse Tal-ku packs her winter petticoats, so that when the rains come she could shake out its brilliance and hold it up. But she is eleven years old and out for adventure. She rides bareback, her skirt hitched up, her knees pressed into the warm withers of her honey gelding. She takes long breaths, inhales this sunlit day.

Now Tica lags behind because there is so much to see this morning. She thinks she might be her grandfather's squire as she rides along this beach, a squire like Sancho Panza. She and Grandfather have read much of *Don Quixote* on this visit, and she imagines her grandfather as the gentle, chivalrous knight riding out ahead of her, his thick silver braid

---

* In *Las sergas de Esplandián,* Garci Rodríguez de Montalvo described a mythical island called California.

falling down his straight back, his crimson sash flying at his waist, his long legs settled firmly into his saddle.

She is too young to appreciate the irony of *Don Quixote*. She hears only the romance and the funny parts that make her laugh out loud. She longs for glorious pursuits out into the countryside, rescuing shepherdesses, meeting enchanted Moors.

In fact, California might have been the Spain of Cervantes' time, idealized, without the misery, the last frontier of Spanish chivalry in the collapsing Spanish Empire. "Their island was the strongest in all the world, with its steep cliffs and rocky shores." So Montalvo had written of his mythical California, and it was largely true. Each vast rancho became its own feudal state, isolated from its neighbors by the enormity of its own land grant boundaries and the huge distances between, the lack of roads, an unfriendly ocean. Unmolested by the absentee governments of Madrid and Mexico City, served by a population of indigenous people the *Californios* called *Costeños*, the Coast People, these peaceful kingdoms evolved into a feudal society dictated largely by isolation, the needs of the cattle, and the customs of the Catholic Church. But Tica knows none of this. She looks for adventure.

Tica's horse's muscles snap beneath her. No time to dig in her knees. Too fast to see more than a blur. A dark shape rears up from the dunes on her right — "*Ores*," the Coast Indians call him, Old Bear. His rotted fish dinner slops from his jaws.

Her horse shies, twists to free himself of her. She grabs his mane, slips, loses her grip, slides beneath him. The horse leaps up, grazing her in the ribs with one hind leg. He hangs in the air.

She hits the beach face down, mouth choked with sand. Clutching two fistfuls of sand, she looks up at Old Bear; he, head down, squints back at her, mangey, foul-tempered.

She trespasses here. Tica feels the savage territorial presence of this grizzly. She thinks, "I fell. I am a child…and skinny," she pleads, an afterthought.

The whistle of a rawhide *latigo* slices the air behind her. She feels the hooves of her grandfather's horse pound the sand. She watches Old Bear look up nearsightedly, drop his stinking dinner in surprise, and wheel around, lumbering off at amazing speed toward the canyon.

3

Grandfather looks down at her clenched fists full of sand and laughs at her. Laughs at her! "Ay, little Tica, you were not attentive."

"I was," she gasps. "I was, Grandfather. That horse is the very Devil's grandson." She stumbles to her feet, spits sand, staggers over to the gelding, who stands meekly ten yards away. She slaps him viciously with the end of her braided horse hair reins. "*Ka-hai*," she hisses at him in Kalinta, "wood louse!"

Her grandfather laughs again, leans forward against the finely woven serape that cushions the pommel of his saddle. "Then how unlucky for him that he is ridden by the very Devil's granddaughter."

Tica lunges for the gelding's back from the uphill side, determined to mount him on the first try, kicks her feet in the air as she inches over onto his back. The beach reels beneath her. "If I had been in a saddle, I would not have fallen off," she grumbles.

Her horse skates sideways.

"If you had been in a saddle you would have had no warning at all. In a saddle one learns nothing. Did you not feel his muscles tense?"

"But not in time, Grandfather."

"*Paciencia, paciencia.* You will. Someday your legs will know without your telling them. They must learn to think for themselves, your little legs. Now, let us go up into the deeper sand, and your horse will not be so rambunctious."

They ride north then, up the bay, angling away from the water to the sand that is fine and deep. Her gelding fights his way toward the hard, wet sand, and Grandfather Castro shows her how to put pressure on his side and turn him back again.

"But at times he fights me and will not give in, Grandfather."

"He will always be stronger than you, just as the bear is. You must not fight him. You must outwit him, little Escolástica." He calls her by her Christian name. "Come, I will show you. There is more than one way to kill a flea."

Grandfather pulls his knife from his tall boot top and hands it to her. This is Grandfather's most prized possession, a fine Toledo steel blade with an inlaid handle. Tica holds it reverently.

"Now, dismount and cut a stout branch from the dune willow. There. Just so. Give yourself time. Be sure your horse watches you.

Now, peel it slowly. Slowly now; shave off every leaf and nodule. Stand in front of your horse as you do this, Tica. Be sure he watches you."

Grandfather slides his knife back into his boot top.

"Now do I smack him, Grandfather?"

"No, Tica. Now you get back up on your horse gripping your willow stick. And because you ride a horse of great intelligence and experience, you will have no need of the stick at all."

The girl laughs out loud and relaxes her grip with her knees, but the horse stands still. Grandfather is her treasure. She knows he thinks it important that she ride as well as her brothers. He does not make a baby of her when she falls. He will not tell her mother.

"All *Californios* must be horsemen. The land is too enormous to walk in," her grandfather says.

And Grandfather should know. Did he not walk over the Sierra Madre from Mexico when he was just six years old with Comandante Anza, walk most of the way because the younger children had to be carried and the Apache had stolen so many of their horses? Did he not walk in the snow when his boots were nothing more than woven patches of rawhide and bacon rind? Six months their journey took. She has heard the stories many times: the Expedition of 1775, the first civilian expedition to California.

She does not always understand Grandfather. He talks of the past, but he warns her to look to the future. By the future, Tica suspects he means the West. To the West she sees only a thin horizon, a glare upon the waters of the vast Pacific Ocean. Still, everything he says resounds in her, like the gruff bell of the mission at Santa Cruz, like the waves that crash against the first rock out beyond the point. He is her knight. She follows him devotedly.

They ride on up around Monterey Bay, which curves crescent-shaped like the horns of Grandfather's cattle, north to Point Soquel. The tide ebbs, and the beach stretches seaward almost to the rocks where the "sea wolves"[*] lie sunning themselves. The sweet, grassy scent of sand verbena mingles with the salt smell of wet seaweed.

In the lee of Point Soquel, José Castro reins his mare into the surf, wades her out to the nearest rocks, and leaning down from his saddle,

---

[*] The *Californios'* name for sea lions (*Zalophus californianus*)

pries rock scallops from the wet rocks with his knife.* The girl and her grandfather sit on the warm sand against a weathered drift log, out of the wind, while Grandfather teaches her how to pick the little scallops open at the hinge and suck the juices from the pearly shells.

Tica pulls off her leather hat, ignoring her mother's threats that she will grow up with the complexion of a *Costeña*. Her smooth black braids are indeed an Indian weave, wound by her nurse Tal-ku with otter skin ties, but her face is thin and delicate as a hummingbird's. Her aunts decree that she will be a handsome woman, which is a kind way of saying that, while her cousins are ideal Spanish *infantas*, soft-fleshed, with docile black curls, charcoal eyes and chubby cheeks, Escolástica is all corners. Her skinny arms jut out in sharp elbows. Her thin cheeks make her nose look long. Only her eyes are generously sized. They shine turquoise green, like agates washed up on the beach, pale, preposterous in such a modest setting.

Suddenly silver plumes rise out beyond the waves. Great gray backs break the surface, curving, one after another, in fluid arcs. A tail flips up; the sea churns around it.

"*Ballenas.* The gray whales carry spring to us," her grandfather tells her. "They swim from the warm waters of their Mother Mexico. They bear spring with them, and the mild air follows." The old man and the girl sit leaning against the driftwood log and watch the whales until their eyes water from the glare and their horses stamp.

"I would ride one, Grandfather," the girl says quietly.

José Castro does not laugh at her. "You have spirit, little one. A good rider must have spirit." He looks fondly into the enormous green eyes that overshadow her thin face. Of all his grandchildren, this is his favorite. She has a ravenous curiosity and a passion for the land. He sighs, "I hope you do not have too much spirit."

"No, Grandfather that is not possible," Tica says gravely.

The old man is quiet for a time. "Life is hard, Escolástica. Sometimes the only way for a woman to survive is to wrap herself around it, to bend, like the silver spoons of your grandmother. Our California is changing."

"What foolishness," says Tica sharply.

---

* These rock scallops are rare along the California coast today. At one time they were plentiful.

His eyes flicker. "Why is your grandfather so foolish?"

"Grandfather, look." She stands up and catches her horse's head. "Who but a fool would change this?"

José Castro looks at the round white waves and the bright beach stretching before them, decorated with flocks of little white sea birds tossed to the wind, and he wonders if an unseen darkness underlies the light, accentuates its brilliance. He wonders if he himself plays the fool.

He stands and dusts the sand from his breeches. They have still a day's ride ahead of them to reach Escolástica's parents' rancho. Behind them, the hills flame up in swaths of yellow bush lupine and gleaming golden poppies.

"There is such a thing as too much wisdom, little Tica," he says to himself. Tica has romped off on her gelding, dragging a long red ribbon of kelp behind her.

But nothing happened as he thought it would, according to the tale told in this truthful history....

Op. Cit., Vol. 1, Chap. 14, pg. 73

THE SANTA CRUZ
1834

José Castro and his granddaughter ride north along the beach past the coastal finger valleys fringed with redwoods, relics of an even earlier age: Corralitos Valley, Calabasas, San Andrés.[*] Across the lands of José's son Rafael, across the land grant of José's daughter Martina. League after league, they see only their families' land. José Castro looks West, judging the time, out across Monterey Bay and a day washed bright by the turquoise ocean, a day blown dry by the ocean breeze, a day about to disappear; a day in March when the sunshine is as clean as a pane of new glass. He might have reached right through such a day and touched Point Pinos.

They ride for Tica's father's rancho, twelve miles up the coast. When they dismount quietly at dusk in the shadow of the oak tree, Tica's mother stalks the courtyard like one of her savage black hens. "Gabriel," she scolds a *Costeñan* servant, "I sent you off ten minutes ago. Tal-ku," she calls to Tica's *Costeñan* nurse, "*Adelante!* Pick some bay leaves. Not the new growth. It wilts." She glances in the door of the *sala*. "This cursed sand. Tal-ku, shake the rush matting in the *sala*, and put that stubborn hen out of the house. If she persists in nesting in the house, she will end up in a stew, a *puchero*. And send Kuki for beach strawberries. I have no time to make a pudding, and we have run out of

---

[*] These valleys, along Monterey Bay, still bear those names.

raisins. God grant me strawberries, if those fat birds — may the Savior strangle every one of them - have not eaten every..."

Doña María scarcely glances at Tica, takes no notice of the tear in her skirt, sends her running off with the key to the storeroom to get candles and wine.

"Boys, *vamos*! pen up the sheep for heaven's sake. You will have to sleep in the loft tonight."

José Castro divines the signs of domestic crisis and backs his horse out of the busy yard. An *hidalgo* never dismounts, even in his daughter's courtyard, unless invited by the *dueña.*

Horrified, María runs after him. "Father, forgive me," she laughs. "I am driven crazy. May God forgive my breach of etiquette to you. Please dismount. You are welcome in my house. Oh, Father, you must stay." She stands on tiptoe to kiss his hands. "Please stay. It is only that two Americans, *Yanquis,* are coming. She looks up at him, still laughing, holds his hand. "They can be so difficult. They speak hideous Spanish—impossible to talk to...." María turns to her chopping block beside the braziers, picks up her knife and begins to peel onions. It is unclear to her father whether the face she makes is caused by the onions or the Americans. "... so uncivilized." She slices deftly. "Nothing of art or literature or music..." Whack. Whack. "Even their religion is ugly. Where is the Latin? The glory of God?"

José sits easily, enjoying the view from his saddle. He smiles at her. "These same Americans consider us quite inferior, you know, idle, undisciplined, shiftless, remnants of a bygone era.... Not unlike the Sandwich Islanders of Honolulu, a native population about to disappear."

"Inferior!" hoots María, attacking the dried ancho chiles with her cleaver. Her father winces, and his mare steps back. "Truly, Father, they are a dreary, vulgar people. They lack nobility. They are not *hidalgos*. They talk of nothing but trade and money. Their very language is miserly. They use only their lips. They don't open their mouths wide enough. They never talk with their teeth. *Carreta,* a cart, dissolves in their mouths, for instance: *cuweda,*" she mimics, drawling the word out. "They swallow a *rosa* altogether."

José chuckles, lounging on his mare, watching his daughter at work. "I am surprised the *Americanos* feel welcome in your *casa, Hija.*"

María shrugs, "Francisco invited them. Thank God, little Carlos rode ahead to tell me. If they don't fall off their horses, they will be here within the hour."

Tica giggles. Americans, more at home on ships than on horses, often come to grief on the high-spirited *Californio* mounts. She looks at her grandfather, who sits a horse more comfortably than a chair.

María looks up. "Tica, *ahora!* You are as slow as these cursed *Costeños.* Gabriel, come. Take Don José's mare and see to her."

Gabriel, who moments before had been sent off to the marsh to hunt ducks, looks crazily around, waving his bow and butcher knife.

"No, Gabriel, *gracias,* I will care for my mare. Go on with your hunt. Assist the *patrona.*"

Grandfather Castro dismounts, loosens the cinches on his tall bay and slides the saddle from her back. Mares are seldom ridden in California. By custom they are used for breeding, but this is José Castro's favorite mount. He has left her mane and tail long and flowing, like a stallion's.

He is easily persuaded to stay at his daughter's adobe, a busy place, bulging with babies and mischievous boys. Brown tiles perch on the mismatched roofs like tilted hats. Walls shaped by sturdy hands are limed with a mixture of ground seashells to the smooth consistency of beaten cream. María has trained wild honeysuckle to climb the beveled posts of the east veranda, and she wages continual war with the horses for the preservation of her vines, her wild roses and her frilly lemon geraniums.

Cautiously, he leads his mare away from the tempting foliage. He looks forward to the visit of the Americans. They no doubt come from farther down the coast and bring news.

Grandfather Castro is the tallest man Tica has ever seen. Her brother, Toño, has seen a Sandwich Islander he claims was taller, with arms the size of tree trunks, so he says. But Tica believes her grandfather to be the tallest man in the world. Tomorrow the whole household will lie awake before daylight, waiting for Grandfather to lead the morning hymn.

"Rejoice! Rejoice! Oh Mother of God....."

He'll stand in his long white shirt, bellow the hymn in a rusty baritone, his snow-white hair falling to his shoulders in the old Spanish fashion, his mustache and beard white, too. Like some medieval archangel, he'll stand in the doorway at dawn.

Now he rubs his mare, *La Bandera*, with a sack, talks to her, courts her quietly in the formal tense, as if he were her suitor. He unbridles her and sets her loose outside the courtyard to water and graze. She comes to Grandfather at a whistle and follows him about like a lovesick maiden.

"Tica!" shrieks her mother, "Why do you stand there like a brick? Go!"

[T]here's nothing better in the world than to be the honored squire of a knight errant who's out looking for adventures. Now it's true most adventures don't turn out as well as you'd like, because if you have a hundred of them, ninety-nine go wrong and get all tangled up.

Op.Cit., Vol. 1, Chap. 52, pg. 357

RANCHO ARROYO DEL RODEO
1834

The Americans approach *Rancho Arroyo del Rodeo*, jolting stiff and forward in their saddles, bouncing up and down. Their fingers seem to be tangled in their double reins. They dismount without invitation and walk straight-legged, not bending at the knee or elbow. Tica's mother says that their women must weave iron into their woolens to make their men so stiff. But Tal-ku, Tica's Indian nurse, says the Americans have no women.

Tica and her brother Toño retreat to the weaving hut, full now with ragged shearings heaped in baskets and still smelling of sheep dung and grease. Toño is a year younger than Tica, and her comrade. The "Terrible T's," the family calls them, "*T's Terribles,*" inseparable, squabbling most of the time, but fierce in defense of one another.

A fly buzzes about their heads as they peer out at the strangers who have arrived with their father, Francisco Rodríguez, and who stalk forward now to pay respect to their mother and their grandfather.

"They look as if their axles need bear grease," whispers Toño.

The tall man, Señor Harker, bows to their mother, "You are gracious to allow us to arrive unannounced, Doña María." His Spanish is surprisingly pure.

"Friends of my husband are welcome, Don Tomás. Please sit down and refresh yourselves. Or perhaps you prefer to stand." Tica sees her mother smile. Only her mouth moves. The rest of her face remains completely composed. A stranger might think it a demure smile. Tica hears the hidden barb and giggles in her hiding place, brushing away the fly.

The second visitor, a thin young man, jerks his head grimly forward and looks at her mother's arms. Tica watches her mother's long neck arch as the young man speaks. Like many Americans, he mumbles his Spanish without opening his mouth. He is wan, with pale eyes and hair the color of dry grass. Even the horse he rides seems to mistrust him and takes the first opportunity to wander off. Grandfather says you can tell everything about a man by the way his horse behaves toward him.

"I admire your wild roses, Doña María," Señor Harker says. "To have one in bloom already.... I have attempted without success...." Thick chestnut curls crowd his brow. "I offer a small gift, if I may be permitted," he says, "a China rose." His teeth are very white. "It is late in the season for a bare root, I know, but the ship .... If anyone can make it grow...." His brown eyes dance on the brink of thick lashes. "It is supposed to be a yellow climber. One can never be certain."

"*Muchas gracias.*" This time the smile spills over onto her mother's whole face. Her full lips soften at the corners and part in delight at his gift, his excellent Spanish. Her white teeth show. Her mother likes this American.

Tal-ku appears with a pitcher of wine and the turquoise wine tumblers from Guadalajara. She never passes in front of the visitors. "*Mollom,*" she calls Americans, "sea gulls." She approaches the *mollom* obliquely, her slight, shapeless body pulled into itself. Her deep-set eyes, drooping at the corners, look buried in her head, her gaze averted. Her skin is the same violet brown as the adobe in the courtyard. Her small, bare feet seem to disappear into the earth. She wears a coarse cotton skirt and shift the color of mud. She might truly be a *tal-ku*, the fly from which she takes her name; she arouses so little notice in the courtyard. She was born in the mission. She must once have had a Christian name, but she refuses to speak of that time. She returns silently with a willow basket of toasted pumpkin seeds, then disappears into the dusk.

The men sit on carved-back benches in the courtyard, Grandfather, Father and the two Americans, their boots sticking out in front of them, all in a row. Tica and Toño slip out of the wool shed, past the dairy room redolent of their mother's *asaderas*, the pale spring cheeses that taste of grass and should be eaten the day they are made.

Tica hugs one of the wood posts of the *pórtico*, her nose pressed into the cedar, and studies the boots of the men as they sit assembled in the courtyard with their backs to her. Her grandfather's boots she knows well, tall and supple, black as beach tar, boots made in Córdoba, the stitches so fine that Tica cannot count them. You do not get this quality of boot anymore, not at any price; she has heard her grandfather say so. The Americans' boots are brown and thick-soled and clumsy, topped by furry brown pants. It makes Tica itch just to look at them. The pants give off the faint odor of bear urine, which causes Tica to wonder if the legs beneath the pants might be as shaggy as a grizzly's.

Thomas Harker sees her staring. "I also admire the beauty of your daughter, Doña María. Her father says she desires drawing pencils."

He turns to her and bows. "You are an artist, Señorita." He speaks seriously and uses the formal third person. "I admire anyone who possesses the faculty for drawing. Here in California, you will draw what no man has ever drawn before. An historic opportunity." His eyes shine like the polished buckeyes Tal-ku collects in her basket. "I have tucked some licorice in with your drawing pencils, which I hope will please you."

Tica comes out from behind her post and takes the present timidly, with a small curtsy. Then gathering courage she asks, "Please, Señor, do you have licorice for my brother, Toño?"

"For your brothers I have... but that must remain a surprise."

"Please, tell us," begs Tica. "Perhaps you lack the words in Spanish," she goads.

"Tica," gasps her mother, "remember your manners!"

But Harker chuckles and winks at her. "Fair señorita, I will not be baited like an old bear by you. My lips are sealed."

"Tell us," María says, "have you been down the coast? What news have you? Has anything come in from China?"

The other man with Harker is Job Dye. A sad name, Tica thinks, Dye, *Morir*. He spends a good deal of time staring at her mother's arms. American women do not have arms? His Spanish is uncouth and awkward; he has come from a land called Kentucky as a fur trapper.* He followed the Southern route and crossed the same desert Grandfather crossed when he came up from Mexico as a child. He followed some of the same trails.

Grandfather quizzes him closely about the Apache, about the *Sierra Nevada.*

Tica's mother watches the two Americans trying to follow Grandfather's flowery, Castilian Spanish. They defer to him and answer his questions respectfully, but María notices their raised eyebrows and barely concealed smiles. An ironic look passes between the two men. They think José Castro is out of touch, an amusing relic of the landed gentry. They patronize him, lead him on for their own amusement. María can see that, and it angers her.

Three Castro cousins ride in from *Rancho de Soquel* and *Rancho de Aptos*, the ranchos to the south. Tica's aunt wears her good sash, and her cousins' horses wear silver, the elegant trappings of a fiesta. The news of the Americans' arrival has traveled quickly and mysteriously down the coast. The native *Costeños* know. No one knows how.

The *Costeños* carry another table into the patio. Wooden platters of *carne asada* marinated in a vinegary *chile adobo* and grilled over bay leaves are placed in the center of the tables. The Americans cut their meat in an odd crosswise fashion, into chunks, not with the grain the way it grows.

More cousins arrive. Tal-ku and the younger *Costeñan* girls pad back and forth from the ovens, offering bowls of *frijoles* stewed with chile peppers, a platter of roasted ducks filled with bread crumbs and spring onions. María passes one of Tal-ku's fine, coiled baskets lined with ferns, full of beach strawberries. She pours foaming Mexican chocolate into Grandmother's silver cups that are the family pride and her inheritance. The silver is so pure, so soft that every dent and thumb print seems to be embedded in them.

Tica and her cousins and brothers sit at a third table near the *ramada*, under the watchful eye of Tal-ku. They toss crumbs to the scrub

---

* Job Dye's Kentucky rifle still rests in the Monterey State Park Historic Museum, Monterey CA.

16

jays when Tal-ku isn't looking. Toño mimics the Americans, chopping at his meat, holding his nose and talking in a shrill voice.

Tal-ku scolds them, "*U-ru-wa*, grasshoppers, sit still or I will get out your mother's willow wand. And you," Tal-ku turns, "you girls are louder than the gulls on the beach." They hush, silenced by Tal-ku's brooding black eyes and by her legendary powers. Tal-ku has a basket that contains an eagle claw and a dried salamander. Tica and Toño have seen it.

Dusk settles slowly upon the hilltop. The setting sun seems reluctant to leave the pale spring sky. The evening star appears before the last gold streak has sunk into the Pacific. It is warm enough for the party to linger in the courtyard. The thick whitewashed walls of the house and the outbuildings protect them from the ocean breeze. An adobe wall completes the rough quadrangle, enclosing the well and a towering oak, just feathered out now in new pink leaf.

Tica's brothers set a torch to the bonfire in the center of the courtyard, arguing over whose turn it is. The fire sputters, catches a twig here, a scrap of tallow there, then a dry, encrusted oak branch. Suddenly it flames up, illuminating for a moment each log and silhouetting the boys' backs -- skinny, intent figures hunched over the fire as if they have just invented it.

The guests pull their benches closer to the warmth. Tica's father calls for his violin. Toño runs to bring it to him from its special shelf above the *sala* door, his famous, melodious violin. Her cousins begin to sing before he has tuned it, tapping their boots in the packed adobe of the courtyard. The rancho *Costeños* gather, too, edging up beside the smokehouse. They sit on their heels against the dairy wall, drawn by the firelight and the music. The gray, wrinkled branches of the oak beside the well are gradually soaked up by the night sky. María carries out an armload of shawls and *rebozos* from the chest in the *sala*. Then Tica drops to the ground against her mother's knee and sketches by the firelight with her new pencils, an excuse to stare at the woolly strangers, to draw out the evening, to make it last.

During one of her father's songs, she sees Señor Harker whisper to her brothers, sees the boys sneak off toward the well. Suddenly, as the song ends, an explosion rips the courtyard. Tica presses her face against her mother's skirt. The men instinctively grab for their knives; the

Costeños shrink into the shadows. Tica's father and grandfather race for the well just as another series of explosions sounds. Grandfather stops on his heels and turns angrily toward Harker, who realizes at once that he has blundered. He rushes forward, his face red.

"Forgive me, Don José, Don Francisco. I am to blame. I apologize. A present from China for the boys.... Firecrackers, some excitement.... I did not think...."

Grandfather Castro, his hand still on the hilt of his knife, looks sternly at Harker. "We have enough excitement in our lives, Señor. We value peace."

"Don José, my surprise was in poor taste. Please accept my apology." He turns helplessly to María and bows his head. "Doña María, if I frightened you or the children, please forgive me."

He looks so remorseful standing before her that María takes pity on him. "You must understand, we do not like surprises, Señor Harker. It is because here in California everything comes to us as a surprise. We never know. Perhaps you could demonstrate this new invention so that we could understand it."

"Perhaps another time," Harker stammers reluctantly.

But the boys, who had mysteriously disappeared, dart back into the firelight, beg for more firecrackers. Harker looks toward José and Francisco.

"Please, Grandfather," the boys plead. "Please, Father. We will be careful."

Don José relents, and his son-in-law relaxes and smiles. "Señor Harker must supervise you then," he says. "We will see this new invention."

"Not new," says Harker. "It is an ancient invention of the Chinese. They use these little paper packets of gun powder in their celebrations." He carefully pulls a colored string from his pocket. "Now, with your permission, I will light one end of this string with a brand from the fire, and each little firecracker will make a noise. But it is just a noise. Nothing more. Watch."

The group stares fascinated as first Harker and then the boys give a rattling display of their Chinese firecrackers. At the end, Harker asks permission to light a cylinder full of golden sparks that make the stars themselves look old.

When Señor Harker has promised that there are no more surprises, Tica's eyelids begin to droop. She kneels to receive her mother's blessing and kisses her mother's hands, resting her cheek against María's warm fingers. As she leaves the fireside she gives Harker a sketch of himself in his stiff collar and grizzly bear coat. He examines it carefully, holds it up to the firelight. "You have a brilliant eye, Señorita. I will treasure this drawing." And he bows to her and kisses her hand, which so delights and dismays Tica that she runs off to find Tal-ku, begs the Indian nurse for bed. Her ribs ache where her horse kicked her; her stomach aches from too much licorice.

Both gentlemen were wonderfully pleased to hear Don Quijote tell the strange events of his history, and quite as struck by the nonsense he narrated as by the elegant way he spoke it. One minute he sounded like a man of good sense, the next he slid down into foolishness, nor were they able to find the slope that led him from the one to the other.

Op. Cit., Vol. 2, Chap. 59, pg. 662

GRANDFATHER CASTRO'S STORY

"You came with the first expedition?" Job Dye asks José Castro in his faulty Spanish, curious about the old man and his travels. "You were very young." The bonfire has sunk into a deep bed of glowing coals.

"The first civilian expedition to California. Ay, but I was not the youngest by far," says Grandfather, and the grandsons edge closer to the fire, hearing the first strains of a story.

Francisco Rodríguez puts down his violin and joins his wife, stands behind her, wraps his cloak around her, molds her shoulders against his chest. He feels María cave contentedly against him while she listens to her father's adventures, which she can recite as easily as she can her breviary. She feels as soft as the day Francisco married her, her black hair caught in silver combs and shining in the firelight. A sense of well-being floods over Francisco. His marriage to María seems to him the greatest good fortune. Now all the coastline lies safely within their two families' grasp, over fifteen leagues, from Monterey Bay to *Año Nuevo*. The land seems blessed. The cattle fatten, babies come. Every generation secures more of the rich California coast. His sons and daughter sprout like saplings; his wife grows more lusciously beautiful with every child. Five children and the rigors of building a rancho have only modeled her beauty more deeply. She is of the *sangre azul,* the blue blood. Was her French grandmother not married in Notre Dame de Paris to a Spanish aristocrat? María welcomes guests -- even Americans -- into her adobe-floored home as graciously as if it were a palace. He strokes her shoulders lightly as they listen.

"1775," José Castro begins. "1775. Who knows why those first families hazarded the trip, even for such a land? My father was Galician, from the green and fertile plain along Spain's northern coast. Yet he risked the sea voyage to Mexico and then the overland trek to California. Imagine my mother, your great-grandmother, a fair gentlewoman who grew up in France, spoke three languages, played the Spanish guitar. Think of her courage to set off into Apache country with eight small children." He sighs, "But my father was the youngest son, and for an *hidalgo* the land is everything. One must have land."

"Yes," muses Harker. "*Hidalgo,* 'landed gentry.' Always the land."

"I was six, so old I had to ride alone. There were younger brothers and sisters to be carried. Six months on the trail. Land so scorched and dry. Not a blade of grass for the cattle. Bad water. We poured the water through my mother's best handkerchiefs, and still it looked murky. We were coated with dust inside and out. Everything we ate tasted of sand.

"Then, after months of heat: the snow. We children couldn't believe it when snowflakes fell from the sky, covered everything: our horse's hoofprints, bushes, trees. At first it seemed a miracle from heaven. Only later did we feel the cold. My mother vanished three yards ahead of me in the snowstorm. The snow stung our cheeks. Our fingers turned to ice. San Carlos Pass. We spent three weeks getting through those frozen mountains. I don't think you can appreciate how great a feat that was, to lead a civilian expedition. Comandante Anza was a soldier, an explorer, burdened with all those families, pregnant women, little children... Our Comandante Anza was a great man, a Basque."

"He must have been crazy," says Job Dye. "I came across that desert. To think of women and children in that wasteland...." He shakes his head.

"Not crazy, Señor," José Castro says evenly. "Under orders from the King of Spain."

"Why?" asked Harker. "Why send women and children?"

José Castro smiles, "For the land, Señor. The King knew only a civilian population would secure the land for Spain. And, miraculously, when we arrived in California, our number was increased by two. One woman had died in childbirth, but her baby had been saved and suckled by other mothers. Two new babes were safely delivered on the way. Thus, we left Mexico with 240 in our party and arrived in California with 242 souls."

"And you were only six years old?" Dye asks.

José Castro nods. "How old were you when you crossed?"

"Seventeen," says Dye, "and dumb. God knows why I am here tonight."

Francisco fills Dye's wine glass, and Dye sits staring into the fire. José Castro watches the wine loosen Dye's shoulders, but his face does not soften. Tall, slender, with a thatch of blonde hair, he is younger than he first appeared, and tougher -- an iron jaw forged from fear and pain and poverty, José guesses. His blue eyes will be forever squinting over his shoulder. José Castro has seen his face before on other men in California. There lurks something of the coyote in this face.

"Grandfather, tell the señores about the Apache."

José Castro smiles and turns to the boys, but probably he is not talking to the boys alone. "Listen carefully, young *bandidos*. I tell you your short history, your brief heritage. You are *hijos del país*, but it is a land bought for you only yesterday and with much suffering. Do not lose it carelessly.

"The Apache were the great fear. They stood silhouetted, silent as smoke, up on a ridge, watching us. Or the next day on horseback, off in the distance, like a mirage. Twice in the night they crept into our camp and stole horses. We imagined them behind every mesa, every bush. When we reached the canyon of *El Guambut*, even our valiant comandante was afraid. He barked at us to hurry, to close ranks. He galloped back and forth, urged us forward. The walls rose sheer and red on either side of us like the bloodstained walls of a dungeon. El Comandante sent the soldiers first, then the women and children crowded close behind them, and he commanded us to make no sound. He told the mothers to put their babies to their breasts to silence them. The floor of the canyon was dark and cold. The sun never shone there. Behind us came the men, then the stock animals, then more soldiers. All morning we rode through the canyon, crowded together, silent. Padre Pedro fingered his beads, prayed noiselessly. A cow bawled once, and the sound echoed up the canyon. The walls rose higher as we neared the pass; the canyon narrowed. Four long leagues. The canyon grew so deep, so black that stars shone above our heads in the middle of the day.

"We could feel the Apache up above us, behind every rock, but we never saw them. My older sister Encarnación told me that in other raids they had scalped the women and mutilated the men, but they took the children alive and kept them. Father told us later that the men had vowed to kill their wives and children by their own hands rather than let them fall into the hands of the Apache.

"We never saw an Apache that day, but they were there. When we reached Pima territory a few days later, the Pima Headmen rode out carrying two bloody Apache scalps stuck on short sticks. They had taken them in battle the day we rode through *El Guambut*."

"I know *El Guambut*," Job Dye says, then closes his mouth and stares into the coals.

Someone throws another oak log on the fire, and it hisses, pops, flames up. A bench creaks. Back on the hills a coyote yowls its eerie, uneven song.

José Castro continues. "When we reached the Pima village, we had to ride single file between two lines of Indians, their men on one side, their women on the other, hundreds of Pima who had come to greet our comandante. For us children, it was like riding through the Canyon of the Guambut all over again. The Pima stood naked and silent, close enough to touch us, and they stared. They had never seen white children. We tried to ride soldier-straight through their ranks, but the line of Indians seemed to stretch forever out across the plain. My sister, your Great-Aunt Martina, cried when they stroked her hair, and Father had to take her up on his horse."

Grandfather stretches his legs out straight, crosses his arms, drops his chin, lost in thought. His grandchildren lean forward, studying him, but they dare not interrupt his reverie.

"Then we reached the lands of the friendly Yuma," he says after a pause, "and when we rode into the village of the great chief Palma of the Yuma, we children were no longer so afraid. The Yumas wove a shelter of fragrant piñon boughs for us. My mother hated them crowding around us, peering under her petticoats. They smelled of rabbit fat and urine, and they painted their faces red, which frightened the babies, but we loved the Yuma. The day we arrived in their village they dug up melons, scores of melons they had buried in dry sand to preserve them. They broke them open on rocks and we burrowed our heads in them -- so sweet! We ate until our stomachs ached.

"And when we had to cross the Colorado River, Chief Palma himself showed us the way, where the stream divided into three. He took off the navy blue military coat that the comandante had given him and waded into the muddy current leading my horse so that it would not struggle and drown in the deep water. When the current swept a little girl from her father's arms in mid-stream, a young brave climbed out on a wet snag, balancing on his hands and feet, caught her by the hair as she swept downstream, and dragged her to shore. The father was so grateful that he cut the brass buttons from his coat and gave them to the young brave. We cried when we had to leave the Yuma and set out across the frozen desert. Only my mother was glad to leave."

There is no moon. Outside the circle of the fire the stars are strewn in such abundance that they blur into milky strands across the spring sky. It seems to María, as they sit around the fire, that they inhabit a bright golden island in a dark, silent sea.

"He who retreats is not running," answered Don Quijote, "because let me tell you, Sancho, courage which isn't solidly based on wisdom is called rashness, and anything that rashness accomplishes can be traced to good luck rather than to bravery. So I'll grant you that I retreated, but not that I fled…."

Op. Cit., Vol. 2, Chap. 28, pg. 498

MONTEREY
1836

María insists. Twenty days after her infant Natividad is born, she must be baptized by Padre Vicente Sarría at the Carmel Mission, and Tica must receive her first communion before Padre Sarría dies of heartbreak or is shipped back to Spain.

"It is not as you remember it," Francisco cautions her.

"No," she says. "Padre Sarría baptized me in that mission when it was a glory to God, with statues of the Holy Mother and the infant Jesus. Their crowns were silver, and their haloes were gold. My daughters must receive the blessing of Padre Sarría before it is too late. He is the last of the Spanish '*Fernandinos,*' a college-educated priest from a good family. This Mexican 'secularization' is just another name for robbery. They have taken the land right up to the door of the chapel. These new Mexican priests are all peasants. They know nothing. If we wait, there may be no mission at all."

Tica can hardly stand still as Tal-ku braids her hair. Monterey! She has ridden down the coast to the various ranchos of her family, but never so far as Monterey.

They ride the coast road, taking the journey in two easy days because of the new baby. Their horses wade through June fields of pale green bunch grass and pink clarkia. Pink sand verbena hesitates on the verge of the sand dunes. Wild rose and azalea bloom in the gullies. The ripening hills swell round and golden, full-hipped, creased with the green shadows of the redwood canyons.

The boys spy a herd of elk and race off after them. Tica joins the chase, through a grove of oaks, hanging from her stirrup straps to duck under low branches. The elk outrun them and disappear over a ridge.

"I'll race you back to Father," calls Toño, and he and Tica whirl their horses and gallop back, neck and neck, hunched low and forward, snapping their *reatas* on their horses' flanks. Their father refuses to declare a winner. Their mother is irritated that Tica sped off in the middle of learning a new prayer from her missal. Toño and Tica are left to argue it out for themselves as they ride along. At their uncle's adobe they rest the night, their uncle and grandfather joining them on the trip the next day.

Although she has glimpsed Point Pinos far off across the Bay, Tica hasn't imagined anything so hectic as the *pueblo* of Monterey tucked in the lee of the point at the southernmost corner of Monterey Bay. Three sailing ships, with sails drying, lie at anchor off the beach. Beneath the *Presidio* on the hill, houses scatter in crowded confusion. Panes of glass sparkle in their windows. Tica has never seen glass windows. Foreign sailors in baggy trousers and stiff hats dot the beach. Here comes a man with poppy-orange hair. Two thin men pass by chattering in a strange nasal language, without stopping for breath. So many people. A pack of dogs runs on the wide white beach, barking at sea gulls. The bones of a whale stick out of the sand in the shallow surf. An ox cart lurches by, its wooden wheels squawking against its axles.

They go first to Thomas Harker's store. He has become a good friend of Tica's father since his first visit to the rancho two years before. ("He is a tradesman," Francisco says, "but Americans look upon trade differently. Even gentlemen enter the trades. He has taken the young man Job Dye into partnership with him.")

Harker's store is a tiny white-limed adobe with two slits for windows. It sits not a hundred yards from the water's edge, just behind the customs house, welcoming the inbound ships.

"Señora, señorita, the whole family," Harker greets them with his merry, vivid smile and great courtesy.

Once her eyes grow accustomed to the dark, Tica discovers the most astonishing assortment of treasure she has ever seen. "It is like climbing inside grandmother's bridal chest, *Mamá*," she whispers.

"Ay, Tica, *cuidado!*" her mother says, for every inch of space from floor to rafters is so crammed that it is difficult to move without stepping on something. Job Dye, Harker's young partner, stoops in one corner weighing nails. Casks of wine and spirits are stacked in rows along the back wall. Before them are crates of crockery packed in straw, barrels of molasses. On top of these are heaped piles of coffee sacks, boxes of spices, tea tins. From the rafters hang chairs and cartwheels spoked with cobweb, long strings of shoes tied together. Shelves of fabrics, papers of pins, crockery jars full of peppermints, soap cakes... Tica stops. There before her, on top of the desk, in a gray tinware frame, stands her sketch of Thomas Harker.

"We must choose a calico for you, Tica, and we need shirting," María says.

"No, Mamá," groans Tica, "I am too dizzy." She sits on a wine cask with her head in her hands, overcome by the frenzy of odors that she mistakes for the smells of England and Spain and China, the very lands themselves, invading the cramped store. In fact, it is the smell of straw and spilt coffee beans and water-damaged ginger that she sniffs, the spillage of ordinary trade. "There are too many calicoes to choose from. I did not know so many flowers existed, even in springtime."

"Come, Señorita, we will find one to match your enormous eyes, a blue-green of the baby blue eyes in the meadows," Harker says.

"I would prefer the blue-green of the ocean," says Tica.

Harker laughs, enchanted by her. "These *Californio* women are strong-minded," he says.

Tica and María spend the afternoon surrounded by luxury and abundance. María is intoxicated by the satins and ribbons, the exquisite thin porcelain dishes, the candied ginger -- a storeroom of plenty in a spare, simple land.

After the agony of choosing a calico for herself, Tica is relieved when they set off over the hill through the pines for the nearly deserted Mission San Carlos Borromeo a league away. The mission stands alone on a grassy hillside, looking out over the Carmel River and the deep, protected Carmel Bay, nestled between Point Pinos and Point Lobos to the south. But, of course, the mission buildings themselves face contemplatively inward.

"*Bienvenidos, hijitos,*" Padre Sarría greets them sadly, vaguely, limping out into the courtyard on his gouty foot and giving them each a tottering embrace. He has shrunk inside his loose gray robe. He has the thin, transparent look of a man so near death that he casts a pale shadow in the empty patio. His hands are already cold.

María's heart aches for the old man. Not all the progress in California has been good. The Spanish King, the Spanish priests imposed civility upon the land. These new Mexican governors with their latest crop of Zacatecan priests are rabble. To have allowed the churches to fall into ruin seems to her to be the abandonment not only of religion but of tradition and art and music and beauty. A sense of neglect pervades California: an impotent church, an absentee government, a relaxed morality. The *Californios* are a flock without a shepherd. Her husband fails to grasp that it is not only the religion that is crumbling, it is the civilization.

A dirty stone fountain spills water from its green mouth, and the smell of rosemary fills the dilapidated cloister. While their parents and Padre Sarría talk in the shade of the ruined walkway, Tica and Toño sit on the edge of the fountain with Tal-ku and the baby, catching polliwogs in the mossy pool.

They spend the night at the mission, dining with the frail priest on hard-boiled eggs and watery soup laced with olive oil from the mission's old press. Tal-ku cooks. There seem to be no neophytes left in the compound. Padre Sarría's news is confused and ominous. "I expect to be ordered back to Spain any day. Already I am under house arrest. I am not allowed to say Mass. Perhaps I will not even be called back. They say a new governor will be sent, bringing more families hungry for land. They will confiscate what little remains of the mission lands. My *Costeños* will be forgotten. They will be the forgotten people... It was I who taught them patience. Patience is for the dying," he says.

When Tica files into the chapel behind her mother the next morning, her hands clasped in prayer as her mother has taught her, she seems to enter a vaulted cave of gold. Candles for the carved cedar chandeliers are scarce, so the light is dim, and the gold of the peeling *reredos,* the wood carvings behind the altar, barely gleams in the gloom. The church smells of mildew and mouse droppings and mud nests. Thomas Harker has risked the ride over from Monterey to be present at the ceremony at Francisco's invitation. Foreigners are mistrusted these days and sometimes followed.

Padre Vicente Sarría totters out of the vestry and up to the altar, looking like a faded angel in his shabby white vestments. His thin voice echoes in the stone chapel, as if he were already far away. "... *Corpus Domini Nostri...*" The quavering Latin is shattered by the clank of spurs. A tattered band of Mexican soldiers from the Presidio marches down the aisle.

"This is not allowed by order of the Mexican Government. Mass may no longer be...." The first officer hesitates. Francisco Rodríguez and Thomas Harker have turned on the soldiers. Grandfather Castro and Rafael Castro join them, and the four men stand shoulder to shoulder between the soldiers and the altar. Tica, kneeling at the altar rail, peering up, sees her father's face frozen in rage. The soldiers quail before his silent fury, and Francisco turns his back on them, motions to Padre Sarría to continue the Mass. "...*Corpus Domini Nostri Jesu Christi custodiat animan tuam in vitam aeternam. Amen.*" The soldiers rustle impatiently behind her. Padre Sarría's voice sounds more and more distant as he hastily fumbles to administer communion and baptize Natividad. He raises the cross to his lips, blesses them and flees out the side door of the chapel.

Without a word, María looks at Francisco, takes Natividad in her arms, and, holding her rosary before her, head bowed in prayer, brushes past the soldiers, who grudgingly make way for her. She motions for her children to follow and marches out of the church. As Tica turns to follow her mother, Harker presses something into Tica's hand. María hands her baby to Tal-ku, waiting terrified outside the door, then mounts her horse and, taking the baby back in her arms, leads the way up the hill behind the mission. She never spurs her horse. She never looks back. Tal-ku and the children ride behind her single file for an hour in complete silence. After they are safely over the hill Tica opens her fist and looks down. Señor Harker has given her a tiny silver cross clinging to a silver chain.

Tica is too awed by her mother's ramrod back to ask about her father or her grandfather. No Mass is allowed in the mission without permission of the governor. What will become of Padre Vicente Sarría for disobeying the orders? The Mexican governor is already angry with Tío Rafael, her uncle, for siding with the men who want independence. She worries about Señor Harker. Foreigners are being deported for less reason than attending a Mass. Plots against the Mexican government are hatching everywhere. The soldiers are nervous and unpredictable. She clasps the chain around her neck and rubs the cross as she rides.

Her mother turns north inland, avoiding Monterey. They cross a low chaparral-choked ridge, following a trail Tal-ku knows that leads to her childhood home along the Salinas River. When they stop so that María can feed Natividad, they lead their horses well off the trail into the purple manzanita brush, where they would not normally stop because of wood ticks and tarantulas. María sits back in the brush, nearly invisible against the gray sage, and nurses her baby with her eyes turned southward. "We will spend the night with the Borondas," she says. "Your father will join us there."

"Will the soldiers let him go? What do they want?"

"Who knows? They are vultures. You must learn to be as brave as your father, Tica. The cowardly fear courage more than cannon."

All afternoon they ride along the ancient trail that looks better suited to jack rabbits, Tica thinks. The brush scratches at her legs, the deer flies bite and a scrub jay follows them, flying from bush to bush, scolding. Tica's horse slides on the shale.

"Pay attention, Tica!" her mother says sharply. "Don't lag behind."

They reach Toro Creek at dusk, thirsty and tired. One of the rancho *vaqueros* has sighted them, and José Boronda rides out to greet them, taking the baby in his own arms. "María, may the saints help us. What has happened?"

"José, it was horrible. In the middle of Mass…" She lowers her voice and rides ahead, talking earnestly. Tica drops back beside Tal-ku for comfort.

"Tal-ku, I fear for Father. What will the soldiers do to him?"

"Who knows?" Tal-ku spits in the dust. "The soldiers are born out of the barking dogs on the beach."

They walk their horses along the creek, stop to let them drink under the bay trees.

"I wove my first basket beside this creek," Tal-ku says. "From the three rushes. My grandmother taught me to find the black rush and the red rush and the yellow. She showed me how to cut the stems without hurting the plants, because the plants are also alive. She taught me to weave the hole in my basket for the fly spirit to escape. It is the fly spirit, Tal-ku, that gives me my name. The summers were good on this creek."

That night on a pallet curled next to the Boronda sisters, Tica says a very adult prayer taught to her by her mother from the missal, a prayer worthy of a girl who has just received communion from Padre Sarría. Again the next night she prays, for her mother has paced all day, waiting, distraught. And in the middle of the second night Tica hears her father's voice and hears her mother crying and laughing, and she knows that God has answered her prayer, that her father has broken free of the barking dogs on the beach.

All I keep trying to do is make the world see its error in not resurrecting for itself that happiest of times, when the order of knight errantry roamed valiantly up and down its roads.

Op. Cit., Vol. 2, Chap. 1, pg. 357

RANCHO ARROYO DEL RODEO
1836

The Castro-Rodríguez Washday Barbecue is famous up and down the coast. Every other fortnight the neighboring families arrive in *carretas* full of washing and children. They gather in the redwood grove along the creek that runs through *Rancho Arroyo del Rodeo,* Tica's father's rancho, for a washing party that lasts four or five days, sometimes a week. The tall stands of redwoods along Rodeo Creek are some of the most magnificent in the country, and anyone traveling through makes a point of stopping over for the fiesta.

While they grind the amole bulbs they use as soap and scrub the piles of laundry, the cousins catch up on the gossip from the other family ranchos; and while the laundry dries they bathe, then prepare an evening feast along the banks of the creek, each family contributing some delicacy: mushrooms from their forests, melons from their gardens, crabs from their coastline, depending on the season.

Grandfather Castro supervises the lining of the pits with river rock, the base for the manzanita and oak fires that will burn all through the night. Tomorrow the *vaqueros* will bury slaughtered calves in the charcoal pits beside Rodeo Creek. They will embed a thin iron rod in the fattest part of each hindquarters. The rods will stick out of the top of the pit so that Grandfather can gently press them into the meat and judge its firmness.

Meanwhile the young women teeter on redwood planks set out to span the creek, rubbing their linens with sand and bulbs of amole soap and the stiff horsetail ferns that grow along the banks. There is much giggling and chattering, and the creek froths with soap bubbles. Roundups and brandings take place here, too, and although he has relinquished to his son-in-law the responsibility of *Juez de Campo* at the *rodeos,* José Castro still takes great pleasure in supervising the *barbacoa.* There is a knack to it. The pit has to be dug deep into the stubborn adobe. The manzanita root must be used, not the trunk, oak wood must be added and it must burn white before the hindquarters are laid on the fire.

A great whoop goes up behind him. "What in all heaven?" José Castro starts toward the noise, blinded by the smoke of the cook fires. Before he reaches the rim of the creek bed, a huge sorrel stallion charges over the edge with Tica in the saddle fighting to control him. The stallion kicks and snorts, already in a lather, twists up in the air, clenches the bit between his teeth. Her brothers and cousins gallop close behind, yelling and cheering and snapping their reins. The stallion races in blind rage down the steep side of the canyon, scatters the women, plunges through the washing spread out on toyon bushes to dry. The animal tangles himself in the wide skirt of a petticoat, falls, staggers to his feet, trembling with fury and fear. Tica takes her feet from the stirrups when he falls, but she doesn't budge from the saddle. When she has ridden him to a standstill in the creek, she dismounts onto one of the washing boards, strokes his neck, then starts to lead him up the other side of the gully.

"Escolástica Inocencia Rodríguez!" María Rodríguez marches up the arroyo from the cook fires, wielding a wooden spoon. "Jesús María! Antonio Francisco!" She catches the boys as they back over the creek bank. "Bring down the silver you made on this wager. All of you! Carlos! Come down here. *Pronto*!" The brothers and cousins dismount and skulk toward María. "Is that all? I want every *peñique.*" María sweeps the coins up. "This will pay for the damage you did to *Tía* Martina's washing and the fright you gave her *Costeñas.* And if I ever find you wagering money on your sister again, I shall horsewhip you. All of you!

"As for you, Tica, you wild rabbit, you shall give Tía Martina your new petticoat to make up for the one you just ruined. Now rid yourself of that animal and go to work. You have the responsibility of your grandfather's washing. You know that well enough." María's voice rings up and down the gully. Her face is hot. When María Rafaela Inocencia Castro y Rodríguez loses her temper, there is no help for it. The children and cousins all slink off to do as they are told, while the other mothers stand menacingly in the creek with their hands on their hips.

José Castro busies himself with the barbecue, avoids his daughter's eyes, looks away so that his grandchildren will not see him smile. His daughter is right, of course. This cannot go on. Tica's brothers wager on her horsemanship whenever they see the opportunity, claiming she can ride any horse on the coast. That this might be true is no excuse for making money on their little sister.

In fact, she is no longer so little. He straightens up and watches Tica stride over to his washing baskets, a fiery young woman of thirteen. She has grown tall, almost shapely. A streak of savagery runs through her that horses recognize and respect. How men will respond to it, José Castro can only guess. No wonder her mother worries.

Since the death of José Castro's wife, Tica has supervised the washing for her grandfather's rancho. He leans against a bay tree and watches her as she sets to work, sorts through the *camisas* and tablecloths, looks for spots and stains that must be boiled, chatters with Iss-ma and Esken, the old *Costeñas* who were her grandmother's servants.

Iss-ma and Esken still wear the braided rush and buckskin skirts of their people. But Tica is as native to California as the old Indian women. Her eyes can pick out the deer under the buckeye. She can call the ducks down with a feeding call as well as they can, sniff out pennyroyal and *yerba buena* on a hillside. Despite Tal-ku's efforts, Tica's rush baskets are lopsided, but this is because the young girl lacks patience, not skill.

José Castro's generation has clung to things Spanish, typical pioneers. Even his daughter and son-in-law are traditionalists. But his grandchildren are a new breed -- true *Californios, hijos del país*. Their only allegiance is to the land.

He walks over and sits beside Tica on a rock in the creek. "That *melcocha*, that molasses one, of Tío Rafael is quite a stallion, no?"

"I don't like his type, Grandfather."

"No?"

"He is stubborn for the sake of stubbornness. He will hurt himself and his rider, too. I like a horse who fights me because he wants to defeat

37

me, not because he lacks the imagination to do more than hit his head against a rock."

"Ay, Tica, and he is so stubborn?"

"Do you remember, Grandfather? You told me that to train a horse one must hunt like a *Costeño*, slowly, quietly, patiently, for the good points of that horse. Tío Rafael has failed to do this with his horses. Did you not tell him, Grandfather? His horses are as hard-headed as he is."

José Castro sighs. She is already a good judge of horseflesh and cattle. And men, too. What will become of her, this little *vaquera?*

Tica sits on the bank, pulls off her boots and stockings, hitches up her skirt and wades knee-deep into a pool. The best washdays are like this one, when the hills are brown and the days are hot. On these late summer days, the cold creek water trickles from springs deep in the old redwoods, spills down the canyon.

Ever since they were babies, all the cousins have loved washdays. They invent water fights and elaborate games of hide-and-seek and capture-the-flag, with everyone, even the youngest cousin, joining in, sometimes on an older cousin's shoulders. They are the only playmates any of them has ever known. As they grew up, the boys tended to gallop off to concoct impromptu lariat competitions and riding contests. But even her brother Toño can seldom tempt Tica to join them. This is a chance to visit with her adored Castro girl cousins. In a family of brothers it is her only chance to be a girl.

Her two favorite cousins are older than she. Rafaela sings a high soprano, clear as spring water, and plays the Spanish guitar with long nimble fingers. Antonia is plump and brown with shiny, blackberry eyes and a naughty smile. Later that afternoon, the three girls sit by the creek in the long shadows, talking idly, weaving fragrant bay leaf crowns for one another. They construct a miniature village along the creek for the redwood fairy folk who live there, the half-breed fairies they have known all their lives, a mythic blend of Tal-ku's spirit legends and their mothers' stories and superstitions. The fairies have already faded from lack of faith, but they will never be blotted from their imaginations. The girls crouch in the sand, smoothing it with the sides of their hands. Tica builds a little bark house thatched with woven redwood leaves and pebble bordered walks. Already the two older girls talk of marriage. Rafaela's wedding chest is half full with embroidered linens.

"But you would not go away," Tica pleads. She places a pebble carefully along the bordered walk and begins to gather acorn cups.

"But of course! We cannot marry our cousins. We must move away. I will live in a grand house of two stories in Monterey, a house with wooden floors, and eat white flour pastries," teases Rafaela. She picks bay leaves for her sister.

"And I will marry a sailor and live on the wreck of an old sailing ship tossed up against Point Pinos, dining on crabs and sand fleas," says Antonia, laughing.

"And what am I to do without you?" cries Tica.

"You? You will lasso a grizzly bear and marry him."

But the younger Tica does not laugh. She is too revolted by the looming prospect of marriage. Rafaela and Antonia exchange glances and shift the subject to their new ball gowns. They are attending the Governor's Ball in Monterey.

"Then you <u>are</u> leaving," wails Tica.

"Only for three days," says Rafaela.

"But you will meet men from other families, and they will marry you," Tica says disgustedly.

"Don't worry, little Tica. My new gown is a terrible shade of gold, like the underbelly of a salamander," teases Rafaela.

"And mine fits like the habit of a monk," says Antonia, "and drags behind me on the ground, so that I trip on it when I dance."

"We will never leave each other, little Tica. We are cousins." And they put their arms around her because Tica scowls so, and she has tears in her eyes.

Everyone camps at the Rodríguez adobe, the men sleeping in the straw under the lean-to, where María forbids them to smoke their cigars, the women occupying the house. But the barbecue is held down by the creek in the redwood grove.

About dusk Grandfather pokes the beef one more time, tests its firmness against the flesh at the base of his thumb, and declares it ready. The succulent *terneras* are dug up, smelling of earth and ash. María has made a big bowl of her mother's red chile salsa, seasoned with thyme and fresh bay leaves, and this time Tío Rafael has brought ripe corn for the children to roast on the coals, and yellow melons cooled in the creek. Sweat runs down the women's faces as they squat at the cook fires slapping tortillas from hand to hand and stirring the five-bean *puchero* in the great iron stew pot. The boys are sent off to scare away a bear who has been attracted by the delicious smells.

José Castro stands and gazes about him. He thinks there must be no castle dining hall in all of Spain so grand as this redwood grove. He cranes his neck, looks up. The rough, furrowed trunks soar straight into the sky, ancient blood-red columns, delicate foliage floating down from high above his head. The grove is carpeted with fern and wild ginger, and lighted by a long golden sunset over the bay.*

These evenings with his family gathered about him give him more pleasure than anything else in his life. María and her children; Martina and her brood; Rafael and his. Two of the cousins have ridden over from Branciforte, and two of the grandsons have come down the coast from *El Refugio*.

The cooking done, the family gathers around him under the elegant redwoods at their ease on tule mats and blankets. Their laughter mingles with the sounds of the running creek. The girl cousins congregate under their own redwood, which they call "Queen Isabela." A burned-out hollow inside its shaggy trunk is so large that the three girls can all sit inside at once.

Tía Martina shrieks, leaps to her feet, grasps her breast in horror, then looks around the assembled family until she spies Toño and Carlos crouched behind a fallen tree. Scowling, she reaches carefully down into her sewing basket, flips up a corner of her *rebozo*, and, glowering at the boys, pulls out a fat, dappled garter snake that wriggles helplessly in her grasp. "Boys? Have you left something?" But she can't keep a straight face. Her mouth collapses into a mischievous grin and her chins jiggle. She shakes her head. The rest of the family is howling at the joke. Everybody knows when they play a trick they will get the best reaction from Tía Martina. She is the theatrical member of the family. The boys creep out from behind the tree and retrieve their pet. Martina cuffs them both half-heartedly, but they manage to hug her and duck away. Carlos wears the snake around his neck. They scoot off to hunt for banana slugs. Tía Martina will love banana slugs.

After supper Rafaela brings out her guitar, leans against their tree and plays for the girls as they stretch out, sashes untied over their

---

* Today, virgin stands of redwood along the California coast are nearly extinct.

full bellies, arms flung over one another. They sing the songs of their childhood, folk songs, silly songs, lying on their backs looking up into the warm evening. The coastal fog will not come in tonight. They can tell already. The breeze blows down the canyon, an onshore breeze smelling of hot grass and greasewood. It will be hotter tomorrow. From a nearby blanket Francisco's violin joins in the song. Tica loves to hear her father and Rafaela play together. She hears her mother and her aunt begin to sing, tossing the harmony back and forth between them – *"Sobre las Olas," "Las Blancas Flores."* Tica lies in the dark listening to the songs. With sorrow, she realizes that many of the tunes she has sung all her life are about love and marriage.

[A] historian should be accurate, truthful and never driven by his feelings, so that neither self interest nor fear, neither ill will nor devotion, should lead him away from the highway of truth, whose very mother is history,… witness of time past, example and bearer of tidings to the present, and warning for the future.

Op. Cit., Vol. 1, Chap. 9, pg. 46

RANCHO SAN ANDRÉS
1838

In Tica's fifteenth year, the summer seems to turn on itself, to consume itself in its own heat. Day after day the sun scorches the hills. Brush fires blaze, water holes dry up, the earth cracks. September smolders into October. One morning Tica and Toño ride out on their grandfather's rancho, hoping to move the last of his cattle down to the springs that have not run dry. Still no sign of rain. It seems to Tica that even the fog shuns the blistered hills. The redwoods wilt in the canyons. Ferns curl up along dry creeks. An orange haze hangs under the sun. As they start back into the hills, she feels as if they ride into an oven, as if the dry heat sucks the juices from them, suffocates them.

They are headed back toward the last ridge, hoping to catch a few yearlings that have wandered eastward, when her nostrils catch a stray wisp of smoke. In the dry greasewood of the south-facing slopes there is no more terrifying scent. She stands in her stirrups and looks around her nervously. It comes from the far side of the last ridge, she thinks. She can see it now, a whisper of smoke off to their left. She and Toño exchange glances and without a word kick their horses into a lope, hoping that it will be a *Costeño's* fire or an old campfire they can stamp out. They must not get caught downwind of it. They must keep their wits about them. Their father, their grandfather have both lectured them. No horse can outrun a brush fire once it blazes.

They hear the men before they see them, rein their horses in, move up cautiously. Afterwards Tica couldn't say what made them approach so stealthily. Had a brown thrasher whistled a low warning from his hiding place in the manzanita? Had the vapors of evil drifted in the smoke? They hunch low on their horses' necks and peer through the tangled branches of the chaparral. Thorn bush screens her view, but Tica guesses they are four Americans, trappers perhaps, filthy, shouting. They stand around arguing. Ah, a young *Costeño* lies on the ground roped and tied like a steer, tight around the neck, his arms and legs cinched together. She can scarcely see him for the ceanothus. She can understand little of the Americans' coarse, guttural talk, but apparently the boy has stolen something from them. The boy makes no sound. He looks about Toño's age, but Tica does not know him. A Yokut? He might have come over from the inland valleys.

One man grabs a leather thong from his saddle and snaps it across the boy's face. The boy gasps, his only sound, and turns his face to the dirt. The man whips the boy's shoulders until his shirt is torn in shreds and his back is bloody. Then he turns toward the boy's buttocks and whips him again and again in a horrible rhythm. Toño groans and spurs his horse. Tica grabs his horse's head and motions him to be silent. She has no weapon except the long knife her grandfather gave her. They are no match for four men, even these greasy Americans. Tica's stomach shrivels; sweat beads her forehead. They watch hidden in the brush, paralyzed. She has never known this fear. It is the repulsive horror of helplessness. They can do nothing. The boy lies motionless.

The man continues to curse and beat the Indian boy while the other men watch, leaning against their horses with their arms folded, and Tica and Toño crouch frozen in their saddles, afraid to make a sound. After a deep cut with the lash flays a chunk of the boy's skin away, one of the other men takes the whip from the man, slices the bonds of the Yokut and kicks him up. The boy staggers, unable to stand, then scurries off into the brush and disappears. The men seem to be packing up to leave, but they mill around the campsite for some time, kicking up dust, moving saddlebags from one mule to the other.

There is some discussion going on about the Indian. At last the four men mount their horses and set off eastward at a fast trot, dragging their string of mules behind them.

Tica and Toño circle around the clearing, call quietly in Tal-ku's dialect. But they know they will never find him. He will be afraid of them as well. They have hidden like rabbits in the bushes watching, powerless to help. Toño sobs.

Tears will not come to Tica, although she longs to cry. The specter of her own helplessness has shriveled up her tears. All her life she has believed she could do anything. She can ride any horse; she can use a rifle and a *reata*. She has knowledge of the mountains and the rattlesnakes and the grizzly bear and the wild bull. On horseback she need never be afraid. She was wrong. There are things she needs to fear, frightful things over which she has no control. She sits still in her saddle staring straight ahead, stunned by this terrible realization.

[It's] one thing to write as a poet, and very different to write as a historian. The poet can show us things not as they actually happened, but as they should have happened....

Op. Cit., Vol. 2, Chap. 3, pg. 366

MONTEREY
1838

*"Thomas Harker and a union of friends beg
Don Francisco Rodríguez and his family to be
present at a diversion..." December 4, 1838.*

Tica is just old enough to attend the ball. Her cousins delight in the prospect. Her brother Toño thinks it is dumb. Her mother remakes a white satin dress of Rafaela's for the occasion, lengthening it, adding a piece of grandmother's fairy-wrought lace to the bodice. Tica tries it on one afternoon while the household is at siesta, standing in front of the dim little mirror in the *sala*, stooping to see herself. She peers seriously at her image, pulls her hair back with one hand, holds the dress in at the waist with the other. It is difficult to tell. The old glass is veined and spotted. She might look like one of her mother's tall, bony turkey hens.

Thomas Harker is giving the ball in his grand new *casa*, the first two-story house in Monterey. When Escolástica enters the door on her grandfather's arm, she nearly faints with excitement. Spicy green garlands of pine and redwood wreathe the doorways and deep window sills, then wind up the stairway, scarlet toyon berries tucked into the branches. The whole upper floor of the new house has been transformed into a narrow ballroom. To the right, doors open out onto a long, covered second-story balcony facing the bay. The *dueñas* sit in stiff-backed chairs against the other long wall, and at the far end of the room the musicians stand on a low platform: three violins, three guitars, a flute and a golden harp. Tica has never seen a harp. Dozens of candles flicker around the ballroom, making little puddles of light on the windowsills and in the chandeliers overhead, but the light seems to emanate from the women on the crowded dance floor. Their long, wide silk skirts catch the candlelight and reflect it, like Chinese magic lanterns, lavender, pink and pale yellow. Jewels gleam in their hair, dangle from their ears, glitter at their necks. Tica stops at the top of the stairs.

"What is it, little Tica?" asks her grandfather.

"They are all too beautiful, Grandfather," she whispers.

"You forget, Escolástica. You wear your grandmother's diamonds in your hair. You will be the queen of the ball, just as she was when I first met her."

Tica takes courage, although he has spoken sadly.

Indeed, when she steps onto the dance floor the eyes of Monterey follow her. The older generation recognizes her, of course, so like her grandmother at that age. But the girl has blossomed, as young women tend to do along this fair coast. They recognize at once her grandmother's diamonds, and they smile because the diamonds become her, reflect her fiery brilliance. Her grandmother would be pleased. Her grandfather dotes on her.

Tica loves to waltz. She knows that waltzes have been banned by the church for years, but the old Spanish dances tend to be boring and repetitive. The women are stuck in one place with their eyes cast down and their arms at their sides. This new waltz has movement and romance to it. The women move with the men. She and her girl cousins have practiced for hours in the redwood grove. But she has never waltzed on a wooden floor. Her satin slippers glide across the polished surface, and the planks seem to spring in response to her step. Several young men ask permission to dance with her, men who are not even cousins. They smile kindly at her and joke, lead her through the steps she has practiced with Rafaela. Juan Carrillo is there, an elegant young *caballero* from Santa Bárbara. The cousins have heard tales of Juan Carrillo's grace on the dance floor.

Grandfather Castro stands on the balcony talking to Thomas Harker, smoking, watching the dancers, cursing his gout.

Harker is in a pensive mood, despite the festivities. "The governor attends our balls because his wife and daughters insist," Harker muses. "He himself doesn't like foreigners. Neither does his government, it seems."

"How many foreigners actually live here?" asks Castro.

"There are ten Americans in Monterey. There's talk of closing the coast again."

José Castro could add his own concerns about foreigners, but they are, for the most part, groundless. The English are exceedingly courteous. The *Americanos* pay promptly for their hides. One cannot fault them for being so enthusiastic about the harbors, the soil, the climate. Is it that they seem too eager to adopt this new country? They shrug their Californian citizenship onto their shoulders as if it were a new coat, a trifling change that can be altered later to suit them. Is that it? Are they too eager? At times a proprietary tone creeps into their enthusiasm about this land that is not theirs. Sometimes their praise sounds like boasting. But these are the frettings of an old man who is, he must remember, a guest in the house of an *Americano*. "The Mexican government does not seem to like *Californios* much better," says Castro graciously. "My nephew Juanito Alvarado isn't helping the situation, pressing for independence. It is a ticklish time."

"But the Americans are an easier target," Harker says. "I hope the government stays calm until most of the Americans can marry into your *Californio* families and settle down."

"It means converting to Catholicism for most of them," warns José Castro.

"For land, they will forsake their own mothers," says Harker wryly.

José Castro sighs, "The land. Always the land. Apropos, who is that blonde *Americano* dancing with my granddaughter?"

"Do you not remember him? He has dined at your daughter's table. Job Dye, my new partner."

"Ah, yes." José remembers. Dye. *Morir.*

Tica is beginning to understand that breaking colts and dancing with men require similar skills. She must maintain the upper hand. She must encourage them with her voice, but keep them in check with her body. She must rivet them with her eyes occasionally to keep their attention. And for the rest, it is merely a matter of not letting them

49

crowd her or step on her toes. This is a skill she excels at. She has broken many horses on the rancho. She is enjoying herself enormously.

She noticed Job Dye early in the evening staring fixedly at her. She remembers him from the night at the rancho when he stared at her mother's arms. Tica chuckles to herself. There are certainly arms to be stared at tonight, and shoulders, and quite a bit of bosom. All evening, as she dances, his eyes are on her.

Until now, Job has refused to participate in any social occasions in Monterey. His natural caution and his ignorance of society and local custom combined to convince him that he would fail. He knows nothing of music or manners. Gaiety is beyond his ken. What would he say? His coarse Spanish comes from muleskinners and common soldiers. He doesn't care about company. Loneliness, Thomas Harker's patient prodding and the indulgence of the few ladies in Monterey have overcome his diffidence to some degree, but he still views social occasions as fraught with danger. He tends to keep his back to the wall.

Only the sight of Tica on the dance floor could lure him from the edges of the room. She is some kind of damned miracle. From a skinny little tike with green eyes, a tomboy, a hellion, she has fleshed out, blossomed. She is a woman all of a sudden. He can't believe it. Once he joins a line in which she dances, but he doesn't know the steps, and when she laughs at him he gives it up. Now, late in the evening, he summons his courage and asks permission to waltz with her. He's a terrible waltzer. He jolts her around the floor as if she were a broken pump handle, staying very far away from her so that his lead is tenuous at best.

He has obviously prospered since she last saw him. His Spanish still sputters in coarse half-sentences, but when they dance near the candlelight, she sees that there is less of the coyote in his face. He has filled out, and his suit is well cut.

"I am partners with Harker now," he says proudly.

"Ah, in the firecracker business?" she teases.

"Oh, no," he says, "a real business, a legitimate business." He stumbles over the word in Spanish. "A grist mill."

A very good thing, thinks Tica, for a man with so little sense of humor.

Job dances too long with her, a breach of etiquette that has to be remedied by her host. Thomas Harker bows to her and asks her to dance. Job, of course, is ignorant of his blunder. He slinks back out onto the balcony. He is in a cold sweat. His hands shake so that he has trouble lighting his cigar.

"Señor Harker," Tica sighs, when he leads her onto the floor, "it is a beautiful ball."

"The women make it beautiful, Señorita," says Harker, gathering her into his arms. "Do you know you are the focus of every eye tonight?"

"You have a prejudiced view," laughs Tica, "because you are my father's friend."

"You are right," smiles Harker, looking down at her fondly, "I am prejudiced." But Tica looks over his shoulder at the other dancers, only half listening.

When the ball is nearly over, Juan Carrillo asks Tica for a dance. She has watched him all evening, gliding gracefully across the floor. He is from the pueblo of Santa Bárbara. He wears white satin pantaloons, open at the knee to show his snow-white stockings and his fine lace drawers. His short black silk jacket shines with silver embroidery. He is tall and fair skinned, and his hair and eyes are jet black. When he takes the floor with Tica, the two of them forming a double vision in white satin, the other couples unconsciously give way. Here is a man who loves to waltz as much as she. She feels his fingers at her waist, lightly guiding her, senses his moves before he makes them. They whirl around the room in perfect unison, looking straight into each other's eyes, parallel streaks of white. It is a sight to see. They dance two waltzes without changing partners, which is not proper. Even the old women in chairs lined up against the walls cease their talk to watch.

Thomas Harker and José Castro watch the dancers, too, and an uneasy feeling seizes José, a feeling he has had only once or twice before in dense chaparral. He sees nothing dangerous. He hears nothing dangerous. But he senses danger. The musicians play on. The harp embellishes a tune with a descending arpeggio. Perhaps all grandfathers are loath to give up their granddaughters, he thinks. Perhaps I am a doting old fool. And he watches Tica's white satin slippers glide gracefully, twirl, waltz toward the brink.

"Harker, you must promise me something," José Castro says, as the two men watch the dancers. "If you *Americanos* inherit California, you will not forget Escolástica Rodríguez."

"That," says Thomas Harker, rather too quickly, "is a promise I make with all my heart."

Juan Carrillo has studied at the University of Mexico City. Juan Carrillo has read all of Cervantes, even the *Novelas Ejemplares*. Juan Carrillo plays the violin. They whirl around the floor, and Tica feels lifted up by a white wave.

"And what of you, Señorita?"

"Me?" says Tica. "Me? I read, I ride, I dance a little. I am just an *hija del país.*"

"That," smiles Juan Carrillo, "would appear to be enough."

Okay: there's a cure for everything – except death, because he gets to throw his yoke on all of us, no matter what, when we get to the end of the road.

Op. Cit., Vol. 2, Chap. 10, pg. 397

RANCHO SAN ANDRÉS
1838

The winter of the ball, when Tica turns sixteen, the Pacific Coast unleashes a series of cold, wet storms along the Santa Cruz, some of the wettest anyone can remember. In spite of the weather, Tica rides down to her grandfather's rancho for a fortnight's visit. Grandfather's favorite mare, *La Bandera*, is about to foal. Grandfather has promised the foal to Tica, and she wants to be there for the birth.

Every day for a week the old man and his granddaughter ride out to check on the mare, grown swollen and finicky. They debate whether to bring her closer in to the house, but Grandfather says she is nervous confined inside a corral.

"She prefers these south-facing slopes," he says one day. "It is the view, I think, that she favors."

Tica smiles and turns in her saddle to admire the black green pines of Point Pinos off in the distance outlining the southern tip of Monterey Bay. This day they are banked by black clouds from an incoming storm.

"Then *La Bandera* should take note of that storm, Grandfather. It sweeps in from the southwest. A wet one, I'm afraid."

That evening they continue their reading. Tica reads now because Grandfather's eyes have grown weak, but she still sits on a stool at his feet, beside the brazier. They are rereading *Don Quixote*, and they are well into the second book. Sancho Panza has been granted his fondest wish and given an island to govern.

As she turns the page, Grandfather says, "Sancho Panza is like the Americans, is he not, Tica? They want so much to possess California. Did you know that the world once thought California to be an island? It was named after one of those 'abominable books of chivalry' that Don Quixote talks about."

"Perhaps they will be disappointed like Sancho Panza was, Grandfather. Perhaps they will give it up."

Grandfather leans down and strokes her head. "Who knows," he says. "It is an enchanted island, this California of ours. God only knows how her story will end. I will not be here to see it."

Tica rests her head against her grandfather's knee and continues to read so that he will not speak sadly:

During the night the storm strikes the coast and early the next morning Tica and her grandfather find the bay mare struggling to give birth to her foal in the pouring rain. It is clear at once to grandfather that the birth is complicated. The wet mare is already exhausted. Her eyes are glazed with her effort.

Thunder shakes the hills around them, and the sky lowers. The slick hills glow an iridescent green.

"Grandfather, we must go in. *La Bandera* will be fine."

"You go. I will stay with her."

"But Grandfather!" Suddenly the sky heaves; sheets of cold rain blow at them, batter their shoulders, soak through their ponchos, run off the brims of their hats. "Ángelo will stay with her. He has healing hands. I have heard you say so."

Ángelo has said she is too old to foal.

"*Costeños* know nothing of horses. I will not leave her."

And he kneels in the mud at the mare's head encouraging her. It is a foolish thing to do in this weather, but the foal has twisted itself somehow. Grandfather rips off his poncho in the pouring rain, and finally his shirt; the raindrops ricochet off his bare, bony back and splash up in a fine spray so that he seems to be encircled in a pale shroud of rain.

La Bandera is not too old. She has produced six fine foals in her time. She is a good brood mare. There is no reason this foal can't be persuaded out. He eases his arm into her ripped and bloody uterus, gently tugging, pressing, turning with his hand. Of course accidents happen. He is a *ranchero*. He knows this. But she is not too old to foal. He strokes her rump with his free hand and reaches again, feeling gently for the other leg. "*Coraje, Banderita, coraje.*" After a long struggle, he succeeds in grasping both legs, and as the mare lies quivering with cold and exhaustion, he manages to pull the foal in a mess of sac and blood. Tica gags, repulsed by the stench; but the mare revives, struggles to her feet and takes charge of the wet, slimy little thing, licking, whinnying. Gradually, the foal comes to life.

"Well done, old lady," Grandfather grunts, gasping to catch his breath. "A fine daughter you have thrown," he says, "stubborn but beautiful." And he stands with the rain running down his neck and back and into his boots, laughing. "By God, we did it, Banderita," he crows. "Not bad for a couple of old ...." He turns to Tica, "You must name her, Tica. She is yours."

But Grandfather shivers with cold. Tica grabs his poncho and drapes it over his shoulders. "Stupid mare," grumbles Tica, for *La Bandera* has insisted on giving birth in a slippery hollow at the bottom of the south-facing slopes, half a league from the *casa*. By the time Tica catches their two horses and they reach the house, they are both chilled and shivering.

"Where have you been? Do you think you are frogs?" Iss-ma hisses at the sight of them. "The two of you, without the brains of the pill bug. Can you not leave this to the younger men?" the woman scolds as she peels their soaked clothes off them, tugs at Grandfather's boots, wraps them in blankets and soaks their feet in pots of hot water, which irritates Grandfather. Es-ken brings braziers into the *sala* and doses them with madrone root tea, which Grandfather crankily refuses to drink.

"You two crows are always trying to poison me with your brews. A little rain will not hurt us."

They pay no attention to his complaints, rubbing his arms and legs and stubbornly forcing bitter liquid on him. That night Grandfather develops a deep phlegmy cough, and by the next day the Indian sisters say he has a fever.

Tica sends a *vaquero* home to get her mother. María and Francisco arrive the next day, their saddlebags packed with medicines and spices.

María sets to work at once cooking her father's favorite *menudo* stews, mint teas, beef *caldos* laced with garlic and oregano, but Grandfather has little appetite. They spend a discouraging week at the Castro rancho.

"He seems limp," María says. "He has lost his fight. He does not even growl at Iss-ma and Es-ken."

"God alone knows what they are giving him," says Francisco. "Those powders and herbs and tribal incantations."

When her parents leave to check on their own rancho, Tica receives permission to stay with her grandfather.

"Your Tía Martina will be here tomorrow, Tica. You must help her. You must keep his spirits up."

But the next morning a *vaquero* rides down from *Rancho Soquel* with a message. Tía Martina and two of the children are ill. Tica is left alone to care for the old man. Every day she administers her mother's medicines, and Iss-ma and Es-ken dose him with yerba santa and willow root powder. They rub his chest with bayberry. His cough worsens. He is unable to leave his bed.

Sometimes he tries to speak to her, but Tica urges him not to. "Save your strength, *Abuelito*," she says, for she cannot bear the finality of his words.

"I have no strength, Tica. I cannot turn the tide."

One day he murmurs, "My books, where are my books? They are to be yours." And on another, "You must take a land grant. Why have you no land?" He worries about wolves. He hears wolves howling in his sleep. He makes Tica promise to set a guard on *La Bandera's* foal. "When I die, you must take my books."

Tica will not listen. She will not let him talk so familiarly of death. She cooks *pucheros* and yerba buena teas for him. She brings more candles into the small, dark room and keeps the brazier burning. She reads to him from Cervantes, seated on her little stool beside his bed. But now, wherever she opens the volume, the adventures of Don Quixote seem ill-fated, disastrous:

> ....the miserable, toppled body of Don Quijote who, despite the whirlwind of blows falling on him, never shut his mouth, threatening heaven and earth, and the whole pack of scoundrels....And he, as soon as he saw himself alone, went

back to trying to stand up, but if he couldn't do it when he was healthy and in one piece, how was he supposed to manage, thoroughly thrashed and exhausted? And yet he thought himself lucky, for it seemed to him that this was a fitting misfortune for a knight errant, and everything was his horse's fault and still he couldn't stand up, his body was so bruised and battered.[*]

Tica puts the book down. "*Don Quixote* is supposed to be a comedy, Grandfather. Why has it turned so sad?"

Her grandfather smiles at her, but his voice falters, "Because it is also a tragedy, Tica." A spasm of coughing interrupts him. He lies back against his pillows. "You will see. Read it again when you are older," he says weakly, "and you will see."

Tica kneels beside her grandfather and prays for him, clings to his oak bed, resting her head against the carved rail. "Blessed Mother of Mercies," she prays, "bring him through this illness." And she promises the Blessed Virgin everything she owns, and some things she does not, if she will save her grandfather. With her finger she traces her grandfather's cattle brand burned into the seat of her stool. She loves his brand, a hawk soaring on a mountaintop, the most elegant brand of the Pájaro Valley:

Grandfather told her she was his little hawk. She believed that he was her mountain. Now the mountain trembles. Now the mountain threatens to melt away.

He begins to speak of her grandmother, a stern, devout, dark woman whom Tica had loved and feared. He stirs from his sleep and calls

---

[*] *Op. Cit.*, Vol. 1, Chap. 4, pg. 25

Grandmother's name -- "María Antonia, Antonia," he calls -- and Tica looks into the shadowy corners of the room, afraid that Grandmother may be answering him.

José Castro knows he is dying. A darkness has spread over him in the past months, sometimes clouding his mind, sometimes narrowing his vision to a small shaft of light. He has not mentioned this to his children. If he sits down, he can clear his head, but the shadows never retreat entirely. They lurk like a winter storm just offshore, a bank of black cloud, ready to rush over him. The birth of his mare's foal seemed crucial to him, a sign that spring would come again, if he had to pull it out of the dark himself, tear it from its cloudy sac. But now that the foal is delivered and he lies exhausted on his bed, he knows that he has seen his last spring.

If only he could be sure that it was he alone who was dying. His own death is not so frightening. He is a fairly good Catholic. The poor, gaunt crucifix on his wall is an old friend. More and more, he misses his wife and longs to be reunited with her.

Was California perishing, too? Are all dying men overwhelmed with a sense of general doom? The traders and new arrivals to California fill José Castro with dread. It is not so much that they disapprove of the civilization in California as that they fail to notice a civilization exists. It is as if the newcomers step off their ships and look right through the *Californios*, as if the continual sunshine shines through the *hijos del país* and renders them transparent.

José Castro falls to musing on the *Costeñan* civilization he and his fellow *Californios* have overrun. Iss-ma and Es-ken, the women who care for him, are rich in their own eerie heritage. He has seen them call rabbits to arm's length, cure burns and snakebites. They brought his third child, who was born dead, back to life by plunging him in the creek in winter. They are daughters of a Mustak chief. He remembers them when they first came to the rancho, small and straight as reeds, dressed in short, ragged rabbit skin capes and tule skirts, barefoot. They appeared at the gate and signed that they needed food. José's wife gave them food and blankets, and they stayed. They insisted on wearing their native dress, and José's wife allowed them this. "It is their family tradition," she said. "They have traditions, too." She furnished the sisters with buckskin and rabbit skins for their clothes. Often now, José sees them as they stood that winter morning at the gate in their scanty capes, and sometimes it is the faces of the two Mus-tak princesses he sees, and sometimes it is the face of Escolástica.

As he lies dying and the gloom closes in around him, he longs to glimpse the future, but the future seems black, too. And though he fights it for his granddaughter's sake, he is aware that the darkness looms all around him.

Worried, Tica summons her mother and father. The rain has not abated since her grandfather fell ill. "Tears of heaven," her mother calls them, a dismal drumming, the damp chill of the adobe, the smell of mud. Tica's aunts and uncles begin to ride in. Padre Francisco is sent for from Santa Cruz, but now the creeks are flooded.

Grandfather grows thinner until his legs, sticking out from his nightshirt, look like the legs of a bird. His skin becomes thin, too. As if he has been enchanted by one of the sorcerers in *Don Quixote*, his flesh begins to disappear, until Tica worries that he will vanish altogether. When she kisses his cheek, his skin smells waxy. His eyes remain closed. When she calls to him quietly, clutching his hand, weeping, praying he will not leave her, his eyes open slowly, with great effort, but they do not see her. A tear rolls down his thin, sunken cheek.

Still Padre Francisco is delayed by flooding. In desperation, María improvises her own last rites, anoints his forehead with olive oil, murmurs an *Ave María:* "Now and at the hour of our death…"

The room smells of tallow candles and bitter herbs. The low murmur of her aunts' prayers and the drumming of the rain fill her ears, melancholy sounds. Tica kneels beside him, weeps, prays that he will not leave her. She searches his face for hope, and in the middle of the night Grandfather opens his eyes wide, wheezes, then falls back against his pillow, still. Tica reaches for his hand, but she finds instead the empty hand of a corpse. Nothing of him remains. He has vanished. He has sloughed off his body as easily as a snake sheds its skin, abandoning it, thin and transparent, in the dust. She drops his hand in dismay, and sobs against his bedclothes.

Her mother and aunt wash his thin, gray body and wrap it in the ancient priest's vestment given to Grandmother many years ago by Padre Sarría to be used as Grandfather's shroud. Tía Martina and María lay him on the earthen floor of the *sala* with a flat stone beneath his head and a small wooden cross in his hands, according to tradition. Tica's uncles keep a vigil around Grandfather's body, praying and smoking, singing the *Miserere*, never leaving his side, until Padre Francisco arrives for the burial.

His body is buried in a downpour. It is February, and the grass is still short so that the hills spread smoothly out around them, a luminous green against the charcoal sky. The priest trudges up the hill swinging a thurible filled with smoking incense. Behind him Tica's uncles carry Grandfather on a cypress board to the grave. The rest of the family follows in a damp procession, praying a *sudario,* and then come the four cousins carrying the coffin. Rain splashes in the bottom of the grave while the uncles place the body in the coffin. Padre Francisco sprinkles Grandfather with holy water and passes the incense over him once more. *"Requiem aeternam dona eis, Domine, et lux perpetua luceat eis."*

The uncles close the coffin and carefully lower it into the adobe pit. Wet, gray mud sticks to the shovels when they try to fill in the hole. The grave lies under a leafless oak on a hill behind the house, looking out over the Pájaro Valley. He is laid to rest beside his wife and an infant daughter who died many years before. Iss-ma and Es-ken stand beside the grave in their otterskin capes, their hair cropped short in mourning, their faces smeared with ashes.

"I am the resurrection and the life, saith the Lord: he that believeth in me, though he were dead, yet shall he live..." María has told Tica that Grandfather's soul is in purgatory, and that she must pray for him. But Iss-ma has told Tica that Grandfather has gone to be with Grandmother in the place beyond the ocean where the sun sets, which seems to her more likely. Tica knows that, wherever he is, Grandfather is dead, and it seems to her, watching through her tears as the wet clay plops onto her grandfather's coffin, that all the joys of childhood have died with him on this day.

In a word, Don Quijote so buried himself in his books that he read all night from sundown to dawn, and all day from sunup to dusk...

Op. Cit., Vol. 1, Chap. 1, pg. 10

RANCHO ARROYO DEL RODEO
1839

It was Grandfather's wish that his books belong to Escolástica, and she herself drives the *carreta* that transports them in their heavy leather-covered trunk studded with brass. Over the winter Tica spends much time repairing and reading the books. The dry California summers have been cruel to the leather bindings, and the damp winters damaged the pages. She polishes the inside of the camphor trunk with beeswax and otter oil. She lines it with dry bay leaves. She rubs the binding of each book with beeswax, and sews the torn pages. Then she stacks them neatly inside the trunk according to author: Cervantes, Dante, Euripides. Some of the books Grandfather has read aloud to her in Spanish: Cervantes, Defoe, Shakespeare. Many he has discussed with her: *Pilgrim's Progress, Candide.* It was his dream to build a library that would educate his grandchildren. He selected each volume for some particular literary or philosophic strength. It seems to Tica that when she sits on the floor of her room, leaning against the trunk, reading, she is closer to her grandfather than anywhere else in the house. When she picks up *Don Quixote*, she can almost feel him beside her.

Her brothers complain. Their mother insisted that they learn to read and write, too. "Why did Grandfather not give me books?" asks Toño.

"Because your grandfather's library is the largest in California. His collection must not be broken," María tells him. "You are welcome to read as many of the books as you can. And if you boys played cards less, you would have plenty of time to read them all."[*]

One day in early spring, while visiting the rancho, Thomas Harker expresses an interest in seeing the books.

"Tica," her father says, "show Señor Harker your grandfather's books while I check on the harness mending."

"But Francisco, I can wait until you..."

"Tomás, you misjudge our little Tica. Although she is young, she is the best educated member of the family," Francisco says proudly. Thomas Harker turns uncertainly to follow Tica.

Señor Harker and Tica kneel before the leather trunk in Tica's tiny room. Above the chest hangs a drawing Tica has made of the Carmel Mission, colored with the pencils Harker gave her. Besides the leather trunk, the room holds only her narrow carved bed, covered with a lamb's wool blanket, a chest and her rosary, hung on the wall. The hard adobe floor is carpeted with a small Chinese rug from her grandfather's house, beige, the color of beach sand, bound around the edges with a border of pale blue. Sunlight falls on the trunk and on Tica's drawing.

Señor Harker says, "Your drawing shows great promise, Escolástica. Do not neglect your art. It is also an important part of your education."

They sit together on the silky carpet in the narrow shaft of sunlight, rubbing their hands over the slim leather volumes, leafing through the fragile pages, as Tica tells Harker the history of each volume that Grandfather has painstakingly collected.

"Voltaire," Harker exclaims, delighted when he recognizes an author. "Petrarch." Fenimore Cooper wrote originally in English, Harker says, and they talk about Defoe's *Robinson Crusoe* kneeling together on the soft carpet, caressing the supple bindings until María stumbles upon them.

"Señor Harker!" Maria says. "I heard voices.... I did not know you were in my house."

---

[*] The collection still resides today, one hundred leather-bound volumes, in the *Casa Serrano* in Monterey, CA.

Harker leaps to his feet, red in the face, "Doña Rodríguez, forgive me. You were out riding when I arrived. Your husband consented to have Tica show me your father's library."

Doña María looks at Tica kneeling before the chest. "So, you are interested in books?"

"Oh, yes, Doña María. I miss them terribly on this coast." Harker's face is the color of ripe toyon berries.

"Perhaps you might bring some of the books into the *sala*, Tica, where it is warmer, so that Señor Harker can look at them while he takes a cup of chocolate."

Tica reads aloud from *Don Quixote*, which Harker has read in English. Harker, whose Spanish is excellent, enjoys it immensely; but it makes Tica too sad to read *Don Quixote*. It reminds her of her chivalrous grandfather. She puts it aside and reaches for Lope de Vega. Her mother, who has been raised on these same books, listens as she tats.

The little *sala* is warm. The raised threshold protects the room from drafts and evil spirits. The two windows are shuttered, their rawhide hinges and latches closed against the spring gales. Braziers stand at either side of the narrow room on the hard adobe floor. The floor is waxed with tallow to a deep cordovan shine and covered with tule mats. Carved oak chairs stand against the creamy back wall under a painting of San Fernando. Elk tallow lamps glow on the Spanish chest.

But to Tica, Harker seems suddenly strange, jumpy, like a horse in a north wind. When her father returns, he seizes the first opportunity to leave them. He is just on his way to Branciforte, he says. He will be late. He has lost track of the time.

Francisco laughs at him. "You Americans are always late for something. What is there that will not wait until tomorrow? Are there two such lovely ladies to pour your chocolate in Branciforte?"

"No, Don Francisco."

"Then you are insulted that I left you so long alone with Tica."

"Oh, no!" chokes Harker.

Doña Mariía bends to her tatting to hide her smile at her husband's lack of intuition. Sometimes he sees nothing but what he sees. Her mother had a saying, "Men lack the whiskers of the cat."

But Harker seems more anxious than ever to be off. As they bid him farewell in the courtyard, he blushes again and fumbles in his saddlebag. "I had forgotten," he says, and he pulls out a little tin box that he thrusts into Tica's hand. Then he lopes out the gate.

Inside the tin box is a tiny set of watercolor paints and a fine camel's hair brush. Tica looks up at the receding figure of Thomas Harker, already just a speck on the road. "Americans are odd," she says, "but I like this one."

[He] decided to turn himself into a knight errant, travelling all over the world with his horse and his weapons, seeking adventures and doing everything that, according to his books, earlier knights had done....

Op. Cit., Vol. 1, Chap. 1, pg. 10

RANCHO ARROYO DEL RODEO
1839

As soon after Grandfather Castro's burial as decency permits, Juan Carrillo requests the honor of calling upon the Rodríguez family at *Rancho Arroyo del Rodeo*.

The handsome dancer from Santa Bárbara coming to *Rancho Arroyo del Rodeo*! Her cousin Rafaela crows at the news, "Most certainly a fiesta..."

"My new dress will never be ready," moans Antonia.

Tica's brothers favor horse races. Only Tica's brother Toño objects. He revolts at the whole idea of Tica in love. "You just sit around all the day, Tica. I have to do everything."

They have been rivals all their lives, evenly matched, crack horsemen, good with cattle. Toño is more musical. Tica is the better student. Tica and Toño. *Los Dos Terribles. Compadres.* Tica doesn't even reply to Toño.

"There is something wrong with her, Mother."

"She will recover, Toño. And you may suffer from the same malady yourself someday, so don't torment her."

When Juan Carrillo rides into the rancho courtyard, the midday glare bleaches everything from Tica's vision except his figure as he dismounts and approaches her. He looks even more beautiful in his riding clothes, more masculine. His flat-brimmed black hat slices his brow, casts a shadow across his face. He bows politely to her mother, then turns to Tica and looks straight at her as he greets her formally. Tica staggers imperceptibly. Her feet have turned to stone.

"You are afraid of him," her cousin Rafaela complains later when they are alone.

"I am not afraid," Tica scolds. But she senses that he has the power of the wild stallion, the power of the bear. And she seems to have lost her will to outwit him.

Juan Carrillo remains at the rancho for a fortnight, and the confusion that he causes is general. Tica wanders in a daze, no help to María in planting the spring onions. "And the peppers. We are already late with the *poblanos*," María fumes. Tica is also scant help to her father, who depends on her. They are hosting the last stage of the spring round-up and branding, a huge affair. Five of the family ranchos along the coast cooperate. There are no fences, so their cattle tend to wander onto each other's land. The *rancheros* start their ride in the south, fanning out several miles inland to pick up the strays that have wandered back into the canyons. Slowly, they move the herd north across all five ranchos, a distance of some fourteen miles as the crow flies, ending up at last at Tica's father's rancho, *Arroyo del Rodeo*, which is bordered by the San Lorenzo River on the north, a natural barrier.

The *rancheros* round up the cattle, branding the calves with the brand of their mothers. There is no time for frivolity. And this Juan Carrillo, although a brilliant horseman, turns out to be a pueblo boy when it comes to cattle. He has spent too much time in Mexico City.

The cousins constantly turn up for picnics. The boys are distracted by schemes for horse races. Tal-ku and the other *Costeñas* are deluged with petticoats to starch, at a time when twenty or thirty men sit at the table for the evening meal.

María watches Juan Carillo's courtship of Tica with a shrewd eye, allowing the young couple only an occasional brief moment alone. In fact, the crowded conditions of the round-up allow for very little privacy for anybody.

"Our daughter is stricken by this young man," she says to Francisco as they prepare for the night. "I recognize the signs. I, too, felt such a helpless attraction."

Francisco smiles, takes the hairbrush from María's hand and brushes her hair down her back. "This Juan Carrillo is much suaver than your suitor was."

"Yes," María says, "You were uneducated in the vagaries of romance."

"I was just impatient to marry you, take you away with me." He kisses her shoulder.

"Yes. This Juan Carrillo seems to be in no hurry at all. He savors the game of courtship as much as he likes Tica," María says pensively. "He is an expert suitor, but does he love her?"

Tica, for her part, has fallen in love. She has given Juan Carrillo her heart, or rather he has taken it and she has been powerless to resist. She does nothing by halves. When he takes her hand to help her across a creek, her hand trembles. When he lifts her from her horse, her knees buckle, and when he dances with her, she can't breathe. Her heart has run away with her.

Tica has never needed help getting off her horse before. All her brothers find her predicament hilarious, except Toño, who thinks Juan Carrillo is a skunk and says so. Tica avoids Toño at every opportunity.

One night as they sit in the courtyard listening to Francisco play the violin, Juan Carrillo touches Tica's elbow. "Come," he whispers.

Tica instinctively looks around for her mother. But María has gone to hear her younger brother's bedtime prayers. Her father is engrossed in his music. She tiptoes through the gate of the courtyard and walks toward the sliver of a moon, which seems to have turned its back on them tonight; just its shoulder shows in the starry sky.

"Tica," Juan comes up behind her, catches her arm lightly in the dark, as if to dance, pulls her around to him and kisses her.

"Ay!" says Tica.

"That is all you have to say, my little savage? Ay?" And he takes her face in his hands, kisses her again, hard.

She reaches out to him, amazed, touches his hair, his cheeks. She puts her arms around his neck and kisses him, tenderly at first, covering his face with kisses. Then she pulls his face to her urgently, presses her breasts against his chest.

"What am I to do with you?" he whispers. "How can I live without you? Come, *querida mía*. Your mother will miss us." He leads Tica by the hand, because Tica can see nothing but him.

From that night Tica leaps at every opportunity to be alone with Juan. Her mother scolds her constantly, but still she lags behind on horseback rides. She beckons him from the smokehouse. She takes early morning walks toward the beach. She knows it is improper. She doesn't care. She wants nothing but to be with him.

Juan rides up alongside Francisco one day at the end of the roundup. Francisco looks at him sternly, "My daughter has fallen in love with you. What do you propose to do about it, *Señor*?"

Juan Carrillo's cheeks color under the brim of his black hat. "I care deeply for her," he says. I would like to ask for her hand in marriage, but…." He hesitates.

Francisco looks at him sharply, "Do you love her? Have you land enough to support her?"

"There is much land, but it is complicated. I must go home and work out an arrangement with my father. I will return in a month to ask for her hand."

Francisco reins in his horse. "Then go at once," he says. "You have stayed too long. This thing must be settled."

Juan Carrillo leaves the next morning, and Tica is numb. "Why can't we marry now?" she asks her mother miserably.

"Because it would be unseemly to marry in such haste. His family must be told. He must see that he has his own land. And you! You have no trousseau at all. Your clothes are in tatters. We will be lucky to be ready when he returns."

Tica attacks her trousseau with vengeance. She and her father ride to Monterey for silk. Thomas Harker pulls down his most exquisite bolts for her, shows her the French ribbon and the handkerchief linens. Tica's eyes shine. Her cheeks are streaked with sun. She is beginning to feel almost lovely. Señor Harker seems to think her pretty as he holds the shimmering fabrics up to her face.

"No, too dull for the green of your eyes," he says. "Not rich enough for your hair." He spends an afternoon with her, picking fabrics. Her father, easily bored by such things, has gone off to the Alvarado adobe to hear the latest news.

"Little Escolástica," says Harker, "why do you need so many clothes? Are you going off to Mexico? Could it be a bridal chest that you are…?"

Tica blushes. Her mother has strictly forbidden her to say one word about her marriage to Juan until they are officially betrothed. But Thomas Harker's bright eyes seem to look down inside her. She takes his hand in both of hers. "Señor Harker," she whispers, and tears of joy shine in her eyes. "I am so happy," she says, nearly kissing the tips of his fingers in her ecstasy.

Looking down at her, feeling his hand held in hers, it seems that he, too, might cry. "May you have a long and blissful life, my dearest Tica," he says hoarsely. "Now," he slams several bolts back out of the way. "We must find something very, very special." And he reaches for the white *peau de soie* just arrived from France.

Tica returns laden with purchases and gifts from Harker's store. She sets to work at once cutting out her chemises and petticoats. María fears she will lop off a finger in her haste. María works at her loom in the courtyard while Francisco sits beside her, bringing her up to date on the gossip in Monterey. He hands bobbins to her as she passes her shuttle back and forth. They talk to the rhythm of the treadle.

"... a strange conversation with Thomas Harker, by the way. He seemed very interested in Tica's future."

María chuckles at her husband's innocence. "Now the other wool," she reaches for the bobbin. "Did you not know that Señor Harker is in love with Tica?"

"He said nothing to me," Francisco grumbles.

"Did you think then that it was my cooking that brought him out so often?"

Francisco frowns. "He should have announced his intentions. These Americans, they are so reticent, even Tomás."

"Perhaps he could see with his own eyes that fate was taking a different turn," María says, leaning into her loom with a long flowing motion, as if she were spinning spider-like from her own body.

"Harker says he would court her himself if he were younger. He says she would become restless married to so old a.... And he worries about a commitment to some American woman he met on his last voyage to the Sandwich Islands. He says the American woman is someone more his age and temperament, someone congenial, who will be content to grow old with him."

"That doesn't sound like love," muses María. "He sounds as if he would dig his own grave. He can't be much more than thirty." Back and forth she sways.

"He says he would be better off safely married. Only then can he easily dance at our daughter's wedding fiesta."

María pauses in her weaving, tucks her hair back, rests her hand on her husband's sleeve. "Harker is a good man. My father held him in high regard. I hope we do not err in allowing this young Carrillo to...."

"Allow?" asks Francisco. "To forbid it would be like forbidding the chaparral to burn upon the hillsides. Do you not remember, María?"

María sighs and drops her shuttle in her lap. She stares into the shaded corners of the courtyard, full of intimate shadows and dusky memories. "I remember when you rode onto our rancho. I nearly died of joy. You were magnificent."

"Harker says he will go to Santa Bárbara to meet this American woman's ship. While he is there, he will inquire into the family Carrillo and their finances. Carrillo is an old and respected name in Santa Bárbara."

Tica creeps out of the house soon after the morning hymn. She shivers in the first gray light, pulls her wool shawl more tightly around her. The summer fog is in, and a cool, damp cloud drapes the rancho. She saddles her horse quietly in the round corral, and, once away from the adobe, lets him run in an easy lope toward the beach. The adobe lies a mile from the ocean. She rides out across the gently rolling dunes, blanketed with gray-green salt bush and sand verbena, following Arroyo Creek to the marshes and on down to the beach. She skirts the hollows where the straight, black cypress stand, their tattered branches flagging out behind them in the western winds.

She rides as if to a rendezvous, but in fact it is solitude she seeks. It is almost possible, she thinks, when she is alone on a gray beach looking out at the calm water luminous as an oyster shell, for the ocean breezes to blow through her, scouring her of the present, the tedious day-to-day stitching and grinding and churning and waiting.

Only then is there room for her memories to bob calmly to the surface, like the giant kelp on the surface of the sea. Her last year, her sixteenth year, has been one of partings. She lives on remembrance.

Here on the beach, this empty wave-washed sand, there is room to remember.

As she rides along the beach, she can hear her grandfather's voice, as low as the rumble of the rolling waves. It is strange the things she remembers about her grandfather. Frailties really. Quirks. When she thinks of him, she thinks of him as a great *hidalgo*. When his words come back to her, they are wise words. But when she remembers him, actually remembers, it is the scar on his cheek she sees, the deep crease where his horse had kicked him, or the plume of wayward white hair from the peak of his eyebrow that shot up straight, giving him one queer, surprised eye. She remembers his gouty foot up on a stool, his bony, wrinkled foot and inflamed big toe, swollen and tight. When she strives to see him in his saddle, like the drawings of the great equestrian statues he has shown her, the picture fades.

As she sits staring out to sea, searching the horizon where the gray sky dissolves into the gray-green ocean, she can feel Juan's arms around her. She cannot recapture his voice, much as she tries. And he is a blur of partial images, as if his face, being too smooth and perfect, has rolled right through her mind, failing to imprint itself on her memory. Only if she rides alone like this along the beach can she hope to feel him near her, feel the pressure of his hand in hers, the burn of his lips on her neck.

Every morning she rides out like this, early to avoid Toño, and though her mother looks anxiously at her as if for signs of fever, she does not question these silent rides. She and her mother seem to have a new vocabulary with which to communicate. Though they seldom venture to put it into words, they each love a man, and some things are understood between them now.

"Tica, this dress becomes you."

"Do you think..."

"Yes, he will."

"It has been so long..."

"The ships are not dependable."

"You don't think..."

"No, you will hear soon."

The bustle of the rancho, to which she was once the main contributor, oppresses her, and her face becomes somber enough to still a room when she enters. Tica begins to watch her mother curiously.

She has never taken notice before of María as a wife. She sits in bed every night of her life, brushing her hair while her husband watches. Tica is embarrassed, flustered if she interrupts this little ritual when she comes to wish them good night and ask their blessing. "May God be with you," she mumbles, her back already turned, headed for the door.

"Now what is wrong with our daughter?" Francisco asks. "Is it so upsetting for you to brush your hair? Has she not seen you do this all her life?"

María smiles, "Yes, but she has never seen you watching me, my loved one, never really noticed. It is you who embarrass her."

A month passes, and no word reaches her. Harker leaves for Santa Bárbara to meet his fiancée, promising to send word by return ship. Two months go by. Tica becomes defensive. "Something has happened. He is ill, or he would be here by now."

"Yes, probably." Her mother's voice lacks conviction.

"Of course, that is it," Tica insists. "Or his mother is ill, and he cannot leave her."

"It may be."

Tica fumes. This wretched land, cut off from the world, an island in the Pacific, beached on desert, run aground on the sharp spines of the Sierra. She sits isolated on the rancho. The world could end, and this island called California would be the last to hear it. And when the news did come, it would arrive as a series of conflicting rumors.

"Take care, dear Tica. Your fingers are already bloody where you have pricked them."

María watches Tica, prays for her, worries over her. Tica's fears are few and desperate. María has seen enough of life to know that danger comes from many directions; her fears are jagged uncertainties, a maternal terror of the dangers that slice obliquely and cannot be parried. María has seen a mother grouse hurl herself hysterically at a man to protect her brood. She knows that instinctive horror -- not alarm for oneself, which can be met head on, but for one's child.

In the name of all that's holy, what makes you think there ever were or now are real knights errant?

Op. Cit., Vol. 2, Chap.31, pg. 515

RANCHO ARROYO DEL RODEO
1839

One morning a fortnight later, already the beginning of June, Thomas Harker rides into the rancho courtyard.

"Toño," María calls, "ride out for your father quickly. Quickly."

"Mamá, I do not know where he is. He went out after wolves. The cows were bawling last night."

"Well, find him. *Vaya*. Jesús, you go, too."

A glance at Harker's shoulders as he rides into the courtyard tells her there is trouble. When she invites him to dismount, he looks nervously about the courtyard.

"Tica is out on her morning ride, Don Tomás. She prefers solitude to our inferior company, it seems. Good morning. How goes it with you? Please sit down. Take something to refresh yourself."

"Doña María," Harker takes her hand and bows, "the news is not good."

"He is dead?"

"No, unfortunately."

"Oh, no." María leads Harker under the grape arbor in the courtyard, where they speak earnestly.

He has never really looked at María Rodríguez closely. Being an unmarried bachelor, he has been careful not to. The dappled light of the arbor illuminates her beauty. Unlike her daughter's, María's eyes are black. Hers is the light and dark luster of Goya and Ribera. Her blouse is embroidered in bright, luscious blossoms, rose and lavender and orange and green, glowing against her suntanned cheeks, her open neck. Her skirt is hand woven, soft to the touch. She is probably only a year or two older than he, although she has already borne five children. She possesses the open intelligence, the easy charm of the California women that combine to make them breathtakingly beautiful. A coarse seaman's joke on the coast is that the purity of California women depends solely on the number of brothers they have, a ridiculous jest. The women he knows are very chaste, but their clothes have no buttons. Their blouses tie with drawstrings. And like their clothes, these women have, all of them, an open, direct smile, an attractiveness that is very misleading to stuffy Americans just off a ship.

María questions him calmly, carefully, takes the blows he deals courageously, though he can feel her aching for her daughter. "This will not be easy, Don Tomás." María says.

"May I tell her myself?" he asks.

"She may hate you for it."

"I know."

María pats his hand gratefully, spies his new wedding band. "Don Tomás, in these troubles I had forgotten. You are married. Your little American from the Sandwich Islands..."

"Yes, we were married on an American ship in Santa Bárbara."

"Before you knew about Carrillo?" María asks.

"No, I knew," he says. "Rachel had arrived, and...." Harker bows his head. His face reddens.

María pauses. "May you be very happy together, Tomás. I congratulate you."

And they sit together under the arbor thinking of all the things that have not been said between them.

"Señor Harker, *estimado* Señor," Tica gallops into the courtyard, leaps off her horse into his arms. "Tell me. Tell me everything, dear sir," she cries, her cheeks flushed with excitement. "I saw your horse. I knew you had come."

He takes her arm and leads her to the arbor, where her mother sits. He sits beside her, still holding her arm in his.

"Juan Carrillo loves you, Escolástica, but he cannot marry you."

She pulls her arm away, but she holds her tongue.

"His family is in serious trouble financially. All of their land is mortgaged to trading firms in Santa Bárbara. Their debt is staggering. The only solution is for Juan Carrillo to ingratiate himself with the Mexican comandante in Santa Bárbara so that he can gain a government post."

"But..." Tica sputters. A glance at Harker's unhappy face silences her.

"When he came to Monterey last winter, he was already promised to the comandante's daughter. He never should have..." Harker breaks off. "When I left Santa Bárbara, the banns for their marriage were already posted."

At first Harker wonders if she has understood. He knows his phrasing in Spanish is sometimes awkward. She stares at him solemnly, stares through him. The morning courtyard is unnaturally silent. A junco drops to the ground before them, hooded in black like some tiny executioner, scratches at their feet. Otherwise, all is quiet. María sits, searching her daughter's face.

Tica stands, "I thank you, Señor Harker," she says formally. "This could not have been easy for you. You are a true friend to my father and to his family. We have been disgraced. He had no right to court me."

"Señorita, I spoke to him. The love and esteem he felt for you were genuine. He was heartbroken at his family's decision. Of this I am..."

"It is finished. Let us speak of it no more. Excuse me." Tica mounts her horse and rides out of the courtyard.

"God help her," says María.

God help us all, thinks Harker.

Tica has pictured this moment often over the last months, the arrival of news of Juan Carrillo: a letter requesting her hand in marriage, delivered by special messenger, who has been delayed by range fires, or delivered by the hand of Thomas Harker. Lately, she has even imagined the arrival of news of Carrillo's death, killed by a fall from his horse. She has tormented herself with a thousand accidents that might have befallen him, reported to her in pathetic, formal phrases from some relative.

But that he lied to her, that he bought her affection with cheap promises, that he planned to marry another woman all along, she never imagined. She is stunned by his treachery. She rides into the hills nearly blind with bitterness, hating Juan Carrillo as she has never hated another living soul. She has been angered by horses she has broken, frustrated by willful young stallions, even hurt. But she has never allowed them to mislead her. She has been a fool. She gave too much to this shadow of a man without demanding something in return. She entered this affair at a dead run, without looking to the left or right. She has courage enough. What she lacks is caution. Her grandfather would be disgusted with her. Her brother Toño is.

From high above her, an eagle stoops, hurtles from the sky, scaring her horse, causing Tica to duck as if from cannon shot. A crack of wings, a screech on the hillside. The eagle rises again just above her head, slowly, flapping to gain altitude. A rabbit shrieks in its claws. "Stupid rabbit, to be out in the open like that," thinks Tica. "May God forgive me," Escolástica Rodríguez whispers, "for my own stupidity." She will not forgive herself.

By the time Francisco returns with the boys, Tica has disappeared. Francisco explodes at Harker's news, "What? To dishonor our family? To betray our hospitality?" Francisco stomps back and forth across the courtyard until his spurs rattle. "This insult cannot be borne. I will challenge him. Our honor demands it," he roars. "I leave today." Harker and María make no attempt to calm him. They seem relieved to see such a clear-cut reaction after Tica's cold reception of the news. And they seem unanimous in their judgment that Francisco must burn himself out. He fumes, "We must find another husband immediately before it is known that Carrillo is married. We must marry Tica at once, or she will lose face."

"Tica will have many suitors," Harker says.

"Yes, but we need a suitor now."

"She will never allow herself to be married off," María warns. "I fear that in her anger she will plunge into the first love affair that presents itself," she sighs. "Perhaps Francisco is right. Perhaps we should seek to guide her choice."

"Should her choice be Californian? Mexican? American?" Harker asks.

Francisco pauses, "A provocative question, Don Tomás." He stops pacing. He seems to be thinking rationally again, Harker observes with relief.

"Don Tomás, forgive me. You have had nothing to eat or drink. Would you take a chocolate? Francisco?"

"Thank you, Doña María. I left early this morning before my house was stirring...." He blushes. "I did not want to wake my...."

María sighs as she fans the braziers. The blessed saints only knew how she erred when she did not encourage Thomas Harker as a suitor to her daughter. He is a warm, considerate man, a handsome man, with shining eyes.

Francisco sits down and stares moodily at the chamfered arbor posts. "Who will win this California?" he muses. Harker does not reply. The two men sit together on the cedar bench silently sorting through their fears and aspirations.

Harker says at last, "I have spent many hours puzzling this problem, wondering what your father-in-law, Don José Castro, would want for his granddaughter.... What will California bring her generation? I have no answers. I do know that my young partner, Job Dye, loves her."

"Yes?"

"He is mesmerized by her. He is rough-cut, but he is strong and stable and young, and he is succeeding financially. He is committed to a free California, but if the United States takes over, he would be in a position to prosper from the change."

"Job Dye. Yes, I remember. He visited once with you. A quiet man. That is not a bad thing. A cold man? Is he not cold? Could he provide enough affection for a California woman?"

"He is hard, it is true, but he is kind. And the few times I have seen him show real affection have been when he speaks of your daughter. It is difficult to imagine anyone not falling in love with Escolástica," Harker says. "She is enchanting. That is, even as a child..." Harker's voice trails off, and he is glad to see María approach with glasses of chocolate.

But Francisco is not listening attentively. He is concentrating on his remembered impressions of Job Dye. He is a partner of Harker's, a good sign. America certainly seems determined to occupy California permanently. American war ships appear more and more frequently in the bay. Francisco is beginning to think that, if foreign domination is a political necessity, the Americans might be preferable to the Mexicans. Perhaps an American son-in-law would be a diplomatic move, a good face-saving device after Carrillo. Tica could certainly control an American. Perhaps it would be a wise move.

"Job Dye!" gasped María. "Not Job Dye." Torn by consideration for Harker, who is his partner, and revulsion over Job Dye, she says, "Not for Tica. He is too cold."

"Tica is her mother's daughter. She could light a fire in a stone," says Francisco.

"No, Francisco, he is not right for her. He would ruin her. Trust me in this."

"You are too old-fashioned, María. Listen. A new age is dawning. We will need American connections. It might be a shrewd political move."

"Francisco, Don Tomás, she is too... too Californian. She is a *Californiana*. Señor Dye does not want a Californian wife."

"I think he does," says Harker.

"<u>He</u> may think he does," says María, "but he does not. Believe me when I say this." A formless panic wells up in María's throat, leaves her mute. She stands gaping at the men, unable to explain why her instincts tell her, "No. Not Job Dye."

Tica rides into the rancho promptly for the midday meal. She is polite but distant with Harker and brusque toward her father, who nurses his anger and humiliation and mulls over the prospect of Job Dye.

Several times at dinner Francisco attempts to broach the subject, but María and Harker manage to head him off. Finally, as they sit in the courtyard before siesta, Francisco turns to his daughter. "I have invited Señor Harker to visit us with his new wife and his partner Job Dye. Señor Dye has a very good future in California. He is building a grist mill at the Zayante. He will be practically our neighbor."

"I do not like him," says Tica.

"Tica!" Her father is humiliated by her lack of courtesy.

"I beg your pardon, Señor Harker. It will be a pleasure to welcome your wife to California." Tica turns to her father. "I meant only to discourage my father from matchmaking."

Thomas smiles at her quick surmising. "Dye is a fine, serious man," he says, "and he is fascinated by you, Escolástica."

"He is an illiterate boor."

"Tica, enough!" roars Francisco. "See to the chocolate."

"There she has a point," Harker says. "Dye is rough around the edges."

"It will take a strong man to control that little filly. We have been too indulgent with her. She grows unruly."

As Harker lopes away from the rancho, he notices a cloud of dust on the road behind him. He reins his horse in, and Tica, galloping hard, soon catches up to him. Her cheeks are flushed from her ride, and black tendrils of hair trail across her forehead. "Tomás, why do you do this to me?" she demands.

Harker is speechless with her familiarity and her rage.

"Why do you thrust Job Dye upon me?"

"Tica, I want only to see you happy. Please believe me."

Tica sits straight in her saddle. Her green eyes glare. "I will not rush headlong into any more traps, Tomás, even yours. If you love me, you will not do this thing." She wheels her horse, spurs it, and she is gone.

Harker calms his horse and sits watching her dash away through the grasses, fleet as some reckless wind. Why does his heart pound as if she has surprised him at some crime?

I'd been saying all sorts of wild and senseless things, showing without much doubt that I'd lost my mind — and indeed I have been aware, since then, that I'm not always sane, but am sometimes split apart and feeble-brained, and doing a thousand crazy things.

Op. Cit., Vol. 1, Chap.27, pg. 169

RANCHO SAN ANDRÉS
1839

Although Harker puts off their visit to the rancho twice, he can delay it no longer. He and his wife and Job Dye are invited for the late summer roundup, the rodeo on *Rancho San Andrés,* Grandfather Castro's old rancho. It is closer to Monterey. The large two-story house can accommodate guests easily. Francisco Rodríguez insists that they come.

Tica rides down early to help air out the empty house. She follows the road up the ridge to her grandfather's *casa* on the hilltop above the Pájaro River, through her grandmother's herb garden, full of blue-eyed blossoms and honeybees. From the hilltop, she can look out as far as the shell-shaped Bay of Monterey that stretches south to Point Pinos and the town of Monterey, north to Point Soquel and the Santa Cruz. The pepper tree Grandfather imported from Mexico rustles in the breeze off the ocean. A Spanish rose winds up the tall, thin posts in the inner courtyard.[*]

---

[*] The house, much damaged by the Loma Prieta earthquake, is currently being restored with the intention of turning it into a State Historic Park.

Iss-ma and Es-ken still live in one of the outbuildings, cooking for the *vaqueros*, weaving baskets, tending their garden. They are delighted to see Tica. Iss-ma's tanned leathery face cracks into a gap-toothed smile. Es-ken's eyes, black as ticks, shine deep in the folds of her face. Tica dines with them that night on earthy, slightly bitter acorn mush and sweet grilled rabbit meat. It has been years since she has eaten acorn mush. Sitting on a tule mat in their little hut, with her knees drawn up to her chin as the women taught her long ago, she falls under the peaceful spell of Iss-ma and Es-ken and of her grandfather's rancho.

The next day her cousin Rafaela, a new bride and expectant mother, comes to the rancho, and the spell is broken. Full of news and gossip, she giggles and chats from sunup to sundown as they supervise the cleaning and the cooking.

The girls unpack a trunk full of Grandmother's legendary white embroidered bed linens, air out the fine cotton pillow shams and bed covers, admire Grandmother's lovely needlework, remember their grandparents. It is a bittersweet day, filled with happy memories and feelings of loss. It saddens Tica to be in this house without Grandfather. The trunks seem to hold a vanished age, full of tradition and beauty and chivalry.

Rafaela is in full bloom. Her bosom is swollen with her pregnancy, her shape slightly rounded, her cheeks dimpled with smiles. Every other word from her lips is "Ignacio." "Ignacio carved a dear bench for me to nurse the baby." Ignacio says the baby will be a boy."

"And what about Rafaela?" Tica snorts, exasperated by the endless hymns to Ignacio. "What about you, dearest cousin? Have you dissolved completely into this Ignacio? Do you not miss yourself? I do."

But Rafaela looks dreamily at Tica. "You cannot understand, Tica. It is a blessed union, just as Father Antonio promised us."

"*Vamos*," says Tica. "And do not look at me like that, Rafaela." Tica can see in Rafaela's eyes that she suffers for her, worries that she has grown hard, that hate flourishes within her like the poison oak spreading red upon the hillsides. Is Rafaela right? Why does pity so infuriate her? Has her hot blood congealed, exposed to treachery? Has a cold crust formed over her molten core?

It is roundup weather. Fog billows in every night settling the dust, refreshing the air. The mornings are cool and dewy. The days are hot.

The family gathers. The men ride all morning, and the women cook. *Ristras* of chiles and onions hang from the beams above the charcoal grills. A roasting calf turns on the spit, beef steaks sizzle, pink beans with yerba buena and wild onion bubble on the fire. The Castro beans are flavored with smoked bacon, a jealously guarded recipe. When Thomas and Rachel Harker and Job Dye ride onto the rancho, the smells from the cook fires draw them up the hill.

Tica's mother rushes to meet them at the gate and opens her arms to Rachel Harker, leading her to a cool, shuttered upstairs room furnished with a painted bed and table. A white embroidered coverlet decorates the bed, and on the pillows lie bouquets of lavender tied with white ribbon. "The bride's room," María beams at her, and orders fresh water and soft soap scented with geranium brought to the room. María takes stock of Rachel Harker even as she helps her take off her cloak: unwell, unsure, unbeautiful; an orphan calf in need of nurturing.

When Rachel has rested, María ties a clean apron around her and leads her by the hand to the cook fires in the courtyard, where with a smattering of Spanish and English she gaily draws her into the festivities. "We must teach our little Rachel how to cook in California. We will withhold no secrets." She winks and hugs Rachel's shoulders, *"ningún secreto,"* and Rachel is soon tasting and stirring and laughing with the cousins, more at home than she has felt since she arrived in California.

Thomas Harker watches from the pórtico and smiles. The Castro women are superb. The women in town have been stiff and suspicious of an *Americana*, have made fun of her behind her back. Out here on the rancho no such snobbery exists. The graciousness of these California *rancheras* is infectious. The babies smile. The men smile, and no wonder.

Tica is nowhere in the courtyard. She is needed on the roundup. She knows her grandfather's enormous rancho better than most of the men. Harker and Dye ride out to meet the *rancheros*. They spot them by the cloud of dust thrown up in the cattle drive and the bawling of the cows for their displaced calves. The drive began at the Pájaro, one rancho to the south. Now headed north, the *rancheros* are just turning the cattle into Pinto Valley, where the *vaqueros* will keep them grazing for the night. Francisco spurs his horse out of the melee and rides to greet them. Tica rides up, her *sombrero* and divided skirt coated with dust, her face smudged and sweaty, flushed with the excitement of the roundup.

"Oh, dear Señor Harker," she says, "I am glad you come to us. We will meet an American wife at last. Señor Dye, did you bring firecrackers this time, or must we provide all the excitement?" she teases. Her blouse is ripped on one sleeve and has come untied at the neck. Her hair flags wildly behind her. Job takes one look at her in the blazing heat of the day, and his heart pounds. He opens his mouth, but no polite response comes out. Dirty, disheveled, Tica seems to him earthy, almost approachable. This is a woman, he thinks. There's no woman the like of her in all the world.

Francisco welcomes the awkward silence. Harker busies himself filling it. Tica sits her horse, takes in the raw emotion on this young American's face. His desire, mingled with the hot sun and the hard ride of the roundup, intrigues her. She finds herself staring at him shamelessly, and he at her. She is breathless. He is mute. The silence stretches like a *reata* between them.

"Don Francisco," Thomas says, "you are headed back to the rancho now? May we have the honor of accompanying you?"

"With pleasure," says Francisco. "I must only speak to the *vaqueros*. Tica, show the gentlemen the way. I will join you shortly." And he turns back.

"Yes, Father," Tica says. "Follow me, *Señores*." Then over her shoulder to Dye, "if you can." She spurs her horse into a hard gallop. She will show these *Yanquis* how to ride.

Compared to the *Californios*, Job is no horseman, but he has ridden more than most Americans. On his trek out from Kentucky he encountered nearly every breed of Indian pony and kicking mule this wild country offers. And he is in love. Fearlessly, he lashes his new horse, a big sorrel. He leans forward in his saddle. He has no idea how fast his new horse is, but he will run it to its knees in pursuit of Escolástica Rodríguez.

Thomas Harker watches in horror as both horses and riders leap forward, obviously caught up in the race, speeding neck and neck toward the rancho. They'll kill themselves, he thinks, or Dye will anyway. Damned fool. And then he reins his own horse back sharply because he realizes he is jealous.

Tica can't believe her ears when she hears hoof beats behind her. She looks over her shoulder to see Job Dye closing the distance between them, riding like a *garrapata*, a tick, tight to the saddle, stretched low over his horse's neck. "We shall see how good you really are, *Yanqui*," Tica smiles to herself, and she turns her horse down a steep gully at a hard gallop. The horse slides down the gully --Tica gives him full rein -- and skids on his back legs to the bottom. She hears Dye right behind her. She races for Corralitos Creek, over the yellow hills, through the oaks, dodging branches. Job edges up nearly even with her. "I'll get him at the creek. He will not know the ford," she thinks, and presses her gelding forward. He has caught the fever of the race, and surges ahead again. Toward the creek they race, very close together, riding flat out through the wild grasses. Down into the creek they plunge, into the ford, both horses lathered now, both riders soaked from the spray as they splash through the creek bed.

Clattering across the creek, Tica edges Dye's horse out of the middle of the ford toward the bear wallow, and he stumbles on a slippery rock, falls to his knees and throws Dye forward into the water, where he lands face down, motionless.

Tica hears him fall, leaps from her horse and runs to him, where he lies stunned. She kneels in the creek beside him, holds his head up out of the water, murmurs prayers, apologies. "Forgive me, Mother of Mercies, I have sinned. Please save Job Dye from my idiocy."

"Amen," says Job, for when he can focus he sees himself in the arms of Escolástica Rodríguez, her soaked blouse clinging to her breasts, her face close to his, her mouth close enough to kiss.

Tica drops his head into the creek and stands up quickly. "You are either courageous or a fool, Señor Dye. I do not know which."

"*Sí*.... No."

"Can you get up?"

"I don't know," he mumbles.

"Excuse me?"

"Yes, I am good," he says in his terrible Spanish. "Please, pardon me, Señorita Rodríguez. You are wet...saving me."

Tica follows Job Dye's eyes to her breasts, which are startlingly revealed under her wet blouse.

"We must hurry back to the rancho, Señor." Tica turns to her horse.

"Yes, Señorita. I follow." Job gets groggily to his feet, mounts his horse and rides a respectful distance behind Tica while she tugs at her blouse trying to dry it before they reach the rancho. Job's head throbs. He feels a knot beginning to form on his forehead. He is a damned fool. He could have killed himself, and his horse, too. What was he thinking? Sweet Jesus, he was thinking of Escolástica's breasts beneath her wet blouse!

What Harker and Francisco think when they reach the adobe ahead of Tica and Job, they do not say. When both riders arrive wet and disheveled, no notice is taken of them. María, fortunately, has her hands full slipping hot rounds of bread from the oven with her long paddle. Rachel Harker notices Tica's arrival with some relief. Obviously she has been mistaken. She had gotten the impression somehow that Harker was attracted to the Rodríguez girl, but this couldn't be. Tica is a dirty, rumpled tomboy, more interested in horses than husbands. Rachel is beginning to like California.

"Rachel," María calls. "Come, let Tal-ku teach you to make tortillas. You must have a *comal*, seasoned properly. Otherwise you can't cook tortillas. We will find you one. Tal-ku's tortillas are as tender as the wings of the angels." Tal-ku says, "Thin as the wings of the fly," but María spares Rachel that comparison.

As dusk settles around the hilltop, extinguishing the embers of a sunset over Monterey Bay, pine torches blaze, and the family gathers for dinner at long tables in the courtyard. By tradition, Alejandro Rodríguez sits at the south end of one table, as owner of the southernmost land grant, the Bolsa de Pájaro, and Francisco Rodríguez sits at the north end, as owner of the northernmost land grant. The three Castro grants are strung between the two Rodríguez grants, and together they extend from the Pájaro River all along Monterey Bay to Santa Cruz.[*]

Tica wears a turquoise silk dress made from the fabric Harker chose for her. The skirt is short, about six inches off the ground in the *Californio* fashion, and the neck low and round. At her waist she wears a sash of bright green silk embroidered with wildflowers. After the heat of the day, she looks cool and fresh.

---

[*] The land grants are marked today by off-ramps on U.S. Highway One.

She takes Job's breath away. He left home a child of fourteen, and in the ten years it took him to get to California he hardened into a tall, slender young man. He is largely uneducated, nearly illiterate, uncultured, tough. He has survived every peril the West has offered, except for Escolástica Rodríguez.

At first when Job reached the coast he assumed these California women were promiscuous, to be taken as he had taken Indian women on his journey west. He was nearly shot for that presumption. The California women were not available; they were simply gracious. And of all the California women Job has beheld, young Escolástica, with her seal black Spanish hair and her round blue-green eyes, seems to him the most entrancing. Memories arise when he is near her: the youth he left behind in Kentucky, his mother, his younger sister Beth. Tears come to his eyes when he looks at her, though he can't remember when last he cried. What possessed him to chase after her today, to frighten her so? He knows nothing of courtship or chivalry, but he wants Escolástica more than he has ever wanted anything in his life. He wants her so much his stomach knots when he's near her. He finds himself squirming beside her at the table, unable to say a word, unable to eat, cold with fear that he will touch her arm accidentally, hot with desire to brush her leg next to his on the bench.

The conversation proceeds gaily without him. He sips his wine and listens to the chatter, staring sideways at Tica's hands on the table. Occasionally she turns to him during dinner. Job Dye is no longer a buffoon in her eyes. He pursued her like a mad man this afternoon. His savage determination, his power, his courage impressed her. And he is a horseman. She looks at him with a new appreciation, which makes him blush and mumble.

Thomas Harker and Francisco Rodríguez, glancing down the table, cannot tell what has happened between them. María suspects at once and is dismayed by Job Dye's avid silences and Tica's unspoken response. She knows Tica flirts with danger, is attracted to danger. But Tica is too young to understand that there are various shades of danger, that not every peril is a quick flash of fire or hoof or fang that can be parried with skill and daring. "Mother of God," she prays silently as she carves the beef, "allow my daughter the time to ripen." María gazes down at her carving knife. "Allow her to learn that a sharp knife and a quick *reata* do not ward off all the dangers of this world. She is a good child. I beseech you, Mother of Mercies. All she needs is a little time."

The following day, Rachel Harker wakes to her first morning hymn, "Oh beautiful Queen, Princess of Heaven," the traditional hymn to the Virgin, led this day by María, joined in by Francisco, then the sleepy children's voices. The thin melody drifts through the open window of her bedroom, repeated through the house as the family awakens, gathers at the windows and joins in the hymn. The sun rises over the coast range, beckoned by the wavering morning song, and the roosters begin to crow from their perches in the spice-scented pepper tree.

Thomas Harker stays back at the rancho to take his wife out driving in the *carreta*, but Job leaves at dawn with the *rancheros* and works as hard as any man on the drive. Tica is impressed. Even her brother Toño notices Job. *Yanquis* often come for the fiesta, seldom for the work.

Job enjoys the day. When they stop for a cold midday meal along the creek, he sits on the bank, his jacket off, his shirt unbuttoned and collarless, rolled up at the elbows. His fair skin is sunburned and freckled. His blonde hair falls forward across his forehead. He grins like a little boy when Tica brings him a handful of blackberries she has picked along the creek, and he laughs at himself as he tries to pronounce the Spanish name for them: *moritas*. His r sticks to the roof of his mouth, refuses to roll.

"I am a child again," he stammers, and then he blushes at his admission. But he feels as if he has regained his lost youth in this one day. As they ride he thinks, "I could do this work. Would I always be an outsider? Could I fit in?" On the way homeward in the late afternoon, Job catches up with Tica. "Are you able to ride with me to the bay?" he asks. "Please. I desire to see Monterey from here. With the permission of your father. Or perhaps you don't like to go...."

Tica's father thinks the view from this rancho is the best on Monterey Bay. Dye should see it. He himself must go directly home to supervise the *asada*, if Señor Dye will excuse him. Tica looks at her father in amazement. He is suggesting they go alone?

Tica and Job follow the creek down to the broad plain of the Pájaro and lope their horses out along the marshes, feeling the cool breeze off the summer fog as they ride. A white egret tiptoes through the yellow tules. Beach grasses inscribe circles in the fine sand. This is Tica's home, this stretch of beach that forms the western boundary of her grandfather's grant, as familiar to her as her family adobe. What is strange to her is the man who rides beside her -- an *Americano* who is comfortable on a horse, uneasy at the table. A surprising man. A headlong man who hesitates to speak. A savage man who blushes easily. Tica smiles to herself as they ride. She has never seen a man blush as much as this fair-haired American. Every time she looks at him, he turns red as clay. The fog bank stretches all along the horizon, and the sun is setting. Job's emotions are in shambles. Since he was fourteen years old he has been a loner, fighting for his life, with only his wits and his strength and his Kentucky rifle. He has survived by concentrating on the problem at hand. He has never, it seems to him, looked up. Until today. Now, in the presence of Escolástica, he sees everything at once: rose hips red as nipples, baby quail scurrying in the brush, and, as they approach the beach, a low pillow of fog lying out along the horizon and the sun setting above it in gold and turquoise green. It seems to him that all the world clamors around him to be seen and savored. In the center, at the heart of every sight and sound, rides Escolástica, blinding him with her beauty.

He blinks. Trying to clear the commotion in his head, he says, "Tell me, please, of your grandfather's brand, Señorita Escolástica."

Tica smiles. The double V. "The tall inverted V is the *montaña*, Mount San Andrés. The smaller V is the *gavilán*, the hawk. Grandfather used to say that I was his little hawk."

"He was a great man."

"I miss him. He was my *montaña*. I could throw myself to the four winds, because I knew where I was by reckoning my distance to him. Do you understand?"

"I wasn't blessed with that," Job muses in English. "I had to count on my own dead reckoning. It must be something to have such strength back of you."

"I think I understand you, but you are strong, Señor Dye."

"Yes, Señorita, I had to be. But it is a kind of desperate strength, not confidence. Your grandfather knew the difference."

"My grandfather liked you, I think."

"Maybe, but he knew the difference. Señorita Rodríguez...."

"*Sí,?*"

"Could you care for an American in the way you did...?"

"I beg your pardon?"

"That is...." He tries again in Spanish, "I am thinking that...."

"Yes?"

"Could we dismount our horses?"

"It is already late, Señor Dye."

But Job has vaulted to the ground and stands gripping her horse's head, looking desperately at her. "I love you. I've never .... I want you for my wife, I...." He falls to his knees in the sand before her startled horse, who shies and nearly steps on him.

Tica gazes down at Job, kneeling before her, head bowed, like some conquered hero in her grandfather's books. She reaches down and touches his blonde hair. He looks up at her in wonderful surprise, stands, lifts her carefully from her horse, holds her high in the air for an instant, looking up at her; then, lowering her slowly until her boots touch the earth, he kisses her.

The thrill of conquest is not lost on Tica. She has felt such rapture herself for Juan Carrillo. She recognizes the malady. She pities Job Dye. She is also elated to be the object of such hopeless adoration. Giddy with triumph, she appears for supper late, her green eyes shining, her raven hair falling about her shoulders. She has not had time to braid it up. She says little and smiles a good deal, which alarms her mother.

"Why did you allow them to ride off alone together?" María demands.

Francisco throws up his hands. "What can happen on horseback?"

But something definitely has happened. María is sure of it. Job Dye sits across the table from their daughter, a permanent shade of pink on his sunburned face. He never speaks. He never takes his eyes off Tica. After supper María takes advantage of a moment alone with Thomas Harker. "I do not like this, Don Tomás."

"Doña María, are you certain he is wrong for her?"

"I thought him cold." She laughs. "Now it is the heat of his ardor that frightens me. And the reckless speed of this romance. It is driven by Francisco's pride and Job Dye's passion. I fear it will end badly."

Harker sighs. "He walked into our bedroom before dinner reeling like a drunkard, bumping into things. He frightened Rachel."

"You must be certain that he leaves with you tomorrow, Tomás. Francisco will insist that you stay...."

"I understand, Señora."

María slips her arm through Thomas Harker's. "I like your Rachel, Tomás. She will bloom in California."

Thomas sighs, touched by María's warmth, "She feels so welcome here," he says. "You are an amazing woman, Doña María." He looks down at her, and his brown eyes melt.

María laughs and hugs his arm. "Pray God, I am amazing enough to cope with your obsessed friend, my foolish husband, and our headstrong daughter."

Tica sits on a bench in the courtyard with María and Rachel Harker beside her. Her father plays the violin, delighting Rachel with a Mozart sonata. Job's eyes never leave Escolástica. If she walks over to the table for the wine pitcher, his eyes follow her. Her lavender dress is cut low in the bodice, which suddenly seems to her provocative. Job's eyes skim her body, taking in every curve and cleft.

She and her mother have often giggled at the tales of the corseted American women. California women are muscular enough to hold themselves together without the help of some martyred whale. But Tica begins to think that perhaps American women have need of such armor against the ravenous eyes of men like Job Dye. She is beginning to feel as if she doesn't have enough clothes on.

She reaches for her shawl, catching Job's pale eyes as she gathers it around her shoulders, aware that she teases him cruelly, that he longs to place the shawl around her shoulders himself, aches to be that shawl, to bury his head in her bosom. She blinks, shocked at what his eyes say. Embarrassed, she glances around to see if anyone else has noticed Job's eyes. She knows that Thomas Harker watches her. Her mother's eyes meet hers, ominous with warning. This romance is dangerous, her mother seems to say. Dangerous. But it is the danger that so dazzles her.

Job rests precariously that night, balanced on the edge of sleep and frenzied dreams of Escolástica. He wakes exhausted by his passion, which persists unmercifully, jumpy with impatience, itchy with promise.

He has no earthly idea how to go about this, but he wants Escolástica Rodríguez. He has to have her. He bumps into María as he comes into the *sala*, tripping on the high threshold, ducking under the doorway.

"*Buenos días,* Doña Rodríguez. *Perdón.* Fine day, Doña Rodríguez. I want your daughter. In marriage. For a wife...." Job is tongue-tied by the very words. He looks ecstatically at María. "Señora, I love her. *Por favor....*" He follows at María's heels like a puppy.

"Señor Dye, please sit down. Take some chocolate. Now, Señor, one moment. It is the California custom for you to talk to the father, my husband, in such matters." She hesitates. "You are Catholic?"

"I am becoming Catholic right away," says Job, without a moment's hesitation.

In spite of herself, María smiles at the ardent face before her. She sighs, "Señor Dye, what are we to do with you? Do you know what you bargain for if you marry a *Californiana*?"

"I marry no Californian. Please, I marry Escolástica. There is no woman like her in all the world."

"She will be no demure American bride."

"No," is all he hazards. The image of Escolástica as his bride leaves him hoarse, bankrupt of the words in Spanish.

María holds out her hand to him. "Go away, Señor Dye. Come back when you are a Catholic."

He takes her hand and bows his blonde head before her as if she has set him upon the labors of Hercules. His bangs fall forward. "I come again, Doña María."

"This I believe, Señor Dye," says María grimly.

That day the rancho celebrates the end of rodeo and the feast day celebrating the Nativity of the Virgin Mary, María's patron saint. Padre Francisco rides down from Santa Cruz to say Mass and bless the rancho. After the blessing, the whole rancho gathers at the round corral below the *casa* to celebrate the day with a bear and bull fight, the last of the year along the Santa Cruz.

Tica is thrilled by these battles. The courage, the fury, the force of these two beasts pitted in savage combat makes her grip the corral railing in terror and admiration.

"I can never decide whom to pray for," she tells Job.

"I am always for the bull," says Toño.

María refuses to let any of her children ride in the corral with the bear, so they are all forced to hug the high rails and watch the drama from the outside. Job stands at the fence beside Tica, scarcely aware that anything is happening inside the corral.

The *vaqueros* drive a huge bull into the corral. He is as dark as burnt charcoal, nearly black, with wide vicious horns. The *vaqueros* finally succeed in throwing him and tying a heavy braided *reata* to his left foreleg. The other end of the *reata* is tied to the right front paw of the mammoth grizzly bear, caught the night before and tied by all four feet to a heavy *carreta* in the corral. He lies like a mountain, very still.

The crowd grows as the *vaqueros* work the wild bull. Many neighbors and cousins have arrived, noisily greeting one another from their horses. Now a silence sweeps over the corral. Even the horses seem to watch as the *vaqueros* back off slowly, cautiously, and at a hand signal from the head *vaquero*, release in perfect synchrony all the tie ropes that hold the two animals down. Tica catches her breath. The crowd has forced Tica to move closer to Job along the fence. Job nearly stops breathing altogether.

The bear and the bull lunge to their feet and face one another, tethered together by the heavy *reata*, pawing the ground, snorting. The bull strikes first. Digging his back hooves in, he charges like a zealot, a blind, furious, mindless onslaught in the haze and heat of the corral. But the bear flattens his enormous bulk just as the bull reaches him, and the bull flies over his mark. The crowd roars in approval. Tica shrieks and grabs Job's arm. This is a noble bull, a sly deceptive bear, a mean bear.

Again and again the bull charges, and the bear flattens himself in the dirt, forcing the bull over him in a cloud of dust. The bull backs off quivering and, with head down, prepares to make a final thrust. Suddenly the bear springs up and roars, leaps at the bull, fastens his teeth on the bull's nose and smothers him in the grip of his bloody front claws. The bull sinks in an instant, bawling and writhing.

Since the bull has fought valorously, the crowd yells for mercy. The bear is pried off and his victim turned loose, but flesh hangs in shreds from the bull's mauled face and his tongue has been nearly torn out. He has to be killed. Rachel Harker, standing on the other side of Tica at the rail, falls over in a dead faint. Tica and her mother help Thomas get her back to the house.

"She became too excited," Tica says. "It was her first bear and bull fight. Was it not a thrilling one, Don Tomás?"

Rachel moans.

By the time Tica races back down to the corral, a second bull has been brought in, a smaller, wiry one with a wicked twist in his left horn. The grizzly, confident after his last victory, rears on his hind legs to meet the new bull, a wall of pure rage, his huge arms stretched out, his long claws bloody from his last battle. He roars. But the new bull, without even stopping to paw the dirt, charges forward, rams his horns into the bear's belly. Quick and agile, the bull presses forward, thrusts again, both horns so deep into the breast of the bear that he collapses, pulling the bull down under him, and dies.

Tica and Toño cheer the bull wildly. Job, who has been looking at Escolástica, finally notices the bull's victory in the haze of dust. The horns have to be pulled out of the bear's chest but the curve in the left one keeps working in deeper every time the bull attempts to free himself. Finally, the wild bull is set loose and he trots off amidst great applause.

Rachel Harker, although she remains very pale, is well enough to leave that afternoon. Job Dye says it's the best bear and bull fight he's ever seen. He doesn't mention that it is the only one.

"Be quiet, Sancho," said Don Quijote. "They may look like flour mills, but that's not what they are. Haven't I told you that these magicians change everything and make it look like something else?"

Op. Cit., Vol.2, Chap. 29, pg. 504

RANCHO ARROYO DEL RODEO
1839

Zayante Creek, where Job Dye has built his grist mill and distillery, is north of Santa Cruz, a short half-day's ride from *Rancho Arroyo del Rodeo*. María Rodríguez has many occasions to wish it were farther away. Every time she looks up, she seems to find Job standing shyly at the gate, as he is now, bearing a sack of freshly ground wheat flour to Tal-ku, or a woven basket of corn meal.

She is growing nearly fond of him. She watches him look over at Tica the way California children look at snowflakes. But to admire a snowflake is not to live in snow-bound mountains. Tica pretends to ignore him, continues to read as he sits beside her, watching her. Does Tica love him? María has her doubts. The uneducated mountain trapper cannot share Tica's thirst for literature or music. He may never sketch with her or appreciate her paintings or learn to identify the wildflowers she draws. His Spanish is so rough that they speak English most of the time. Still, many good marriages have been founded on more substantial grounds than romance.

María studies their profiles as they sit side by side on the bench in the courtyard: fiery Tica, her hair the glossy black of madrone coals, her cheeks burning, her face ever changing. Laughter, anger, tenderness, excitement flicker in her green eyes, even as she reads. Job says something to her, something short and careful. Flinty Job Dye -- a still, sharp-chiseled face, hard to anger, slow to smile. His shock of fine blonde hair and his freckled skin suggest boyishness, but his strong, taut body and his glinting eyes are ice-hard. Tica looks up at him and laughs. Job seems to edge toward her, as if warming his hands. Then he straightens his back, looks away.

Is Francisco right? California is certainly changing. Their sons and daughters will live different lives than she and Francisco have had. Her own hardships on the rancho were offset by the strong, simple pattern of her life -- hand-ground corn, hand-woven shirts, homemade pleasures. Now the pattern grows more complex. Civilization crowds into the California ports, lured by hides and pelts. Her children will embrace a richer life, but also a more tangled one.

And there is about Job, skinny and blond and shy as he is, an undercurrent of power, the power of the flash flood, the power of the rogue wave. There is something about Job Dye that cries out to be tamed.

Californian lives follow the relentless seasons of the cattle. Raising cattle calls for great patience, slow-moving days, persistence. The lazy summer grazing times on which the cattle thrive and fatten stretch out between short, intense periods of birthing and roundup and branding in the spring; round up and slaughter in the fall. The *matanza*, the killing time, is the most hectic season of the year on the rancho.

The *vaqueros* rise with the morning hymn and leave at first light in a vain attempt to beat the heat and the meat wasps, but by the time the sun mounts the hilltops, a cloud of smoke and dust and the stench of tallow hangs around them. Tica wheels back and forth, cutting the cattle into the arroyo to be killed or sending them out to range again. The other *vaqueros* work a steer past her while Tica shrewdly assesses his condition, his age, the sleekness of his coat, the fullness of the hindquarters. A split-second judgment then a shout, "He goes!" and she spurs forward on her black gelding forcing one steer to veer off, crowding the next steer off toward the arroyo, she and her horse turning in a single motion.

Job works with the *vaqueros*, driving the cattle past Escolástica. Work is something he can do. Cattle, he figures, he can learn. His fellow Americans speak of the indolence of the *Californios*. He doubts they've ever seen a *matanza*. Tica's brother Toño has been thrown and is still recovering from a broken arm, so Job's extra help is welcome. Francisco gives him three horses for his exclusive use, just as the other *vaqueros* have.

A wail, then a bawl goes up from the arroyo as a steer is dragged down and Francisco leaps forward to slit its throat. The other cattle, spooked by the cries of the slaughtered animal, mill and break away toward the edges of the arroyo. Jesús and another young *vaquero* pounce on the butchered steer, gut it deftly, rush to skin it while the carcass is still fresh and the hide pulls easily. Torn hides are worthless.

The *vaqueros* squat in the dirt, sweat running down their blood-smeared faces. They work from the hindquarters forward, flipping the carcass, their sharp knives scraping every shred of meat as they creep forward. A carelessly skinned hide will rot. They finish one carcass and spring to the next.

Two older *vaqueros* take charge of the skinned carcasses, separating the coarse *sebo* fat from the delicate *manteca,* the layer of fat closest to the hide, and rendering the fats in great iron try pots. The best beef, the meat of the *terneras*, is butchered and taken to the smoke fires, where Gabriel takes charge of jerking and drying it. Other *vaqueros* lasso the butchered carcasses by the horns and drag them away from the arroyo as quickly as they can to keep the grizzlies and the buzzards at bay. However, nothing can stop the meat wasps, who attack mercilessly, or the brazen eagles, who swoop down and carry meat right off the smoke fires.

By midday the sun is scorching, the dust suffocating. No drop of rain has fallen since the beginning of June, and it is now the first of October. Tica wears a *pañuelo* tied across her face. Sweat trickles down her temples. Job watches her work the cattle, She's hot and dirty; she's irresistible. Francisco has promised that their betrothal will be announced at the fiesta at the end of the *matanza* if Escolástica accepts him. He works as one possessed. It seems to him the *matanza* will never end.

By evening they are all stiff and sore and blood-smeared. The stench of slaughter and rendered tallow clings to their hair, their clothes, their skin. They ride home together from the arroyo well after sunset, too tired to speak, nearly asleep in their saddles. Job grabs Tica's rein and holds her horse back until the rest of the riders round a turn in the trail. Tica suspects that her father winks at their truancy. She knows her brothers have noticed Job grabbing her horse's head. He scarcely waits until the other riders are out of sight before he pulls her off her horse into his arms, tears the *pañuelo* from her neck, covers her neck and her face with kisses. Tica laughs softly, feebly pushes him away.

"I am filthy," she murmurs. But she is as impatient as Job. This tongue-tied American who cannot keep his hands off her is exciting. She reaches up and pulls his face to hers, kisses him, looks into his pale, astonished eyes and kisses him again, presses against him until she can feel his body pulsing against hers.

"Stop that," he says, emboldened. "You are too tempting, you sinner, you." Then he picks her up and carries her off the trail into the redwoods, lays her down in the deep duff. The redwoods tower above her. This fierce young man bends over her, tugging at her blouse. She feels her breasts swell to his touch. She shoves him away, covering his hands with kisses. She must not let her heart run away with her again, but still she aches to have him.

"Marry me, Tica," he begs. "Marry me."

"Yes, yes." She turns away from him.

As she sits silently at the table that night, exhausted by her long day in the saddle, feeling Job's thigh close to hers on the bench, Tica wants him to gather her up and carry her off to bed. It seems to both of them that the *matanza* is overlong.

The last day of the *matanza* Job gallops off to Santa Cruz, promising to return by sundown. He races into the rancho just as the riders return for the evening. The *Costeñan vaqueros* haul the empty lard pot with them, jolting along in the back of a *carreta*. They will feast tomorrow on their favorite soup of acorns and meat scraps cooked in the last lard drippings.

Job is full of news. "I am finished with my instruction. Father Antonio says I take communion next Sunday at the mission. And I have bought us a house in Santa Cruz."

"In the pueblo? A town house?" exclaims Tica. "Job, I will live at the mill."

"The mill is no good for a wife."

"You live there. You work there. I want to be with you."

"It is not an hour's ride from the mill to town. I will be home every night."

"But I will be alone every day," cries Tica. "I will never see you. I won't be able to help you."

"You aren't my miller," Job says, lapsing into exasperated English. "You're my wife. You don't need to help me at the Zayante."

"But I desire to."

"Escolástica, the Americans who live out at the Zayante are a rough crowd. I can't let you live out there with them. I wouldn't trust such men with you for a minute."

"What? Would you not trust me?"

Job draws her toward him. "I wouldn't trust them." He holds her close to him, kisses the top of her hair. "No one could resist you."

"Do not joke, Job. I will not sit home and make lace. I am a *ranchera*. I have never lived in a pueblo. I need more room than that. I will suffocate in a town."

"How do you know? You haven't ever lived in one. You'll find women to keep you company."

"I don't want women. I want you."

"Alberto Robles is carving us a bed of solid oak, a grand bed with high posts..." Job chatters on about the house, about the bed and the table he has ordered; like a blind man, he cannot see her face, cannot see the shadow passing over her, much as the shadow of a cloud passes over the ground casting a momentary chill.

Tica retreats to the kitchen fires where her mother chops a mountain of red chile peppers for the salsa. Tomorrow they will celebrate the end of the *matanza*, with a roasted beef and dancing.

"Mamá," Tica frets, "I'm afraid he doesn't really want a *Californiana*."

"Tica, stir the beans, my love, and add more lard. I smell them scorching. He chooses to live in California, does he not? What else would he have for a wife?"

"He talks about towns and mills. He buys land in town. Why would he not look for a rancho? He says he needs capital. Did Father and Grandfather have capital?"

María straightens up and tastes the spoonful of beans her daughter holds out for her. She pats Tica's shoulder. She worries for her daughter without knowing why. "Be patient with him," she says. "He is headstrong. He is a colt. But he loves you, Tica. He may see the future of California better than we do."

Tica stirs the beans and sighs. "Sometimes I think he doesn't see California at all. Sometimes I think he just sees Kentucky with a coastline."

Women are made of glass
But no one needs to know
If they'll crack or if they'll smash,
For anything can be so.

Op., Cit., Vol. 1, Chap. 33, pg. 213

RANCHO ARROYO DEL RODEO
1839

On a gray morning, November 18, 1839, Tica fords the Río San Lorenzo on her black gelding *El Chocolate* and climbs the steep bluff to the Mission Santa Cruz. The river is in flood from the unusually early rains, and her brothers have risen at dawn to drive three *manadas* of horses across the ford to trample the river bottom and make it safe for the wedding guests. Her godfather, Rafael Castro, rides beside her on a matched black gelding. Both horses are cloaked in black and silver oversaddles and ties. The family stands already assembled at the church waiting for them, and Job gasps when they appear out of the mist and climb the hill toward the mission. According to custom, Tica wears a black velvet gown, embroidered with silver, that hangs a foot below her stirrup. Her rich hair is wound up on her head, crowned with silver combs. On her midnight gelding, she is a bolt of black lightning, slicing the storm clouds on the hill.

After Padre Francisco hears her confession, she retires to the vestry, and Job presents the priest with the dowry of thirteen gold coins and two wedding bands for his blessing. It's a lot of money, but it seems to him a small price to pay when Tica reappears at the altar rail transformed in white peau de soie, her grandmother's embroidered white silk wedding shawl over her shoulders, a long lace mantilla falling about her like new snow.

Padre Francisco marries them at midday in the glow of a hundred elk tallow candles sent from *Rancho Arroyo del Rodeo* for the occasion. Never has Escolástica looked so exquisite to Job, or so unapproachable. The statue of the Virgin Mary above them on the altar seems to him more accessible than this slender child kneeling beside him, holding a lighted candle, her green eyes wide with fright. She looks up at him like a wild creature of the redwoods caught in one of his traps, snagged in a net of white lace. He feels splintered, rough beside her. How can he expect such a finely wrought creature to be happy with a crass, clumsy hick like himself? He is as filled with dread as she.

At the conclusion of the Mass, Padre Francisco gives Tica an abalone shell filled with Job's thirteen gold coins. Tica gathers them up and scatters them at the foot of the altar. Job clutches her arm in horror. What is she doing? Does she reject him? Does she not understand how much money this is?

"But that is the custom, Job," Tica whispers. "I offer them to Holy Mother Church."

"And she blesses you for it," cuts in Padre Francisco quickly. "And I bless you and your marriage in God's name."

The mission bell rings out, an ancient doleful sound that reminds Tica of Grandmother Castro who was godmother to the somber Santa Cruz bell. Now it tolls her granddaughter's marriage.

At *Rancho Arroyo del Rodeo* the wedding guests, swathed in elegant black serapes trimmed with velvet and silver braid, sit their horses in the courtyard waiting for the traditional invitation to dismount. María and Tal-ku have wound redwood garlands around the porch posts and built arbors of redwood boughs tied with milkweed string.

The smell of a rich beef *estofado* braised in two fires with onions and oregano wafts from the *cocina*. Another stew of pumpkin and dried corn bubbles beside it, and Tal-ku turns a succulent veal *ternera* on a spit.

Castros and Rodríguezes have gathered from up and down the coast, and the brandy begins to flow before the riders have dismounted. Lengthy toasts are offered and returned. The Castro cousins unstrap violins and guitars from their saddles and begin to play. Bonfires and torches keep the patio warm, and the dancers are soon shedding shawls and serapes. More toasts are proposed. More food is brought out to fill the trestle tables under the redwood arbors – soft, runny cheeses, crispy cakes of salt cod, platters of beef and roasted geese.

The Harkers have come from Monterey for the occasion, although Rachel Harker is in the fifth month of pregnancy and looks puffy and unwell. Tica recoils at the sight of her. Tica's beloved cousin Rafaela has just died giving birth to her first child.

All day long, black rain clouds have loomed over the western sea, threatening the ceremony. They break at last in the evening over the rancho, causing a deluge that floods the courtyard and sends the guests scurrying.

Job is secretly delighted to have the festivities cut short. He has seen these wedding feasts rage on for days. But when the time comes for them to leave, he cannot find Escolástica. María misses her before Job does, and is frantically searching the crowded house, interrupted at every doorway by a cousin or a nephew.

"Tomás," María says when she meets Thomas Harker in the *pasillo*, "we have trouble. She has disappeared."

Harker feels at once the wintry foreboding that fills María's voice. He presses María's hand without a word and goes off in search of Tica.

Farther along the *pasillo* he runs into Job plowing desperately through the guests. "Thomas, I've lost Tica. I can't find her anywhere."

"It's all right, Job. She's here, I'm sure. We'll find her."

"Thomas, I.... I don't know too much about this business."

"What business?" Thomas looks at him: he is white as blubber.

"This marriage business. I don't want to hurt her. I'm afraid I'll harm her some way. I don't know much about women. I love her so..."

"Look, Job, this is no time...." Harker says crossly. "Just be gentle with her. Give her time. We'll find her." Harker watches Job wander off like some stray dog, then heads out toward the dairy, irritated for no good reason.

Toño heads straight for the room where Grandfather's books are stored. Certainly he will find Tica there. He pauses outside the door, and although no sound comes from the room, he knows that she kneels before the chest.

"It is I, Toño. Do not cry."

The rawhide latch is unfastened. He opens the door.

"What am I to do?"

Toño latches the door behind him, and she buries her head on his chest. He looks down at her nestled against him, hiding in his arms, his big sister, and feels his heart might crack. He pats her head until the sobbing ceases and she is still.

"Come, Tica, it is time."

"I know."

"Do not be afraid."

"It is worse than fear, Toño. It is despair."

"Take a book with you for company, Tica." Toño selects a slender volume from the chest, touches his lips to it, and holds it out to her.

She clutches the book tightly, straightens her back. "I wish his name were not <u>Dye</u>," she says, "*Morir*," and she walks quietly down the *pasillo* to the main *sala*.

For opportunity is the best agent love can have, in fulfilling its desires: it makes constant use of opportunity, particularly when it first begins to work.

Op. Cit., Vol. 1, Chap. 34, pg. 224

THE SANTA CRUZ
1840

In the winter of 1840, nature seems intent upon washing away every human trace from the shores of California. Once begun, the rains pelt the coast until after Christmas. The rivers and creeks flood; bridges and fords wash out. Job's mill is forced to remain idle until the floods recede, so he tarries in Santa Cruz devoting the short rainy days and long stormy nights to his new bride.

Their adobe house stands across the plaza from the mission. Their covered porch faces east across the muddy square toward the mission church where they were married. The walled garden behind their adobe looks straight out to sea. Job has added a fireplace to their cottage in the American style, and a tiny room and kitchen for Tal-ku, who appeared one morning and joined in the hymn from their patio, surrounded by her nets and baskets. "That is no way to make chocolate," she told Tica, and took the muddler from her. No one knows who sent her.

Tal-ku's parents were mission neophytes at Santa Cruz. She was born at the mission, but she won't go near the church and refuses to talk about that time, except to say that her grandmother took her away from there during the great sickness. Whenever she sees the mission priest, Tal-ku's eyes grow narrow and lidded under her straight bangs, and she spits.

Isolated by the fury of the storms, the newlyweds cling together in their damp house and cautiously explore their marriage. Job spends part of every morning splitting the oak logs he has hauled down from the hills. A skilled woodcarver, he delights Tica by carving hooks and shelves and plate racks and a chunky Saint Francis from the soft coast redwood.

Tica relishes the subtle power she holds over Job. She toys with him when they are alone, flipping her skirt up above her knee to button her boot, bending toward him in her chemise to reveal her bosom. She watches his breath catch in his throat at the sight of her, watches his eyes grow hungry. He buries his passion deep, as if fearing discovery, but he is a passionate man, this Job Dye.

Early one morning in January, Job rises early and makes a fire in the fireplace. He comes back to bed bearing a steaming cup of chocolate from Tal-ku. Tica sits up in bed wrapped in warm quilts and coverlets, her hair falling in tangles about her shoulders, caught in the lace of her nightdress. Job sits beside her, sipping his chocolate, looking at her, soft and sleepy beside him.

At first Tica thinks it is the weight of Job on their bed that tips her chocolate cup. Then the books on the wall shelf topple, the floor beneath them wells up, and they bob helplessly on their bed as if they have set out to sea. Outside, a sheep bawls. Dust billows out of the adobe walls. A discordant clang, the clatter of collapsing bricks fills the air. Through the earthquake, Tica and Job cling to the rails of their bed staring blankly at one another.

"Quickly," whispers Tica, "the aftershock, the wave…." She leaps out of bed to dress, in her haste dropping her nightgown, and Job sees her as he has never seen her before. She stands for a moment revealed to him completely in daylight, swelling white breasts, tongue-pink nipples, round hips, a profusion of black hair, and as he reaches out and touches her thigh and draws her towards him, never taking his eyes off her, he knows he will always think of her body in a bright cloud with the earth shaking under him.

Later, when Tica has dressed, they venture out together into the plaza to find that the town has toppled down around them. Tal-ku seems surprisingly unperturbed.

"It is *I-men*," Tal-ku says and shrugs. "The air smelled of *I-men*."

The tower of the mission church has crumbled. Tal-ku seems to be satisfied about that. Grandmother's bell has come down. Garden walls have fallen; roof tiles lie strewn around every building like confetti after a dance. Horses and sheep have broken loose and roam the streets. Dogs howl. The citizens wander in a suspended state of shock. No one has been hurt, it seems; one *Costeño* was knocked down by falling plaster.

Padre Francisco had been about to see to the ringing of the mission bells, but he had been late as usual. All were safe. The blessed saints be thanked.

The populace drifts toward the beach, mindful of the tidal wave that might follow. The men drag the small dinghies farther up the beach and remove a few tools from the hide houses, but there is little else they can do. The spontaneous gathering is rocked by frequent after-shocks, an occasion for old women to cross themselves and say a prayer and for old men to pour a little *aguardiente*. Stories begin that will be embellished further as the day wears on, of near misses and cracking walls. The Buelna sow gave birth to a litter of ten piglets in her panic. Tía Isidora was trapped in her bedroom and had to crawl out the window in her nightgown.

Job chats with his neighbors, laughs out loud, giddy with excitement.

"Too much *aguardiente*?" Tica asks. But she thinks it is not the *aguardiente*.

Tica knows within days that she is pregnant. Her breasts awaken, her nipples prickle, her stomach turns capricious. Her body stirs itself, and she observes her own belly with the amazement of a foreigner. She speaks to no one of this, but Tal-ku, part weed, part witch, will guess soon enough. She reads Tica as she reads bird tracks in the dust.

Job will be proud, shyer with her, perhaps, more timid. The passion she sees sunken deep in his eyes is already difficult to coax to the surface. She sometimes misses the *desespercido* who dragged her from her saddle during the *matanza*. He seems to think wives are more fragile than other women, to be put in the little redwood niches he carves for her. The saints only know what he thinks of mothers! Still, he will be pleased and proud, and she must tell him.

Why then does she sit in the window looking smugly at her own belly, giving no sign? Why does she wake in the night, full of dread, not knowing where she is, and then rub her own stomach like a talisman until she falls asleep again?

She goes often across the plaza to the ruined mission church to pray for her child. Although the mission has been stripped of its lands and its power five years earlier, Padre Francisco stays on, a lecherous old drunk now, who slurs his Latin and slobbers salsa on his robes. Mercifully, he prefers the rectory to the chapel, and the heels of Tica's boots tap an unechoed beat in the long, empty aisle. The vaulted ceiling is high, pale blue, the blue of the first spring sky, and the walls are white as foam. A sea green plaster wainscoting tipped with golden waves runs around the narrow chapel, and although the waves are chipped and cracked, Tica feels, when she kneels at the communion rail, as if she is sinking into the sea.

In the left niche, surrounded by bright, childlike paintings - wild roses and baby blue eyes and yellow sand verbena - stands *La Purísima*, a statue of the Virgin brought from Mexico by Padre Junípero Serra. The young Virgin stands bareheaded, smiling down at Tica, and Tica knows they share the secret of Tica's child. This Virgin is no queen of heaven, dressed in brocade and gold lace. This is a simple country girl.

Her bare feet touch the earth. Tica never tires of visiting the humble little statue robed in blue and gold.*

It is Tica's first lesson in concealment. She never noticed before how secretive the Virgin looks, how smug, as she clasps her hands over her swollen belly with a proprietary smile. This is her child she carries, she seems to say; and so long as her pregnancy lasts, it is hers alone.

Job stoops over his workbench in the courtyard. He has bought a new chisel so that he can carve a shallow pattern of oak leaves into a bench he is making for Escolástica. Slowly, carefully he pushes down on the chisel, brushing away the curls of redwood, so that he can see the outline of his pattern emerging. Tica might be beginning to love him a little, he thinks. Job is ignorant of love. He tries to remember how his Ma was with his Pa, but his Pa died too young, and his memories of his mother are of her bent over, with her back to him, over a stove, over a washtub, over a sick younger child. He can never see her face.

He strokes the deep red heartwood of the bench, musing. There are small signs. At first Tica fled the room when he shaved, repulsed by

---

* She can still be visited today in the mission chapel.

the sight of his bare chest. Now she seems calm. He has been patient with her, gentle. He wants her to love him as much as he loves her. A good hunter sits still and waits for the game to come to him. He is a crack hunter. He waits for her. He watches her. He asks her to read to him out loud because he knows she loves to read. He brings out her sketch pad and poses for her so that she can draw his likeness because she is a natural artist.

He sighs and looks across the courtyard into the shadows. Sometimes he hears her chatting gaily with Tal-ku in the kitchen, and he feels more lonely than he ever felt in the deserts of the Río del Norte. With him, she has grown quiet. Some of the wild spirit has died down in her. A good thing in a wife, he thinks, or he hopes it is a good thing. He is ignorant of wives. He hopes that she is pregnant. A child would bind her to him. He hopes she will love him. He is so ignorant of love.

Late in the afternoon of April 23, 1840, a dust-smudged *Costeño* child races up to the kitchen door, frightened, out of breath. Tal-ku listens to the news he brings, gives him bread, wipes his face, and leads him in to Tica, who sits reading in the failing afternoon light.

"Your husband sends me from the mill," the child gasps. "The soldiers have taken him. They have taken all *Yanquis*. He tells you to return to the house of your father."

"What soldiers?" demands Tica.

"Big soldiers. With guns," stammers the boy. "On fat horses."

"What language did they speak, *tontito*? Did they speak Spanish? English? Which way did they go?"

"They spoke like you, Señora."

"God be thanked then. Tal-ku, see that *El Chocolate* is saddled at once."

"Señora, you cannot ride. In your condition, it is better to walk."

"Never mind my condition," snaps Tica, furious that Tal-ku knows already of her pregnancy.

She strides down the street to the local garrison in town, but the comandante knows as little as she.

"The orders came from Monterey," he says, flustered by her fury. "The prisoners will probably be taken there. It is rumored that a priest heard something in confession, a plot to kill all Mexicans...."

Señora, I apologize for your husband's arrest. Perhaps it was a necessary precaution. These *Americanos*..."

"You would deprive my future child of his father? You would steal the father of a Castro-Rodríguez?" thunders Tica. "Do not mumble to me of *Americanos*. I go to Monterey."

The following day Escolástica Rodríguez de Dye rides at the head of an impressive procession into Monterey. Her father, Francisco Rodríguez, and her uncle, Rafael Castro, ride beside her. Her brothers and nine of the cousins collected from the family ranchos they passed on their route south follow in splendid array.

The Castro men are unusually tall. They sit erect in their saddles, their dark hair braided down their backs, their stiff black hats straight across their brows. They look neither left nor right. They wear their best black jackets trimmed in silver, and the sashes at their waists are crimson silk. Their horses' harness shines with silver, their spiked spurs rattle. They have dressed for effect. The Castro horses are famous. This day the family rides bays that look nearly matched, with flowing black manes and tails. These are doubtless the horses of San Andrés, the southernmost Castro rancho on the way to Monterey. Every head turns as they lope along the *Camino del Pueblo de San José*, passing directly through town without pausing to greet friends or rest their mounts, and up the hill to the fort.

The comandante watches their approach with dread. They carry swords. They mean business. His dozen soldiers are a mangey lot of half-starved conscripts. They are no match for the horsemen headed up the hill. He guesses that if there were violence, the entire town would rise against him and his soldiers.

Job sees them over the low wall of the battlements, where the prisoners are being held. There is not enough room inside the tiny fortress. Escolástica looks so magnificent at the head of the horsemen that he is left breathless, his heart throbbing. She wears her black velvet wedding suit. She rides forward.

"With respect, Comandante, there has been some mistake," she says without dismounting her horse. "You hold hostage my husband, a Catholic, father of my child."

She sits iron straight in her saddle, wearing a flat brimmed black hat, borrowed from her brother probably, but black curls have escaped around her face. Her jet earrings flash when she turns her head to look at Job. "You hold the father of a Castro-Rodríguez," she repeats in a clear, firm voice. "You will do me the courtesy of releasing him."

And that is the first word Job hears about Tica's pregnancy.

The flustered comandante bustles up to the horsemen and bows, "Greetings, Señora Rodríguez de Dye. My compliments to your esteemed family. Would you honor me by dismounting and coming into my rooms for refreshment after your long journey?"

"Thank you, Comandante, we will remain where we are until my husband is released."

And Tica sits her horse for six hours, refusing refreshment or rest despite Rachel Harker's pleading and her father's offer to stand in her stead, until at dusk a frantic comandante, acting without authority, releases Job Dye.

"May God protect me from my foolhardiness," the old soldier moans, and Tica and Job retire for the night to the Harkers.

Tica's bones ache. She had not realized how tender she had become, living in town. She needs Job and Toño to help her dismount. Her face is ashen with fatigue. Job, in spite of his own exhaustion, is frightened by her pallor and hovers over her, fumbling to help her undress, tearing the bed apart in an effort to turn down the sheets and blankets for her, until she laughs wearily at him.

"You are a clumsy nurse, my husband. I must watch you or you will drop our infant child."

"Oh, no," he kneels by the bed, presses his forehead against her hand. "Please, oh, no, never..." And he kisses her fingers tenderly.

After Tica retires, the talk is serious. Job's mill at Zayante has been confiscated by the Mexican government. His house in Santa Cruz has been taken. Tal-ku barely had time to pack a trunk and hide it in the hen house before the soldiers rousted her out. There seems little chance that the government will restore the properties to Job Dye.

The political turmoil is such that Harker fears there will be no peaceful settlement: "Graham's band of American riflemen are harassing families along the coast, and only a month ago he barged into the governor's chambers right here in Monterey shouting insults. No wonder so many Americans were rounded up."

111

"This new republic of Texas has had a bad effect on these American bandidos," Job says, "and on Washington, too, probably. It is a dangerous time to be an American."

"And Governor Alvarado is no administrator," sighs Rafael Castro. "He drinks and dallies with the ravishing Raimunda instead of seizing the reins of his drifting government."

Rachel Harker appears in the room with more coffee. "Shocking," she mutters. "He publicly flaunts that horrible woman in front of his wife, your niece, Don Rafael. Disgusting."

The men squirm in their chairs. They all know Raimunda Castillo. It was unkind of God to make a woman so beautiful.; it was too great a temptation. Why Alvarado had not married her, they could not imagine. Had she not given him three daughters already?

They should never have arranged for Tica's cousin, merry little Antonia Castro, to marry him. She had certainly resisted. "He is not a man," she wailed when she saw him, "He is a walrus."

"These *Americanos* are jumping from the woodwork, like fleas, Tomás," Francisco Rodríguez says. "They are everywhere."

Harker turns to Job. "You must come to Monterey. Business is booming here. I could use help. You would be safe.... When is the child ahhh...expected?"

Harker colors at so indelicate a subject. And Job blushes even deeper. He has no idea.

Job is proud if embarrassed, but Tica wears her pregnancy like a military medal. She walks out more; she rides. Everybody in Monterey comments upon her swelling belly, pats her stomach, smiles on her.

"Seems like this child belongs to all Monterey," Job mutters. "These *Californios* show no modesty at all."

While they stay at the Harkers', Job hunts for a house of their own. Tica finds it, a little adobe cottage down the street from the Harkers, the property of Tica's Bonifacio aunts. Job was told it was not for sale. Tica takes the two old maids a basket of fresh sardines, shows them her rounded belly, and the house is theirs. But there is no deed. Does Job own it or not?

The local carpenter refuses to use nails to repair the leaking roof. Nails will rust. He advises rawhide thongs. He speaks no English, so he addresses this to Tica, ignoring Job. His own house!

Frustrated, Job nearly shanghais a carpenter off one of the American ships in port, offering him double pay, and the two Americans hammer from first light to dusk, replacing rotted beams and patching the shingled roof of the little adobe cottage while the neighbors shake their heads: "Nails will rust. He should use tile on the roof instead of shingles."*

Before he can finish the house, Tica announces that she and Tal-ku must return to her father's rancho for the birth. If Job felt estranged by Tica's pregnancy, he feels utterly ostracized at the birth of his first child. Word is sent to him when Tica goes into labor. But when he arrives, having ridden half the night, nearly killing his horse to reach her, his way is barred by Tal-ku. Tica's mother and her Tía Martina attend her, along with Tal-ku. Job sits for an entire day on a hard bench outside the bedroom, feeling like a damned fool, angry that his mother-in-law seems to think this birth is none of his affair, hurt that Tica has not demanded to see him, yet afraid that he may be called upon to help in some way.

His father-in-law finally takes pity on him. Francisco gets out his pear brandy. "Ay, yes," he says, "I had forgotten." He rummages in a cupboard for two cups. "The child may be yours..." Job reacts as if stung by a meat wasp, and Francisco remembers how undependable the subjunctive can be in English. "Yes, yes, it is certainly yours," he says, "but the birthing time belongs to the women. They celebrate the fact that it is something we men cannot do. Come sit with me outside while I mend this bridle. Tica is strong. She will be fine. Castro women birth easily."

In the evening of September 19, 1840, María Isabela Dye is born. Moments later María leads Job in to see Escolástica, lying pale but proud against the pillows, the little bundle already nestled against her bosom.

"You are well?" he asks, kneeling beside her.

"Yes, Job. Do you want to hold her?"

---

* The restored house has become a historic site. The nails did rust, but a few have been preserved in the Monterey State Historic Park Museum, Monterey CA.

"No. No, I'm afraid I'll break her. She's happy there."

"She is beautiful, no?"

"Yes, Yes." But Job is thinking it is Tica who looks heart-breakingly lovely. She glows in the candlelight. Her eyes shine with happiness.

The baby's birth is registered at the Mission Santa Cruz, and there she is baptized under the smiling gaze of Tica's favorite statue, *La Purísima Concepción*. Her name seems to be a foregone conclusion. Job is not sure why, but Isabela is a pretty name. Why not Isabela?

Tica thinks that even the blessed Virgin's infant could not have been so miraculously beautiful. Her baby looks like one of the little angels at *La Purísima's* feet. Tica, gazing down at the sleeping infant nestled against her chest, feels connected by deeply buried roots. This child is a part of her. Her heart has divided like the bulb of some wild spring lily, so that now she has two hearts: the one beating a slow, contented rhythm in her bosom; the other a light flutter in her arms. The babe is a *Californio* angel, dark, with none of the father's blondness. When she takes the baby to her breast, Tica thinks there can be no greater joy than these tiny lips nuzzling against her swollen nipple, this small, thirsty sucking of her.

It amuses her that Job seems to find nursing a baby embarrassing. He leaves the room whenever the baby suckles. "Americans are strange," she says to her mother. "They are disturbed by the natural cycle of things."

"This strikes me," said the priest, "as a very good story, but I can't convince myself that it's really true, and if it's invented, then the author has made a serious mistake, because I can't believe there's truly a husband who could be as foolish."

Op. Cit., Vol. 1, Chap. 35, pg. 239

MONTEREY
1840

There are walls in Monterey now. Tica can see changes. And where there are no walls, there are coyote fences lashed together with rawhide. As a hermit crab crawls into a larger shell, the once scattered little pueblo has retreated behind higher walls, shut itself in.

The little procession rides along the sandy bay road, bordered now on the land side by walls. Job carries the ten-day old infanta Isabela, swaddled in wool, asleep in his arms. He looks so proud, Tica thinks, at the head of his little *asamblea*. Tal-ku follows, and a *vaquero* from the rancho leads two pack horses laden with gifts and clothes for the baby and a few salvaged furnishings for their new house.

Her grandfather's tales of Don Quixote flit through Tica's head as they ride, and she smiles. Is Job a Don Quixote, embarked upon some new quest, she wonders. Surely, she is no Sancho Panza. Since the birth of her first child, men seem to her touchingly, pathetically vainglorious. Even her father seems less consequential compared to her mother, who has borne six children. Childbirth has filled her with an unseemly sense of superiority. May God forgive her, she does not feel like one of Grandmother's silver spoons. She is not inclined to bend herself to life's shaping as her grandfather once advised. Her horse fights for his head, and she pulls him up sharply beside Job.

Monterey is beginning to look like a pueblo. The Señoras Rachel Harker and Antonia Alvarado, Tica's cousin, are having a civilizing effect on the ragged little port. There are sandy streets now, laid out crookedly between the walls, and planks over the worst of the gullies. Gardens are beginning to escape over the walls: a blazing purple bougainvillaea, a pink rose, a peach tree.

American drawing rooms are corseted with furnishings the way American women are corseted with whalebone. The windows are closed tight. Tica feels she can hardly breathe. The Harker's drawing room is stuffed full of legs -- table legs, chair legs, piano legs. Every table is crowded with porcelains and picture frames. Every chair is loaded down with cushions and shawls. The walls are covered with flowered paper and paintings and maps and cabinets. There is no room to walk. She longs to sweep clear a path for herself and her baby through Rachel Harker's sitting room. Job is forever backing into things. The Harker house is by far the largest in Monterey, and yet Tica feels the most cramped in it.*

As soon as they can politely excuse themselves, Job and Tica retire with relief to their own little adobe three doors away. Job has applied a thick coat of white lime inside and out. Tal-ku opens the shutters in both rooms and spreads fresh rush mats on the redwood plank floor. A clay pot full of Rachel Harker's roses fills one deep windowsill. Tal-ku and the *vaquero* are already unpacking their trunks.

"A perfect baby, little cousin. I envy you." Cousin Antonia Castro de Alvarado sits watching Tica nurse her child in the Dye's tiny *sala*. Antonia is already twenty-three, and married Governor Alvarado several months before Tica's wedding. Tica is troubled by her older cousin's thin face. She knows Alvarado has sired several daughters by his mistress. Antonia remains childless.

"They will come," Tica says. "They will all be sons." Antonia had been the plump, pretty older cousin overflowing with gaiety and witty charm. Now she sits in the corner, frail and gray as a deer mouse. "Ay, Antonia, what has he done to you? Are you ill?"

Antonia smiles at her seventeen-year-old cousin. "He is not a cruel man; only disappointed, I think."

---

* A similar house, #464 *Calle Principal* in Monterey, is now open to the public on Friday, Saturday and Sunday. It still feels cluttered.

116

"He is the most fortunate of men," rages Tica. "He should thank God for his good fortune."

Antonia laughs bitterly. "Yes, yes. 'Good fortune.' I wonder what amount of 'good fortune' it takes to satisfy a man."

Tica seizes her hand. "We must see each other every day," she urges. The hand of Antonia is as cold as sea bass.

Job bursts through the door one evening, "Tica, is it true that you took off your boots on the beach today? Mr. Cooper says he saw you barefoot on the beach."

"Would you prefer then that I wade in my boots and ruin them? Boots are expensive. I was dipping Isabelita's toes in the bay."

"It isn't proper for..."

"Why live beside an ocean if you cannot touch it?"

A few days later: "Tica, did you race the Estrada brothers on the beach road? Mr. Stokes says he saw you racing today."

"I won."

"I can't have you seen racing horses."

"Then tell your friends to stop spying and mind their own business."

"It isn't proper for an American wife..."

"I am not an American wife, Job."

And the following week: "Tica, you can't dance with common sailors at a ball."

"He was a lieutenant."

"I wasn't there to introduce you. Your cousin Antonia had dragged me off to dance. You are a wife and mother now."

"Neither condition affects my feet, Job."

Job complains to Thomas Harker, "Thomas, I don't know what to do with her. I love her so much, but she scares me. She's so unpredictable. What should I do?"

"Rejoice in her, Job. The rest of Monterey does."

"That's what I'm talking about!" Job sputters.

"Job, she is a wonderful wife and mother. You know that."

Tica complains to Harker, too. "Don Tomás, my husband fell in love with a Californian, but he desires an American wife."

"Escolástica, my dear, it is only that he is so proud of you and Isabela."

"Then pride is an uncomfortable yoke, Don Tomás."

"Belle," Job calls his baby daughter, and when he holds her his cracked hands tremble at the touch. Her fingers are angel-wrought, tender little tendrils that clutch his own clumsy thumb, all five delicate fingers wound around his one. He begs Tica to draw their daughter's hands, her face. His tiny Belle seems to him a miracle. He is terrified of losing her. Suddenly Monterey seems full of dangers to him, cold drafts and treacherous rip currents and shifty Indians. He worries that Tica and Tal-ku are not careful enough of Isabela. They allow her to crawl in the beach sand. They put her outside in her little cradle. They dip her feet in the chilly salt water of the bay.

Tica seems to him flighty as a young mare. The more he tries to control her, the more she pulls away from him. She muddles him, frightens him. She does not obey him. She doesn't even know the meaning of caution, of moderation. He worships her, but in God's name, why can't she be a wife like other men's wives, like Rachel Harker?

Tica tosses aside her mending. "Antonia, dearest cousin, I feel so restless on these spring days. It is time for the rodeo and the branding. I feel cooped up like a chicken in the walls of Monterey."

"Let us take a picnic, a *merienda* to the hills," Antonia says. "Don Tomás just received new watercolors from London. He ordered them especially for you. He told me so. Go see him. He will cheer you."

Later in Harker's store, Tica lovingly fingers the tiny silver tubes of paint. "Don Tomás, they are too expensive. I cannot accept them. We cannot afford such luxuries."

"They are not a gift, my dear Tica. They are a commission. Would you paint a picture of the pueblo for me? It has become quite a respectable town now. I think it merits a portrait."

Thomas Harker smiles his dazzling smile at her. He does not mention that he has been asked by the Commodore of the American Fleet to provide a plan of the town and its defenses in the eventuality of war. In fact, he is more concerned with Escolástica than he is about war. He has seen her stamping, flinging her head like a young filly kept too long on tether.

"A view of the town from the hills would be nice," he says, "and I hear the strawberries are already ripe."

The painting occupies Tica for several weeks, until her cousin Antonia complains of spending every afternoon on the damp, grassy hillside. Even with her books to occupy her, Antonia grows stiff and broody. She says that the baby will catch a chill, but Tica insists the shadows will never be right if she doesn't paint on site. Her lack of formal training frustrates her. The clarity of the scene pierces her eye, but somehow, when she floats the colors onto the paper, they muddy to opaque, dirty washes that make her want to scrub the painting with a fist full of horsetail fern, bite her brush in two.

"I want it to look like a clean spring day, rain-washed. Do you understand me, Antonia?"

Antonia looks up from her book. "Yes, yes, Tica."

"But the hills must be new green, that keen, glowing green of rebirth, of the resurrection. Do you know?"

Antonia holds her finger to her place on the page. "Hmm..."

"And the light must come from the bay. I cannot make it emanate from the bay. The bay looks like a dirty well hole."

It is difficult to read with all the muttering and scolding and the desperate crumpling of expensive sheets of paper. Tica is nearly in tears, Antonia can see that, stomping around the meadow as if she might kick the whole scene into the sea. It's a serene spring day, quiet but for a hushed, washing sound, part wave, part wind. The hum of an insect breaks the calm; then, as if realizing his mistake the fly careens off and all is peaceful again, except for Tica, her little storm cloud cousin.

Still, a month later Tica is proud when she appears at Thomas Harker's store with the watercolor rolled and tied with a scrap of white ribbon. She has tucked many of Thomas's favorite characters into the picture. She has stood Harker himself on the new veranda of which he is so proud, dressed in his dashing uniform as American Consul. She has painted Antonia seated beside her cousin Encarnación Cooper in the center of the scene. Antonia is a round little figure, slyly announcing her first pregnancy. She has placed her cousin Joaquín riding down the *Calle Principal,* and she has drawn herself behind Job on his huge buckskin, galloping along the high road, her hair blowing in the wind. Wickedly, she has drawn herself in riding breeches.

Thomas Harker unrolls the painting, holds it up, carries it to better light, turns away from Tica so she cannot see his face. After a moment he manages to say, "It is a jewel, Tica, a masterpiece. You must sign it."

"No, Don Tomás. My painting must speak for itself of all the gratitude and affection I feel for you. You are a good man, Don Tomás." And she leaves him, as she often does, with his eyes watering and his heart twisted in a knot.[*]

Before the watercolors are finished, Governor Alvarado moves his wife Antonia and his finally growing family to *El Alisal*, a fertile rancho along the Salinas River that he purchased from one of Antonia's uncles. Tica rejoices for her cousin Antonia. Alvarado seems to be settling into married life. He has moved out to the rancho. He spends less time with his mistress in Monterey. Antonia grows plump and radiant again. Once she conceives her first son, another pregnancy follows. "I love babies," she says. "I want never to be without a baby in the house. They make my husband sweet and docile."

Tica laughs at her. "You will be overrun with babies. Your house will be like the houses on the beach that are overrun with rats. There will be babies in the rafters, babies living in the walls, babies everywhere you step."

She is lonely without Antonia in Monterey and almost envious of her marriage, which is growing thicker, richer, like a well-woven blanket, Tica thinks. The contentment shows in her cousin's lovely round face, wreathed in smiles, and in Alvarado's figure. He is no longer the puffy, dissolute old lecher Antonia was forced to marry. His step is firmer. His eyes are clearer and full of happiness when he looks upon his gay wife and her round stomach. Will Job ever wear that smile of contentment? Tica wonders. Can she and her child ever bring him such satisfaction? Or will he always wear a hunted look?

---

* The lithograph rests in the Oakland Museum. The location of the original watercolor is unknown.

Thomas Harker never added Escolástica's name. Even when he hired a lithographer to refine that watercolor and a second one that Tica painted for him, Harker protected her identity as carefully as if the paintings were love letters. In the lithographs, the town walls have been straightened, Tica's figure is changed to that of an Indian, a natural mistake. The figure is small and wild and rides astride. But even in the hand-colored lithographs, the light emanates from Monterey Bay. It is a fine spring day. The hills are new green.

Your grace, if these misfortunes are what you harvest, when you practice knighthood, please tell me if they go right on happening, or if they take place only at limited times, because it seems to me that two harvests like this will leave us useless for the third.

Op. Cit., Vol. 1, Chap. 15, pg. 77

MONTEREY
1842

"Tica, I've got bad news." Job stands awkwardly at the door.

Tica looks up from her loom. This foggy morning the house seems snug, impervious to bad news. Isabela plays at her feet with a faded rag doll who has led a perilous life -- one arm askew, a tear, neatly mended, on her cheek.

"Tica," Job sits beside her at her loom, knowing that she has not fathomed his tone; she is still half distracted by Isabela's chatter and the pattern in her wool, a soft white stripe rippling across the piece.

"Escolástica, your mother..."

Finally, she focuses on his face. But the morning is so peaceful, so ordinary, Wednesday. She cannot believe that anything momentous could perturb this foggy morning, when even she is content to sit indoors and weave. Job's expression is out of place. "Would you like coffee, Job? I will go and..."

He restrains her. God, he doesn't know how to do this. He is too clumsy. His Spanish isn't good enough. "Tica, your mother has had trouble with the baby. The baby is dead, Tica." He plunges on, "Your mother..."

Tica looks blankly at him, not understanding, refusing to comprehend, making it harder for him. He takes her hand away from the loom, squeezes it too hard. She winces.

"Your mother is dead in the night, Tica." He blurts it out, badly, bluntly, desperately. She sits silently, stares at him, lips parted. She does not even cross herself.

"No," she says, for she does not believe her mother could have died without her feeling so much as a shudder of forewarning down her spine. She does not believe she could have sat snugly in her fog-bound house while her mother, torn and suffering, bled, died. And she felt nothing? "No," she says, angry with Job.

It is by the confusion on his face, his uncertain mumbling, that she sees it is the truth he speaks. She pulls her hand from his clenched fist, pushes away from him, grabs her shawl and rushes from the house. Isabela starts to cry.

Job calls to her in English, "Tica, don't go." He is hurt that she turns away from him. If only she would let him hold her, comfort her. Isabela is crying. "Hush, child," he says gruffly, then turns and picks her up, holds her, strokes the back of her curly head, looking out after Tica's retreating figure.

Tica walks quickly across the pueblo to the dilapidated Presidio Chapel. Her mother had great difficulties carrying her last child and feared another pregnancy. Tica's heart shrinks. Her mother, her laughing, scolding, vibrant mother, is dead at forty-two. As Tica walks, she recites her rosary. "Holy Mother…." The praise of babies that her cousin sings echoes in her head, answered by a grim descant, the realities of childbirth that have taken her mother.

How could God have given her mother another pregnancy when the last had been so precarious? The damp chapel is chilly and still. The Virgin in the side chapel stands silent. "Holy Mother, have you no help for me?" The Virgin Mother stares mute. The sight of the poor bleeding Christ on the crucifix only reminds her of her mother's suffering.

Tica and Job and Isabela ride north at once, meeting Tica's aunts and uncles along the way, converging the next afternoon upon *Rancho Arroyo del Rodeo*. They find Tica's father and younger brothers numb with grief. Francisco has hardly left his wife and infant daughter's side since their deaths. He kneels heartbroken beside their bodies in the *sala*, and when Tica and the family arrive, he collapses into his daughter's arms.

María and her daughter are buried in the redwood grove beside "Queen Isabela," the towering redwood tree of Tica's childhood, the scene of so many happy washday barbecues. On a foggy morning the family files into the shadow of those giant trees, treading upon a carpet of wild ginger and bleeding heart. As the fog clears, the trees themselves seem to weep. Padre Francisco from Mission Santa Cruz intones the service, and the creek sings a mournful response.

It seems to Tica that in all her happy memories beside this creek her mother stands laughing at the center, a wooden spoon in her hand. It was she who told the fairy stories, stirred the bubbling bean pot, she who was home base in games of hide and seek. She was the touchstone.

A week later, when Tica and Job and Isabela leave the grieving Francisco, Tica carries in her saddlebags her mother's pride and her inheritance, Grandmother's silver spoons and the dented silver cups.

Since her marriage, Tica has seen little of her mother, though she has been only a day's ride away. When she gave birth to Isabela, her mother knelt beside her, confident, calm. Now Tica is alone. All that was solid and certain seems to be falling away from her. Like the bell tower in the earthquake, she seems to waver, without beams or scaffolding to buttress her.

Later, at home, she attempts to explain this sense of loss to Job, weeping uncontrollably, clenching her rosary beads to her breast. He tries to take her hand, but she pulls away from him, holding fast to her rosary, shaking with sobs. Job grows defensive. "Escolástica, I am here. I am your husband. You don't need your mother or anybody else. Lean on me."

She looks up at him through her tears and knows that he cannot understand, that she can never make him see, that he is the earthquake that shakes her. She is inconsolable.

Added to her sense of loss is the isolation Tica feels in Monterey. The insularity Tica complained of on her parents' rancho seems to her even more acute in Monterey. The rancho was its own island, spacious, self-sufficient, ordered by the seasons of the cattle. Monterey seems to her a flimsy little town, sliding off the California coast, open to the sea, utterly dependent upon what washes in with the tide. Even the wharf that Thomas Harker is proudly building at his own expense looks spindly seen from the hill. The wharf ventures a few steps out into the bay, like a bony old woman lifting her skirts. From the tea cup boats that row up to this wharf comes the news and commerce of the world to Monterey. Montalvo's description of their mythical island as the "strongest in all the world, with its steep cliffs and rocky shores," seems ludicrous to her now. During these troubled times, the fear is not so much what will happen to Monterey: the fear is that Monterey will be the last to know its own fate.

Job is determined not to be taken by surprise again, as he was in Santa Cruz. He haunts the waterfront, collecting rumors, quizzing common sailors for a sign of movement of the navies. Job can't afford to start over again. He lost his trapping business when all his hides were stolen in Santa Bárbara. He lost his mill when the Mexican government confiscated it. He has to make something of himself. Tica must be proud of him. He and Harker sit by the hour in Job's little *sala* plotting and speculating on their futures.

During this unsettled period, a fever invades the town. It rages all summer, visiting nearly every household. Tica is uncomfortable with illness, even impatient. Her mother would have been better at this, she thinks, as she visits neighbors, gritting her teeth against the stench and the endless wail of babies. Then in late August baby Isabela falls ill, and eventually Tica catches it. Poor little Isabela, burning with fever, dehydrated by diarrhea, cries for her mamá, and Tica staggers in to her, ashen-faced, doubled over with stomach cramps. "Holy Mother of Mercies," she prays, "help me," but the face she sees is her own mother's. Tica can do little except watch the suffering of her daughter. She presses wet compresses to the child's head until her own head swims and Tal-ku leads her back to bed.

Job sends for the doctor, but the town is of two minds about the doctor. He is an excellent card player from Mazatlán. His medical credentials seem to be more dubious. Tica refuses to let him touch Isabela. At last, after Tal-ku's ministrations, Isabela's fever breaks. She sleeps a cool, peaceful sleep for twelve hours and wakes up hungry. Tica's fever hovers longer. She lies listless and thin for another fortnight, refusing food, haunted by a great sadness over the loss of her mother.

In the early autumn of 1842, just as she is beginning to recover her strength, forcing herself to get up for Isabela's sake, she and the uneasy townspeople are stunned to see two American war ships sail into the bay with their cannons run out. The townspeople collect on the beach, squinting out to sea. Thomas Harker and two other members of the *Ayuntamiento* set out in a leaky rowboat to find out what it means. A Commodore Jones dressed in full regalia meets them at the rail and, looking down on the men in their damp dinghy, announces that a state of war exists between Mexico and the United States. The men laugh aloud. This is a joke, no? The Commodore bristles. He does not invite them on board. He demands the immediate surrender of Monterey. He will not listen to reason. He will not agree to come ashore to read the most recent American newspapers that make no mention of a war. He is determined to score a glorious victory on the sleepy town.

As soon as Harker returns to shore, Job races up to the house breathless and angry. "Get the baby ready, Tica. You and Tal-ku'll have to get her to the rancho. Thomas says this Commodore is an ass and an idiot."

Tica has already ordered the horses saddled. Even in her weakened condition, she recognizes the danger. For the first time in weeks she shakes herself out of her lethargy and leaps into action. She has seen the sailors swarming on the beach. She knows as well as anyone that the fort at Monterey is a rickety affair manned by a garrison of two dozen destitute soldiers who spend most of their time stealing chickens from town to supplement their weevil-infested rations.

The new Governor Alvarado is out at his rancho. No one is in charge. The Monterey *Ayuntamiento* meets hastily; Harker and Dye are both members of that council, and it is decided the town must capitulate as gracefully as possible and then try to reason with this young donkey. They ask Tica to stay and help entertain this Commodore Jones.

"We're reduced to charming him to death," says Harker.

Tica watches fuming with anger as Commodore Jones and his entire force march up the street with their American flag waving (a ridiculous flag, Tica thinks, more like a primitive patchwork quilt than a flag,) and their band blaring martial tunes.

Job is angry, too, but for different reasons. "This is bad for Americans," he says.

"It is worse for *Californios*," Tica snaps.

Before Harker can stop him, Commodore Thomas Catesby Jones reads a pompous proclamation to the people of Monterey. Fortunately few citizens understand the entire bombast, but two sailors step forward and lower the Mexican flag in front of a humiliated population. Then, as the American flag is raised, the guns of the warships fire a salute. Every soul in Monterey understands this insult.

"This whole fiasco could make us the most unpopular men in town," Harker mutters as they stand watching the charade. "There is enough anti-American sentiment as it is."

Harker, as official United States representative in Monterey, requests an audience with the young Commodore Jones. Harker, Cooper and Job Dye retire to Harker's house to try to sort out this dangerous turn of events. Tica and Encarnacion Cooper hurry at once to Rachel Harker's patio. They know Rachel will be required to feed and entertain this stuffed bird of a Commodore. They know, too, how insipid Rachel's *Yanqui* cooking can be. They will rescue her from her New England recipes.

"Are you well enough, Tica?" asks Encarnacion. "You still look pale."

"It is typical, really. So inconsiderate, with all the children sick..." Rachel Harker stands back from the cook fires, perspiration trickling down her temples. "The men rush around making grand gestures while we are left to do the work, feed them, forage around in the berry bushes for them, prowl around in the marshes after ducks."

Tica and Encarnación laugh in spite of themselves. The thought of Rachel prowling in a marsh, for one thing, Rachel, who is afraid of rats and the littlest slip of a water snake. The thought of that puny commodore holding court in Rachel's *sala*, for another. Imagine rounding the point with two American warships at battle ready. Ready against what? A sick town? A mud hut of a fort? Who knows if the fort even has cannon balls or ammunition? Certainly their gouty old captain wouldn't remember how to use them if they have. Now the American sailors roam the beach like a pack of rats, waving muskets, insulting every grandmother. Most of the civilians have dissolved into the hills behind the town. The *Costeños* have disappeared without a trace. So Tica and Encarnacion stand sweating over the charcoal fires in Rachel Harker's courtyard. They are true *Californios*, equally disloyal to Mexico and to the United States. They want no foreign master. They are determined that Monterey's hospitality shall put this vulgar oaf to shame.

Through the long afternoon, the men patiently cajole the Commodore. The women in the courtyard can hear the urgency in the men's voices, the impassioned arguments, the explosive replies of Commodore Jones. Toward evening, the women, changed now into their best silks, rustle through the room with plates of cinnamon spiced meat, trays of hot chocolate and flaky sugared blackberry *tortas*. Job smiles grimly as he watches Commodore Jones accept a cup of chocolate from Tica's hand. To be the guest of a gracious California hostess is a thoroughly humbling experience. Will he even notice the hospitality? Perhaps they will not need cannons to bring this arrogant Commodore to heel.

At last, after showing their guest the most recent newspapers in both Spanish and English, and stuffing him with a lavish dinner of roast quail, spitted beef and quince tarts that leaves the women nearly prostrate with exhaustion, the Commodore grumbles that he may have made a "grievous mistake." He promises to call on the *Ayuntamiento* the next morning to offer his apologies. He bows stiffly to the women, turns on his heels and stomps back down to the beach.

"Oh, no," groans Encarnacion, whose husband is *Alcalde*.

"Don't worry," says Rachel, collapsed on a bench in the patio. "Fair is fair. Tica and I will be there, and we have food enough left over to feed the entire United States Navy."

"Which is probably what we will be called upon to do," moans Tica, her stomach churning at the thought of all that food.

"Ludicrous." Tica's riding *látigo* twitches in her hand as the next morning she stands amidst an amused population watching one hundred and fifty American sailors march up the street from the beach to *El Cuartel* with the band playing and the dogs barking. The American flag is lowered. The Mexican flag is raised with its serpent splayed across it, all with appropriate if makeshift ceremony. Tica thinks of her grandfather's pure white silk flag of Spain, charged with the Bourbon arms. The citizens of Monterey bite their lips to control their smiles as Commodore Jones and his officers, sweating in full ceremonial dress, trudge off along the sandy street to the *Ayuntamiento* to pay their respects. It is unseasonably hot for October. Tica remembers her brother's tin soldiers. Let us hope no one loses his temper and kicks over the whole lot, she thinks.

All the same, I told him nothing of what we were really up to, because that might have been dangerous.

Op. Cit., Vol. 1, Chap. 41, pg. 270

MONTEREY
1843

"James Dye," says Job, holding his infant son proudly.

Tica laughs. "Chames? Djames? What kind of a name is that? Poor little infant."

It is the eleventh of March 1843, and she has remained in Monterey for the birth of her second child, assisted by gentle Rachel Harker and Tal-ku, who disapproves of nearly every move Rachel makes during the delivery. When Rachel cuts the umbilical cord with an ordinary boiled knife instead of the quartz Tal-ku offers her, Tal-ku can stand it no longer. When Rachel discards the umbilical cord, Tal-ku gathers it up in a basket and disappears with it.

"James, I want his name to be James," Job says, in English, "but there isn't a sound like that in Spanish. You know what they do to my name. Danged impossible language. My grandfather's name was James."

Tica sighs, "Djames! Well then, we will call him Jaimito," and she dozes off.

Job kneels beside her bed. "Now I've got to apply for land, Tica. Our son'll have his own land."

"A rancho?" It seems to Tica, in her weakened state, a dream. "We could live together on a rancho? I could be useful again. Oh, Job!"

"Tica, you are plenty useful here. You care for me and my children...."

"But on a rancho I am capable of great things, Job. We will have the most glorious rancho in California, you will see. Of course Mexico will grant us a rancho. How could the governor refuse a Castro y Rodríguez? I will apply at once as soon..."

"No, Tica. I want this to be my land grant, a Dye land grant. I am a naturalized citizen now, a Catholic, by God. They should grant me land in my name."

"Do not be angry, Job. Whoever's name. I long for a rancho." And again she falls asleep while Job stands at the foot of her bed baffled by her wild, elusive beauty. With each year and each child, Tica grows more gorgeous. Her dark hair seems to thicken. Her green eyes loom larger against her sun-tanned cheeks. She is still tall and slender, but now, at the age of twenty, her edges have softened into a womanly voluptuousness that disquiets Job. Her fiery spirit makes him nervous. Whenever there is excitement in Monterey, Job dreads that he will come home to find Tica in the lead: *meriendas*, picnics, horse races, balls. Doña Escolástica is likely to be at the center while he is left on the outside, prowling the edges of the gaiety, proud of her beauty, jealous of her charm, threatened by her impetuosity.

"No man in Monterey can ride this horse," Governor Pico boasts, his pride and his penchant for wine talking for him. He lists as if he were on a boat. For the Mexican Governor Pío Pico this is a rare trip to Northern California. He has brought with him a famous stallion that he purchased at great expense in Northern Mexico. The stallion, named Ten Thousand Dollars, is a gigantic gray and requires three soldiers to saddle him. Governor Pico holds forth at a dinner in his honor at *Casa Estrada*: "No man in Monterey can ride this horse."

Jacinto Rodríguez rises from his chair, "With permission, Excellency, any Rodríguez in Monterey could ride your horse. I wager even the women of our family could ride your horse."

"That is a poor joke, Don Jacinto."

"Not at all." The men of Monterey assembled at the table exchange knowing glances. "I wager my cousin, Escolástica Rodríguez, could ride your little horse to a standstill."

And the bet is on. The cousins take care that Job Dye does not hear of it, but the next morning they accompany Tica to *El Cuartel*.

Ten Thousand Dollars is fitted with a woman's saddle for the first time, which makes him more rebellious than ever. He snorts and shivers, stamps his hooves. A crowd begins to gather around *El Cuartel.*

Fat little Governor Pico perches on the top step, mesmerized by the striking young woman who stands in her black velvet habit before the pitching stallion, serenely peeling a willow branch with a long bone-handled knife. Erect, calm, oblivious to the growing crowd, she meticulously peels the willow branch. The stallion begins to watch her, too. He watches every motion of her knife as she shaves off each strip of bark, each nodule. A strange silence comes over the crowd as they watch and wait. Then Tica steps forward without a word, takes the reins and vaults lightly onto the stallion's back before he has time to pull away.

The stallion shoots off, followed by a handful of runners, and only when a roar rises up along the street do Job Dye and Thomas Harker run out to see Tica streaking down the street on the great gray. They watch helplessly as the stallion races toward the beach, out toward Point Pinos, with Tica fighting to maneuver him into deeper sand. Horse and rider disappear over the dunes, and, as Dye and Harker reach the shore a few minutes later, an eerie silence hangs over the crowd.

Job is paralyzed between terror and outrage. The bettors, avoiding Job's eyes, look anxiously out toward the dunes. The minutes pass. Is there cause for alarm? The governor begins to wonder whose fault this will be if the impetuous young woman is killed by his horse. After all, this was not his idea. He shifts uncomfortably on the steps of *El Cuartel,* looking toward the dunes. There is no sign of his expensive horse or the woman who rides him. The cousins begin to look at one another. This is no longer a joke. Somebody should go after Tica. She may be hurt.

"If anything happens to her...," mutters Job. Harker, standing beside him, shrinks from the thought.

Just then, the huge stallion reappears higher up the beach, headed toward them now, with Tica still on him, using her willow whip occasionally to keep the foaming steed at a gallop. As the horse and rider approach *El Cuartel,* Tica draws him in and brings him to a halt. Then, with a flick of her willow wand, she makes him place his front hoof on the very step where Governor Pico stands, speechless. No one notices the tiny tear in her skirt.

"A fine horse you have, Excellency." She flicks her willow switch, "He wants a little prodding now and again, but he has a good heart."

"He is yours, Doña Escolástica," Pico says, his voice choked with admiration and relief. "Ten Thousand Dollars has met his match. I beg your permission to present him to you as a tribute to the women of Monterey."

But as the governor turns and retires into *El Cuartel*, he murmurs to his aide, "I will still wager there is not a man in Monterey who can ride that horse."

"How dare she?" Job's fright has turned to fury. "How dare she enter a wager without my permission?" Harker, who has maneuvered him back to the store to calm him down, is beginning to regret it. "How dare she do something so dangerous, so humiliating?" Job unpacks barrels of china cups, and Harker shudders as he watches him thrash his way through the straw.

"Easy, easy, my friend. You will break them all. She is a high-spirited woman, Job. Would you have her ride burros?"

"What about her children? What about me?" A china saucer comes perilously close to destruction.

"You wanted a Californian, Job. Do not try to make her into a Kentucky bride. Do not try to break her spirit. You might as well try to tame the waves at Point Pinos. Rejoice in her. The rest of Monterey does."

"Christ! She's not the rest of Monterey's wife."

Job adores her all right. It is not that he doesn't love her. But he wants her to be his wife. Rachel is Thomas Harker's wife. Even Antonia is Alvarado's wife. Tica belongs to nobody, it seems. It's like trying to take a red-tailed hawk as a mate. She is not unfaithful. She is simply not his in a way he can count on. Things slip away from him in California: his mill at Zayante, his house at Santa Cruz. When he tries to exert his authority over Tica, she flares up and out of his reach.

Tica is aware of his predicament, but she is unsympathetic. "Why is it," she asks Thomas Harker one day when she finds him alone in his store, "that American men feel they must own everything: their land, their houses, their children, even their wives? God did not sell me to my husband like this barrel of flour!" She kicks it with the toe of her boot. "He joined us together as man and wife. I do not wish to own him. Why should he wish to own me?"

Harker looks up from his ledgers at her, removes his reading glasses. "Tica," he sighs, "come sit beside me, and I will try to explain to you how it is to be poor, to be cold, to be hungry. How it is to grow up in a land that isn't so bountiful. He is an ambitious man, your husband. He strives to barricade himself against the poverty and hunger and loneliness he knew as a young man." Thomas takes her hands in his. "It is difficult for you, growing up in a family where hospitality and love are a way of life, where the land itself is generous, it is difficult for you to understand what he comes from, how afraid he is that he will lose you."

"Then why does he vex me so? He is jealous of every man in Monterey. He is jealous of my cousins! He is jealous of my horses. He is even jealous of you, Don Tomás."

"He will mellow," Harker says, dropping Tica's hands, unwilling to examine too closely the reasons Job has to be jealous of Thomas Harker. "Perhaps this new land grant will settle him down, make him feel secure. He has become a trusted member of the *Ayuntamiento*, a great honor for an American. Perhaps this will help."

"I've understood every word your grace has said," replied Sancho, "but just the same I wish you'd smear up a doubt that this very moment popped into my head."

Op. Cit., Vol. 2, Chap. 8, pg. 39

MONTEREY
1844

"Little Butterfly," Tica calls her daughter, *"Mariposita."* Tal-ku says Isabela's spirit power is the butterfly, just as she told Tica long ago that Tica's spirit was the hawk. At four, Isabela flits through her world on open wings. She skips along after her mother through the high tules of the fresh water marshes, where dragonflies whirl past them on blue-singed wings, where pollywogs and minnows worry the surface of the ponds. Escolástica tries to teach her to call the wild ducks to her feet with the low, clacking call that Tal-ku taught her. But Isabela laughs to see her mother kneeling in the mud, and the ducks flare up when she raises her arms and chuckles delightedly. They settle down again, the shiny green ducks. They are not afraid of her. She sings their names, sometimes in Spanish, sometimes in Tal-ku's dialect, as she trips along, looking back for her mother, calling to her.

Escolástica understands, now that she has children of her own, the way her life was entwined with her mother's, even though the two of them were different in temperament. Her mother was quiet as well water, while Tica is volatile as the salty waves off the point. She often finds herself in silent conversation with her mother about the most trivial things, Isabela's lost tooth, the way to cook beans, conversations they never had in life, conversations that have the curious authority of prayer.

Escolástica sees that she is the center of her daughter's life. It is that center point she craves. It is, in miniature, what her own mother enjoyed on the rancho. She sees now that her mother was the axis around which the vortex of life whirled: María fed the rancho, clothed the rancho, healed the rancho's sick. With her wooden spoon in one hand and her missal in the other, her mother reigned over the rancho.

Of course, her father never knew it; none of them did. María had been careful to pluck each of them out of the whirlpool from time to time, like a caddis fly set upon a large rock to dry and flutter and make a show of strength. "You must ask your father's permission," she would say, or "When do you begin the *matanza*?" she would ask. When Father planned to travel down the coast, María would fly into a frenzy of preparations, but once he left, his absence caused hardly a ripple in the life of the rancho. Her father was a strong, able man. She and her brothers had towered over her mother. So it was not a question of physical power; it was a question of locus. On the rancho, in the church, her mother was the pivot point. Escolástica is snagged between missing her and longing to be that center herself. Only in Isabela can she capture a hint of that concentric pattern in their lives.

Isabela wanders out onto the rocks and gathers sea shells while Tal-ku, with Jaime tied onto a cradleboard on her back, collects mussels and builds a fire on the beach to steam them. The three women sit on the sand like Tal-ku's people, with their knees drawn up, scooping the mussels from the fire with Tal-ku's looped stick, eating them, drinking the delicious liquor in the shells and munching on fresh tortillas Tal-ku has buried in the coals.

Little *Mariposa*, little butterfly. A gentle, whimsical child, Isabela has none of her mother's restlessness or savagery. Where Tica rebels and fights, Isabela floats, full of smiles. Escolástica marvels at her daughter's perfection. Together they race on the beach, gather abalone shells to line their garden walks. Tica teaches her daughter to ride bareback as she was taught, and together they ride astride on Escolástica's black gelding *El Chocolate*, Isabela snuggled up timidly before her mother on the superb horse's back, Tica's petticoats flapping. But she is careful that they walk around Point Pinos out of sight of Monterey before they mount him, so that Job never hears of their escapades.

One day as they walk the beach, Tal-ku says, "The true butterflies are stirring in the butterfly trees. Isabelita should see them."

"What are you talking of, Tal-ku?"

"Doña Tica, have you never seen the butterflies? It is one of the Spirits' great mysteries."

They set out over the brow of the hill behind Point Pinos along a deer trail through the heavy beach chaparral, Jaime tied on Tal-ku's back. The hill is steep and sandy, and the ceanothus scratches.

"Mamá, let us go back and get our horses," Isabela whines. "It is too uphill. Our horses are missing us."

"Hss, little Isabela, you will wake them," Tal-ku says. "We are nearly there. See, already they hang in the trees."

But Tica and Isabela can see nothing in the black pines. Then a ray of sunlight pierces the fog, and where Escolástica expected a wing or two, she sees mounds of butterflies, branches heavy with the tiny fluttering bodies, golden heaps of them on the ground. As the fog begins to lift, the sun catches the melted yellow wings, the shiny black flecks. The air around them sparkles as if someone has tossed gold coins. They stop, afraid to walk for fear of treading on them. The forest floor is littered with buttered scraps of wings. Isabela reaches out her hands, laughing in delight, and the butterflies reel about her dark head.

"They are always here?" Tica asks.

"No, no. The butterflies follow the geese from the north and sleep here in winter. When spring comes, they wake and return to their homeland."

"Tal-ku, how do you know these things?"

"This is my people's land," says Tal-ku softly, "The eagle gave it to my grandfathers."

The women kneel quietly in the forest and watch the butterflies take flight. Escolástica feels as if they crouch inside a whale oil lamp, watching the light flicker on around them as more and more butterflies waft up into the sunshine.

"But how did you know they were beginning to fly?"

"At the creek. The washerwomen know."

Tica knows this to be true. She knows Juan Alvarado often sends soldiers to Washerwomen's Creek to confirm rumors. She has heard Job quiz Tal-ku on troop movements when she returns from the creek. She has seen Tal-ku's veiled eyes, heard her grunts of ignorance.

"How do they hear, these washerwomen? I will not tell, Tal-ku, I swear."

"Many of my people still have a taste for dried abalone. The inland tribes send a few people to gather them, not here -- it is too dangerous here -- but farther down the coast where the cliffs are high. The inland people talk to the coast tribes, who talk to Kalinta, and so it goes. After my grandmother stole me back from the mission, our whole village came to fish and gather abalone. It was our rodeo."

"Thank you, Tal-ku. Isabela will be blessed by the spirit of the butterfly. Even Jaimito may someday remember."

Tal-ku smiles, "Jaimito has seen much on my back. He has learned things his father will never know." This Tal-ku says with bitter disdain. Her wrinkled face, staring up at the butterflies, looks sewn from cowhide. Her old sack dress looks stuffed with straw, but when she reaches out and sweeps Isabela into her arms, she moves like a young woman. The abalone shell in her pierced ears glimmers. When her eyes darken with bitterness -- or light up with mirth as they do now when she teases Isabela about stepping on the butterflies -- Escolástica wonders how much older Tal-ku is than she.

Isabela cries out in anguish, "Look out little butterflies. Take care!"

A kinship exists between the two women that Tica would never try to explain to Job. Kneeling in the gold-flecked forest, Escolástica knows she has more in common with Tal-ku than with Rachel Harker. Tal-ku possesses the canny intelligence of the hunted doe, the fleeting grace of the chased fox. She hides in the open the way the rabbit does, blending with the chaparral, motionless as the hills, silent as dust. And Tal-ku responds to invisible dangers in a way that strikes fear into Escolástica, although she herself does not feel threatened. They are both *Californianas.*

"The eagle gave this land to my grandfathers," Tal-ku says. When a group of foreign men come into the house, Tal-ku calls them "*mollom*" (sea gulls) and freezes against a wall, her face averted, her body turned, her arms pulled into her no-color dress. Escolástica senses the fear and is unaccountably frightened herself.

Rachel Harker's fears are of another ilk. She stands awkwardly before the gilded mirror in her parlor. She is a plain, timid woman. Her disappointing image mocks her in the glass. She fell hopelessly in love with Thomas Harker in the confines of their ship on the ocean voyage to the Sandwich Islands, seduced by his shining face, his eyes glowing in the gloom below decks. Now she faces two challenges: this energetic man with his bold dreams, and a great savage coast studded with dangers and opportunities of every kind.

In fact, everything about California frightens Rachel Harker -- its Catholicism, the Indians, the grizzly bears, the whales, the drunken sailors and the Californian women. The women! Next to them, Rachel feels like a pale porpoise beached on the sand. She leans forward, studying her image in the mirror. These vibrant California beauties seem to bloom even more brightly along the coast. Their songs grow gayer, their clothes more colorful, their lilting Spanish more vivacious. Their bodies snap as they walk. Their short skirts blow in the wind.

Rachel turns away and looks out the window. Sometimes she hates them all. No, that is not quite true. María Rodríguez had been her salvation. She fell into María's arms on her first visit to the rancho, shortly after her arrival in Monterey, sobbing her whole miserable story, much of which María had guessed: Thomas Harker's child was conceived on the ship, born out of wedlock. María held her, comforted her, told her that the death of Rachel's premature infant daughter was not God's punishment. "God does not kill babies," María said. "They are fragile creatures. God saves every baby he can."

After the death of her baby, Rachel arrived in California puffy, unwell, unwed. Although the priests and the people of Santa Bárbara were kind, she never got over her feelings of awkwardness and ugliness around the Californian women. She had not told Thomas Harker about her pregnancy. He had heard about it accidentally from the ship's captain. Thomas stepped forward honorably, impulsively, and married her shortly after the baby died.

Rachel became pregnant again with a legitimate child, a son, and Harker treated her with every kindness. Some of the pain of her infant daughter's death eased, but not the feelings of inadequacy. Her skirts are too long (they drag in the sand, soiling the hems.) Her feet are too big. She looks down at her boots. Why are Californian women's feet so tiny?

Her coloring is so pale that the old Bonifacio sisters continually inquire after her health. Her Spanish is mumbled and clumsy. She cannot open her mouth enough. Californian Spanish is a smiling language. The lips move, the wide vowels ring musically, the consonants click like castanets. She has no knack for gaiety, and therefore often finds herself sitting silently, hopelessly forlorn while her crowded *sala* rocks with laughter.

She sits down beside the window in the parlor and opens her Bible to her bookmark, but she does not read. Now, as Thomas lavishes his energies upon the house, enlarging, ordering furniture from New York and importing carpet and porcelain from China, Rachel feels even more isolated from the women of Monterey. There is certainly an undercurrent of animosity among them. Being mistress of the most pretentious house in town has not endeared her to them. She continually hears the conversation trail off when she enters a room, not that she can follow the rapid Spanish anyway. She feels the stern barrier of the Catholic Church held up like some medieval reliquary to bar her way. With a curious insensitivity to such subtleties, Thomas presses ahead, gently scoffing at her when she mentions her discomfort, serenely assuming that she is as proud as he of the house. And she is proud. It is only that it seems so utterly his house.

As her family grows, she finds herself isolated even from her children, two adorable little boys, Tom and Will, and two pretty girls, Rebecca and Betsy, who all speak fluent Spanish. She can hear them now chattering in the patio. It seems to her that she, Mrs. Harker, remains the single señora *Yanqui* in town. She tries again to read, but the children's chatter distracts her. Even little Betsy gurgles in Spanish now. The heavy weight of isolation settles on her like some drab, unbecoming cloak.

The sight of Escolástica striding up the street rouses her. She puts down her Bible and pats her hair in front of the mirror. While Escolástica is a good friend, she frightens her, too. Tica's ripening beauty chokes her. When Tica enters the room, Thomas's eyes disturb her. She can tell that her timidity annoys Escolástica. Rachel is afraid to ride the *Californio* horses; she is afraid to take the children on picnics in the hills; and she is afraid of snakes.

"Do the little ones want to go to the beach?" Escolástica asks, once inside the house. Rachel says, "Yes" although she knows they will come back covered with sand and Betsy will wander too near the water, and the seals terrify her. But Escolástica is a friend, offering a relationship precariously balanced on fear and loneliness.

"It isn't too cold out?" she asks.

"No, of course not," says Escolástica, hurt by Rachel's seeming aloofness. Is it a sense of superiority Rachel feels, she wonders, with her fair skin and her soft hands and her college education? Tica envies Rachel her cultured husband, whose manners and tastes are much more nearly Escolástica's than Job's, who for all his energy and determination is an uneducated man. His manners are embarrassing. He can scarcely read and write English, much less Spanish or French. He is gruff and stiff, a boor in polite society.

The two women might easily have been even greater friends had they been more honest with one another about their lonely marriages, but pride and mistrust and modesty prevent them from sharing. Each nurses her own fears in private.

"Ah, don't be so surprised, Sancho, my friend," said Don Quijote, "because you've got to understand that these devils are terribly clever…[W]herever they go they carry Hell with them."

Op. Cit., Vol. 1, Chap. 47, pg. 313

MONTEREY
1846

John Charles Frémont makes Escolástica's flesh creep. He first appears in Monterey in January of 1846, quite alone, claiming to be a scientist. But rumors fly before him. The washerwomen say that he has arrived in California with sixty armed and desperate criminals who shoot anything that moves. One of the Rodríguez cousins sees the band in the valley of the Sacramento killing Yokut and raping women.

Escolástica is repulsed by his greedy eyes, his raucous voice. "A carrion crow, my grandfather would call him. He is not to be trusted, Job. He treats us with disrespect. He sneers at me, even as he bows. I do not like this man. Is he not a crow, *saarai,* Tal-ku?" But Tal-ku has disappeared.

Both Thomas Harker and Job Dye seem intrigued by Frémont, although they profess dismay at his disregard for the *Californios*. They talk long and excitedly into the night after Frémont's first visit. Rachel joins Escolástica in her distaste for the man, shrinking from his violent temper and his scarcely disguised cruelty. He took a whip to a *Costeñan* child right outside her door when the child failed to hold his horse properly. He drinks too much and becomes vulgar. And he has moved into Rachel's house at Thomas' invitation. As a result, Rachel's *Costeñan* servants have evaporated, and Job's insistence that Tal-ku help at the Harker's is met with mute resistance until Escolástica finally steps in.

"Job, Tal-ku knows what kind of man this is. She has heard things."

"That is stupid washerwomen rumor."

"You are quick enough to believe washerwomen rumors when it suits you. Tal-ku will leave for the hills, too, if you pick on her."

In March of 1846, as if to mock the hospitality he has been shown, Frémont rides back into Monterey with sixty rough, bearded, ugly men. The "scientific expedition" receives permission to camp on William Hartnell's property outside town, making the entire community anxious.

Tica has just left to visit her cousins on their rancho north of Monterey. The aunts are petrified. They are positive she is in mortal danger. Their rosary beads click incessantly. The whole town freezes in wary expectation of a crisis, which comes soon enough.

Four days after Frémont's arrival, on a mild spring morning, Escolástica and her three young cousins are out in the garden of Angel Castro's rancho planting peppers. The combination of warm sunshine and damp earth delights Tica after a winter cooped up in the town of Monterey. The two younger cousins chase around the garden barefoot, pelting each other with dirt clods, their skirts hiked up, their black curls flying. They are only eight and ten; Tica hasn't the heart to scold them. María, the eldest of the three girls, is digging holes with a sharp stick for the little seedlings when suddenly she straightens.

"Tica," she says softly, "*Mira,* look."

Tica looks behind her to see three heavily bearded men galloping up to the garden. It is too late to run back to the house.

"Quick," she whispers to a *Costeño* working beside her, "Find Tío Angel. Don't let these men catch you."

The *Costeño* melts into the brush at the back of the garden and disappears.

"Rafaela, Manuela," she calls sharply, *"Aquí,* come here. Now! *Ahora!"*

The little girls look up, astonished at her tone of voice. Then, seeing the men, they scurry behind her. Their sister María grabs both of them by the hand.

"Morning, ladies," the red-headed man says. "We're just looking for a little recreation. Thought we'd join in your game."

The two other riders laugh and dismount, leering at the young girls. They wear filthy rawhide pants and shirts. Their stench carries into the garden. They tie their horses to the rail of the fence, laughing, each arguing over which girl is his. They barge through the garden gate.

The fierce whine of a *látigo* stops them. Escolástica has grabbed her long rawhide whip and stands before her cousins wielding it.

"Ow! Stop that, you...." yells the red-headed man, holding his right hand.

One of the other men turns back to his horse to grab his rifle. "Ouch!" he cries, as Tica lashes at his wrist when he reaches for his rifle. "Why, you damned bitch," he says. "You broke my wrist."

"Get out," Tica says in a low voice. Whap! With sharp cracks of her whip she begins working them back away from the garden, away from their horses and scabbards, as if they were wayward cattle. Crack! She slashes at their ankles. "Get out," she yells, seething with fury. "Animals."

"You God-damned little greaser. We'll take you first, all three of us," roars the red headed man. "You'll pay for this." But they continue to back away. One man reaches for his knife, and Tica cracks the tail of her whip across his hand.

"Get out! Get out!" she screams, wild with rage. The three cousins cower in the garden while Tica advances on the men, snapping her whip, leaving red welts on their cheeks, cutting the backs of their ragged rawhide shirts when they turn away, whipping their buttocks and their legs furiously. She is so livid that she fails to hear hoof beats behind her until her uncle reins up with four *vaqueros*.

"What is this?" roars her uncle, and the three men turn to see the horsemen.

"We were just.... This little bitch attacked us," he says in English, which fortunately Tío Angel doesn't understand.

"*Sinvergüenza!* Tío, they intended to violate your daughters in their own garden. Shame!" Tica screams, shaking with rage. "They should be castrated as we do the cattle."

"Get out," says Angel Castro. "Get out, or I will see that my courageous niece's wish is granted." He points north.

The men haven't completely understood the exchange, but they back cautiously toward their horses, cradling their bleeding hands.

One of them needs help mounting. They ride briskly off, glowering at Escolástica.

"Follow them," Tío Angel says to the *vaqueros*. "Be sure they leave."

The little nieces run sobbing to their father.

"Father, without Tica," María gasps, "God only knows!"

Angel dismounts and gathers the girls in his arms. He looks over their heads. "Tica, thank God you were here. Thank God your grandfather taught you to use the *látigo*. Are you all right?"

Tica drops the whip and bursts into angry tears.

Angel Castro rides into Monterey the next day, his face white with fury. He gallops straight to the cuartel, shouts for his nephew José Castro, who is the new comandante. "My daughters, your cousins," he bellows, "were cornered in their own vegetable garden by three of Frémont's villains. Only Escolástica's skill with a *látigo* saved my children from rape. A *Costeño* managed to sneak off and find me, or God only knows.... By the time I reached them, the three younger ones were hysterical, and Escolástica was so outraged that she wanted to castrate the three men there and then!" The old man is shaking with fury as he dismounts and falls into his nephew's arms. "Get Frémont's men out of the country in twenty-four hours, or I will see to it that my heroic niece's wishes are fulfilled," he gasps, "and every loyal man in my family will join me."

His own cousins! Young José Castro is outraged. Within the hour, he leads a mounted force to Frémont's camp with written orders from the Mexican government to leave California immediately, on threat of arrest. Job joins them. He does not share Harker's enthusiasm for Frémont, having recognized at once that he is a fraud. He claims to be an explorer, but knows nothing about the wilderness. His mountain guides have confided to Job that Frémont is a romantic adventurer, out for his own glory.

"I'm going out with Castro," Job tells Harker. "The scum! How dare they attack Escolástica!"

"I'd better come, too," Harker says, "or you're likely to kill someone." Secretly, Harker resolves to urge Frémont to control his men and leave the area before real violence breaks out.

Before he leaves Monterey, Frémont bursts into *Alcalde* Diaz's office interrupting a complaint about the theft of a chicken and shoving

Ignacio Gómez aside. "I demand that you protect us," he roars. These Mexicans are making outrageous threats! They threaten to castrate my men. By God, I want them thrown in jail."

Alcalde Díaz, who has held his job for many years, looks calmly at Frémont over the rim of his glasses.

"I know the families well, Captain Frémont. They are proud, earnest young men. I would take any threats by them seriously if I were you."

Frémont glowers down at Díaz. "Do I understand that you will do nothing to protect my men?"

"Captain Frémont, the Castro and Rodríguez men are superb cattlemen. I have watched them chase down, rope, tie and castrate a calf in less than five minutes. I doubt that anything in the world could protect your men if they were adequately provoked. I advise you to move your company out of the area with all dispatch."

Frémont sweeps the papers from Díaz's desk and leans over him. "Washington will hear about this, Díaz."

"That may be. But I can promise you all of California will hear about this incident before Washington does. If I were you, I would tell your men to leave the California women alone."

Frémont glares for a long minute at Díaz, who meets his eye benignly. Then he turns and strides out the door, yanks the reins from the Indian who holds his horse, vaults into his saddle and gallops off. Díaz retrieves his papers from the floor and stacks them neatly back on his desk while he tries to suppress a smile.

Ignacio Gómez and Manuel Jimeno have not followed the entire exchange, but they understand at once the gist of Díaz's advice. They clap each other on the back and bow to the *alcalde*. "Never mind about the chicken, *Alcalde*. We'll have our wives cook it tonight for your dinner." They leave Díaz's office arm in arm, laughing.

The town seethes with hatred for the barbaric American invaders. Tica has returned to Monterey and watches anxiously from her window. She realizes that her children are in extreme danger in Monterey. Her family's ranchos up the coast are at once a refuge and a trap. If the American bandidos head north toward San Juan Bautista, as they seem inclined to do, the ranchos will be picked off and pillaged, one by one. Rumors of atrocities perpetrated by Frémont's men are rampant.

Job returns that evening at Harker's urging. He is worried. Frémont's band have vanished and José Castro's new proclamation names them a band of criminals, calling for volunteers to hunt them down.

"They are not criminals and they aren't foreigners," Job says. "They are Americans."

Tica is aghast at Job's reaction. "They <u>are</u> criminals. I saw them. Would you have your daughter raped in her own garden and your son murdered and not allowed a decent burial? Do you take pleasure in watching these foreign heathens pillage our land?" She stares at him in disbelief.

"They are Americans, Tica."

"They are foreigners, sea gulls!" she hurls at him. "You only claim to be a citizen, a Catholic. But your son and your daughter are true *Californios*. They will never submit to foreign..."

"Silence, Escolástica."

"And I will strike a blade in Frémont's heart before I see our children...," she screams at him.

Job grabs her clenched fist. "Tica, calm down. They are coarse, terrible men. I'll agree with you. I only mean that American rule's no worse than this Mexican rule, and a damned sight better than the French or the English. Even your uncle General Vallejo says so. Calm down, Honey. I won't let anyone hurt you or my children."

Escolástica sobs uncontrollably. He holds her, but he cannot soothe her. Tal-ku's words rage in her ears: "This is my people's land. The eagle gave it to my grandfathers." California is slowly ebbing away, and she feels powerless to stop it.

"Are you listening to yourself, husband?" replied Teresa. "Never mind all that....You go on and do whatever you want to... but let me tell you, not with my help, and I won't agree to any of it....both an honest woman and a broken leg belong at home."

Op. Cit., Vol. 2, Chap. 5, pg. 376

MONTEREY
1846

Rachel Harker is throwing clothes into trunks when Thomas arrives home that evening. She hardly notices his presence. Dresses hang on every chair. Linens crowd the tables. Rachel issues orders, sends the children scurrying for shirts, hairbrushes, petticoats.

"What in heaven is going on?" he asks.

Rachel looks up from her packing. "I am packing to leave, of course. You have booked us passage to San Francisco, haven't you?"

Thomas laughs, "Rachel there is no need. We will calm this situation down. Mexico is too disorganized to wage war way up here. The *Californios* can't decide whose side to be on."

"There will be war, Thomas," Rachel interrupts him, "or there will be such hard feelings that your children will be unsafe in Monterey."

"At worst the Americans will take over California. I don't favor war, as you well know, but American rule could be very advantageous for..."

"Thomas," Rachel interrupts him again, standing very straight. "What you fail to comprehend is that your children are not American. They can scarcely speak English, Thomas. Their lives will be in mortal danger. The Americans will see them as *Californios*. The *Californios* will resent them as children of Americans. The older children's loyalties will be torn."

With a sixth sense of which Tal-ku would be proud, Rachel Harker sniffs out danger for her children. She ruffles like a grouse.

"You do as you please, but I demand that you send us to San Francisco. You have influential friends there, and there I can speak the language."

Demand? Thomas gapes. Rachel's eyes crackle.

"But what will I do without you and the children?" he asks, amazed at her, horrified at the prospect of being alone.

"Get into mischief, probably. But I must take my children to safety."

Thomas looks sharply at his wife. She stares directly back into his eyes. She knows that he has entered into huge land negotiations with Frémont privately. She knows that he has received secret orders from President Polk. She knows he is an impulsive man, a man consumed by ambition. But she is leaving, and she means it. Her previous fears have been for herself. Now she fears for her children. She looks at her husband with such fierce resolve that she seems to him for a moment quite beautiful. The next day he reluctantly books passage on an American ship leaving for San Francisco, where they will arrive by the week's end.

The women may be right. Rumors fly: In Sonoma, Vallejo has been captured by Frémont's American rowdies. The Mexican flag has been replaced by one sporting woolen underwear and a shaggy pig-shaped animal that reminds the populace of Frémont's coarse unshaven gang, who have hair on their bare chests and even on the backs of their hands. Frémont's men wear pants made of animal skins and hats of coyote fur. They behave like animals. Frémont captures Rosalia Vallejo Leese's husband and terrorizes the poor pregnant young woman, threatening to burn down her house with her children inside it if she doesn't follow his orders. He heaps insults on her, steals from her, orders her to deliver her young maidservant to the officers of his barracks. He and his men are a pack of loathsome, savage animals. It is rumored that other Vallejo women have been raped and imprisoned in their own homes.

Castro is said to be countering with brilliant military maneuvers, said to be liberating Sonoma, said to have been killed by treachery. Frémont steals horses from every rancho he passes, although this is not a serious problem because he lacks the wit to steal the bell mare of the *caponera*, as well.[*] He and his men also steal saddles, which is infuriating, and *aguardiente* when they can find it.

Frémont is rumored to be on his way back to Monterey. Every story has three or four versions. Even the more prominent women of Monterey wander over to Washerwomen's Creek seeking news.

On July 2, three American warships loom suddenly out of a dense summer fog. With shortened sail and flags flying in the breeze off the fog, they ride the flood tide and cast anchor in an empty bay. Their masts and rigging tower above the little town. José Castro has ridden off to Sonoma with his force to try to free the Vallejo family. The harbor lies perilously unprotected. Escolástica watches the sailors climb like monkeys up the rigging to furl the sails. They swarm the deck, rushing back and forth. Then suddenly a thick bank of incoming fog hides the ships from view. Even the sounds of the sailors are muffled in the mist. An anxious silence blankets the town. The fog rolls in. The streets are empty.

Thomas Harker rows out to the flagship at once to find out what has happened and to plead with the commodore to take control before Frémont tears up the whole country.

Commodore Sloat has never heard of Captain Frémont. "Frémont," he says. "What does he think he is commanding? None of my dispatches mention a land force." Sloat himself has no orders to take over California.

"If you don't establish order," argues Harker, "the whole country will explode into war, and it will be left for England and France to pick up the pieces. You know they are waiting for any excuse to move in."

---

[*] It is the custom in California to tie a new horse neck to neck to a bell mare for a few days until they get used to each other. As this process is repeated a *caponera* is formed, and a horse will never desert his *caponera*.. Therefore, the *rancheros* need only to bring the bell mare with them and stampede the stolen herd to retrieve their stock.

"I have no orders to occupy California," says Sloat. "In fact, I was specifically ordered not to offend the inhabitants. We cannot risk another Catesby-Jones disaster."*

"You must seize control. You have the authority. Frémont has none."

After five days of frantic pleading by Harker and a delegation of merchants and *Californios* who are convinced that order must be restored, Commodore Sloat reluctantly demands the surrender of Monterey to the American government. On July 7, 1846, on a cold, foggy morning, two hundred and fifty well-drilled sailors land and march to the customs house. The women and children of Monterey line the sandy lane. The women are dressed in black, their dark *rebozos* drawn tightly around their faces. The children peek from behind their mothers' and grandmothers' skirts. Old men stand glumly off to the side. Most of the young men are still off with José Castro.

Escolástica clasps the hands of her two children as they watch the parade go by. From under her cape, little Isabela pulls a tiny silk American flag and waves it as the sailors pass.

"Where did you get that?" asks Escolástica.

"Father gave it to me," says Isabela proudly and waves the flag.

Juan Alvarado strides over to where they stand. Glaring at the child, he growls, "You are no niece of mine," and slaps her hand. Isabela howls.

Commodore Sloat is very close to them now. Tica clasps the child to her. "*Silencio, querida.* Wave the flag. It is your father's flag. Wave it." But Escolástica's face is grim as she watches the Mexican flag lowered and the American flag raised over Monterey. She had no great love for Mexico, but the American flag seems to her to signal an ominous change. She fears that the thunderous twenty-one gun salute from the fog-shrouded warships tolls the end of Escolástica Rodríguez de Dye's California.

Job bursts into the *casa* at noon, out of breath, excited. "Commodore Sloat has chosen me to take the news to San Francisco. I go at once. I ride the ocean route, by your father's rancho. Don Rafael goes inland

---

* Thomas ap Catesby Jones captured Monterey in 1846 under the mistaken belief that the U.S. and Mexico were at war. The local population was outraged. Jones was later relieved of his duty.

just to be safe. One of us'll be in San Francisco tomorrow with the news."

He takes her hands. "California is ours, Escolástica." And in his proud face Escolástica sees that his Mexican citizenship and conversion to Catholicism have been only temporary disguises, exotic trappings he donned for the fiesta. The fiesta is now over. "California is yours," Tica thinks. "California is yours."

As the household scurries to pack Job's saddle bags, Escolástica pens a quick note to her father and one to her cousin. Job takes down his long Kentucky rifle and he is gone, racing up the sandy beach road, riding toward the Pájaro. In her note to her father, she writes:

"California has fallen to the Americans.
My husband carries the news like smallpox
from town to town. Do not despair, dear
Father. Our California was strong enough
to survive the Mexicans. She will outlast
the Americans, as well."

Escolástica takes Isabela's hand and walks over to the Presidio Chapel. She kneels on the cracked tile floor and prays to the Virgin Mary that her assurances to her father will prove true.

When she returns home, she finds an impatient Thomas Harker waiting. He thrusts an invitation at her. "Doña Escolástica, Commodore Sloat is giving a dinner tonight in my honor aboard the flagship." His face glows with pride. "Because of your husband's service.... Because Rachel is.... That is, it would be..." His words tumble out in his excitement. "Would you do me the honor of accompanying me?" He bows his head, embarrassed as a schoolboy. Tica smiles bitterly at his discomfort.

"Don Tomás, is this an occasion I should celebrate? I am not so sure as you and my husband. Would my grandfather, your friend, have welcomed this change, Don Tomás?"

Thomas looks at her and feels his heart flare up. He turns away and walks to the door of the *sala*, gazes out at the ships lying at anchor. "Why must you ask the difficult questions, little Tica?" he murmurs. He turns to her, longing to take her hand. "I do not know the answer. I know only that your grandfather knew the winds were shifting. He

153

was too good a *ranchero* not to feel the storm building. He made me promise that I would protect you if the winds favored the Americans."

"But why did you pretend to be *Californios* when you were all Americans in your hearts? Why did you become Catholics, marry our women -- not you, Tomás. Pardon me. Your fellow Americans, Job and all the rest. Why did they pretend to be *Californios*? Was it only for the land?"

"Tica, it is never so simple. Why do you and your father and your grandfather pretend to be Mexicans when you are *Californios* at heart? You have no allegiance to Mexico. Why do you pretend?"

Tica turns away.

"California beckoned us, Escolástica. California seduced us. We fell in love with California," he says. "But surely you know that Job did not marry you for land. It was not only the land that drew us."

He breaks off, goes out onto the veranda. When she follows him, he says, staring at the bay, "Will we spoil the California we love so well? Will we pluck California as we do the golden poppies on the hillsides and then watch her wilt in our hands? I pray we do not. Sloat is a grave and responsible man. Perhaps he can lead the way."

The flagship *Savannah* shines on the occasion of the celebration dinner. Is it "spit and polish," Escolástica wonders, or a display of naval might? She and the other guests board to the spirited tunes of a brass band. Every rail gleams. Every seaman's face shines as they line the deck saluting the guests. But the dinner is a great political coup for Commodore Sloat. Governor Juan Alvarado and his wife, Antonia, come to town for the occasion. Monterey's finest citizens attend. Escolástica wears a deep emerald gown that makes her eyes look green as agates plumbed from the sea.

Rotund Antonia hugs her fondly. "You are in mortal danger, Cousin," she whispers. "Every sailor's eye is upon you. Even Commodore Sloat is perturbed by your beauty."

As Thomas's guest, Tica is seated to Commodore Sloat's right. He seems a shy, reticent man, ill at ease with the conqueror's role, and Escolástica likes him for that. He is curious about the famous California horses and has heard of Escolástica's horsemanship. Turning to her, he says, "In the United States I am considered a fair equestrian myself, but in California I would not be fit to hold your horses. I would like someday to ride out with you. I understand you are the premier horsewoman in California."

Escolástica laughs. "Then you have been talking to my cousins, Commodore, who are up to no good," she says, "but it would give me pleasure to ride with you."

Sloat questions her about the breeding of the California stock and the ingenious system of *caponeras*, the small herds led by bell mares and trained to stay together.[*] He neither flirts with her nor demeans her, and she takes heart in the gallantry of her American captor.

The man on her left, Walter Colton, she likes at once. He is a chaplain on one of the ships, a former professor, a literary man with a warm smile and a delightful wit. He seems embarrassed by the occupation of what he calls, "an enormously civilized country." She tells him about her grandfather's library. They discover a mutual affection for Scott. The chaplain sends to his cabin for a book of poems by an American with the curious name of Longfellow, and offers to lend it to her. The wine, the stimulating conversation, the admiration make Escolástica quite giddy.

She and Thomas are rowed back to shore. The fog has swept in again, and no sooner do they leave the flagship than they are enveloped in a cool mist so thick they can barely make out the backs of the oarsmen. Escolástica loves the summer fog. It is moist and delicate, embracing the coast in a refreshing cloud after the heat of the summer days. She pulls her shawl closer to her and feels her cheeks licked by the cool, delicious air. Thomas reaches over, spreads his cape around her shoulders and draws her toward him. She turns to him, sensing rather than seeing him in the dark and the fog. They are invisible, even to themselves. "It was a lovely evening, Tomás," she whispers in Spanish. And she kisses him.

And again.

As if they both have jumped headlong into the sea, they kiss, exploring the depths of one another in the dark. Then, suddenly aware

---

[*] According to William Heath Davis, these *caponeras* consisted of approximately 25 horses. The bell mares were usually calicos, *yegua pinta*. William Heath Davis, *Seventy-five Years in California,* San Francisco, Howell, 1929

of the sound of the oars' slap, they stop but continue clinging to one another, wrapped in fog.

American Consul Thomas Harker walks Doña Escolástica Rodríguez de Dye to her door. It is cruel coincidence that her *casa* is only three houses away from his; the fog is thick, making the world seem dreamlike. It is happenstance that Escolástica has sent the children to the *Casa* Bonifacio for the night and allowed Tal-ku to go abalone fishing farther down the coast. Job would never have allowed it, but Job is embarked upon his glorious ride. Rachel is safely in San Francisco. If Thomas had had the night to reflect, if Escolástica had not been titillated by the exquisite wines and the heady conversation....

But Thomas does not pause for a moment to reflect, and Tica scarcely pulls him through her door before she sheds her gown, abandons it in the middle of the *sala* floor, a pool of emerald satin, and leads Thomas to her bed.

Perhaps if the *Californio* women had worn complicated corsets, if Thomas Harker's consular uniform had had a dozen more irksome little gold buttons... The buttons only make Tica frantic. Thomas has never felt such shoulders, such full, delectable breasts. As she pulls at his tunic, her hands trembling, he slips Tica's chemise down around her hips, stares at her shadowy form in wonder. Aroused by his fingers on her naked hips, she is even more beautiful than he imagined, suppler, smoother. Flushed with desire, he stares at her and realizes that for ten years he has waited restlessly, hungrily, to have her.

Thomas stalks his *sala* the next morning waiting for a respectable hour to call upon the Señora Dye. Of course, that is the end of it. He was drunk. He took advantage of her -- an unforgivable breach. He will apologize promptly. It is a somewhat delicate subject, but he can trust Escolástica's intelligence and tact. She is a lady. It must never happen again. But as he marches down the street to her *casa*, his heart races. He is dismayed to find her already gone, probably to early Mass at the chapel. He cannot see her. He will have to wait an hour before he can see her. What if she does not come directly home?

And she has no intention of coming directly home. She has no desire for company. After Mass she rides along the beach north of town. The fog is still in, and she is relieved to find herself lost to view from the pueblo. She avoids company not because she is ashamed, but because her radiance will give her away.

"I love. I am loved. Surely the whole town will see it written on my face, imprinted on my cheeks the way the children imprint the gold dust of little gold-backed ferns on their foreheads."

She has prayed that morning for forgiveness, but she feels no remorse. It is a night she will treasure as long as she lives. She hopes Tomás will not smudge her memories with ashes of repentance. It was a rare, magical night in a world about to disappear. Why she knows this she cannot say, but she knows with inner certainty that an American California will envelop her like this summer fog. She will not be persecuted or punished; she will simply vanish, as she has this morning in the gray fog. And her California will vanish with her. Is her love for Tomás an act of vengeance? She does not know. She hopes for one more night with him, one more glorious night. That is all in the world she hopes for.

When she returns home late in the morning, Thomas rushes out of his *casa* full of firm resolve, gallantly lifts the señora from her horse, and, touching her, suddenly aches to gather her up in his arms.

"Put me down, Don Tomás," she says quietly. "The whole town is on the street this morning. Dear God, you will devour me with that look." She laughs quietly, intoxicated by her power over him. "*Paciencia,* Tomás. Nibble at me; do not gulp."

"Tica, I.... It cannot be."

"Tomás, who can stop it?"

...and if indeed there's anything worthwhile missing, I'd blame it on its dog of an author, rather than on any deficiency in the subject itself.

Op. Cit., Vol. 1, Chap. 9, pg. 46

MONTEREY
1846

Commodore Sloat sends his compliments later in the week. In the absence of her esteemed husband, would Escolástica have the kindness to accept the Commodore's invitation to a ball four days hence, celebrating the annexation of California to the United States of America? And would she do him the very great honor of leading the Grand March with him?

Escolástica's new white lace ball gown, ordered from Paris a year ago, has arrived the month before, a gift from Job for her twenty-third birthday.[*] When she dresses for the ball, Tica twirls around her tiny *sala* for Isabela, who shrieks with excitement. She feels spun from sugar in the frothy white gown, like some delicious French confection from Thomas Harker's shop. She is beautiful. Thomas will think her delectable. His lips will part, the taste of her still on his tongue. He is a passionate man. His mouth betrays him.

Did she know this long ago, that his warm, jovial cordiality masked a hot-blooded sensual man, much the way quiet coals betray a hotter fire? Tonight Tomás will be tortured by civility. Tica will be exhilarated by danger.

---

[*] The ball gown is included in the Costume Collection at the State Historic Museum of Monterey CA.

The main *sala* of *El Cuartel* has been cleared and hung with dark green garlands of cypress and pine against the thick, creamy walls. It is an ink drawing, Escolástica thinks as she stands on the threshold, India ink on heavy French paper. California is a land of pencil grays and pastel yellows and umbers. The shocking elegance of white -- starched white, lace-white, milk white -- only tumbles into California in clouds or on the crests of waves. Scraps of white are secreted in wedding trunks, but white is an unexpected luxury in a drab landscape. Yes, pen and ink, she thinks -- the wrought iron sconces and the black mustaches, the pitch green pine against the whitewashed walls. Ivory candles light the sconces, and the ladies of Monterey have added their own silver candlesticks on the deep sills.

Young naval officers form two lines, between which Commodore Sloat and Escolástica enter the ballroom to lead the Grand March. The men's dress uniforms and gold braid compliment Escolástica's white lace gown. The officers wear long trousers instead of the more becoming Spanish breeches, but as Mariana Munras floats by in the arms of a shy officer she is thinking that the American occupation might not be as onerous as her father claims, despite the trousers.

Even the older *Californios* are softening. The increased business the fleet has brought to Monterey is a boon to the merchants. The promise of duty-free imports delights the Malaríns and the Estradas. Commodore Sloat's diffident and courteous manner has impressed the Bonifacios and the Vallejos. Furthermore, his fatherly devotion to Escolástica Rodríguez de Dye pleases everyone, as the Castro and Rodríguez families are old and respected aristocracy and related to nearly every Californian family from San José to Salinas. Escolástica's beauty and accomplishments are a source of honor to them all; she is one of their own daughters. In the absence of her beloved mother, María Inocencia, they accept Escolástica's accolades with a mixture of parental pride and amusement.

Now they watch the Commodore bow stiffly to her, begging the favor of a waltz, and see the other dancers recede to the corners of the floor as Escolástica dances with the bow-legged Commodore, floating on his rigid arm like a lively white wave upon the ocean. Thomas Harker seethes with envy.

The days following the American occupation have been frantic. With Job Dye away, Harker is short-handed. The American sailors on shore leave with six months' wages in their pockets pack his store; Sloat cleverly paid them as soon as he occupied Monterey.

The nights have been agony. If Harker visits Escolástica, he is tortured by remorse. If he doesn't, he is racked by desire. Her passion terrifies him, rivets him. He has lost the lead in this affair run wild. She has seized the moment in a way that seems to Thomas almost suicidal. He damns himself for his indiscretion. He blames her for her wild abandon.

He stands that night on the sidelines of the dance floor, his eyes fixed desperately upon Escolástica as the junior officers with coltish awkwardness beg her for a dance. He could run each young man through with his own ceremonial sword. Thomas knows he must not dance with her, must not touch her, but before the first hour is over, she is in his arms and his feet are moving. He hopes his feet are moving. All he can sense are her green eyes and her lips, which are slightly open as if she were trying to catch her breath, and moist, as if they had just been kissed. So numb is he that he nearly loses his footing in the middle of the waltz and has to clasp her to him as he stumbles, then nearly drops her in embarrassment.

This uncomfortable scene is observed and relished by the guests at the ball, who in fact miss few of life's little quadrilles. Monterey is still a very small town. Anything that escapes the Estradas' eyes is sure to be noticed by the de la Torres. The unspoken consensus is that any man foolish enough to marry an American woman when he had all of California to choose from deserves to live in torment. *Pomposo*, pompous, the word is similar in both languages. Watching the self-important squirm is one of life's simple pleasures in Monterey.

The guests might add that Job Dye, having married a Californian and having failed to appreciate her, deserves his fate. The people of Monterey are not a cruel populace. They wish no one unhappiness, but they have a fearful lack of tolerance for false appearances. Frontier people seem to have a poor aptitude for respectability, and a little of the frontier lingers in Monterey society. So Thomas Harker spends a miserable evening. Escolástica looks more radiant than ever, and all of Monterey agrees it is the best ball in years.

Two days later Job returns home elated by his trip. San Francisco was thrilled to hear of Sloat's capture of Monterey. More and more Americans are pouring in, he announces excitedly. "I got there second with the news," he says, "on account of all your relatives along the coast who made me stop to eat at every darned rancho." Escolástica knows this is fool's talk, since they also would have provided Job with a fresh, fast horse for each leg of his journey. "But once in San Francisco, we were treated like heroes. A real celebration, Tica. By Joe, an all-American parade. You should'a seen it. Us two behind the fire engine, and American flags every place. You've never seen so many flags. You'd a thought we won California single-handed, the way they treated us."

She knows he wants her to sit beside him on the patio, to draw from him the details of his glorious ride, to make it grander than it was. He needs her, this slender blonde reed of a man, to color and fill in his victories, to shade and rub out the harsh edges of his defeats.

"You can't imagine, Tica," he pleads with her, knowing that she can imagine if she only will.

She smiles vacantly and asks the questions: "Did they give a dinner for you? Were you a guest for the night?" For once, Job's chauvinism hardly ruffles Escolástica. She leaves Isabela to squeal and giggle at her father's stories.

Thomas Harker is relieved to have Job back, who returns with a solemn letter from Rachel, modestly relating the family news. Rachel writes that she is finding many congenial friends in San Francisco, has joined a Methodist ladies' Bible group. The oldest boy has had an attack of fever, but he is better now. Thomas feels his feet begin to settle onto firmer ground. He politely refuses Job's invitation to dine at his house, pleading unfinished correspondence. He avoids seeing Escolástica for several days. Job's enthusiasm for things American seems to draw in ever more business with the sailors, and his aggressive lead in soliciting duty-free items under the new American law attracts the Californian families.

A week after his return to Monterey, Job strides into Harker's store ebullient with his latest triumph. He has been hired as guide and interpreter for Captain Fauntleroy's land expedition into the interior valleys and will be paid generously for his services. He will leave at once and be gone for two months.

"But Escolástica," Harker stammers, "and the children."

"Escolástica'll be fine. She's got plenty of family. You'll look in on her now and again? This here's the chance I've been waiting for, Thomas. I can stock my rancho. Thomas, this is a whole new era. By damn, the two months will fly by."

"Yes," says Harker grimly, "you're probably right." He writes at once to Rachel, sends his letter off that afternoon with a ship bound for San Francisco. It is perfectly safe for her to return to Monterey, he writes. He misses her and the children. Please hurry home, he pleads, before the rains. San Francisco will be too cold for the children once the rains come.

Rachel procrastinates. Their six-year-old son Tom is attending Sunday school. Young Tom will be confirmed the end of August. Why doesn't Thomas come up for the occasion? There are still rumors of trouble with the *Californios*. There is plenty of time before the rains. The summer has been sunny. She has found a dressmaker. They have been invited by a charming Englishman, Captain Richardson, to come over to the *Sausalito Rancho*, and the boys are beside themselves at the thought of traveling by sailing skiff over to the north shore of the bay. Rachel sounds cheery as a little thrush, but remote, as if he had known her years and years ago and then only vaguely.

The words of Rachel's letter swim on the page. Thomas puts it aside. The face immediately before him, vivid, suffocatingly close, is Escolástica's. Not just her face. The small of her naked back where he kissed her as she bent over to remove her ball slippers. The nape of her neck. Oh God! He holds his head in his hands.

Job Dye leaves at once on his mission with Captain Fauntleroy. Rachel lingers in San Francisco. Escolástica seems shoved by circumstance closer and closer to Thomas, until she crowds his dreams, breaks his concentration at the store, runs into him on the street. The tense political situation only fires the air with further crisis.

Frémont has disappeared altogether.

"In every disaster," said Don Quijote, "fortune always leaves a door ajar to offer some relief."

Op. Cit., Vol.1, Chap. 16, pg. 78

MONTEREY
1846

Commodore Sloat's health is failing. After reports of several bouts of sickness, Escolástica is rowed out to attend the ailing man, carrying with her various remedies and liquors offered by the women of Monterey. The patient can hardly lift his head from the pillow when Escolástica arrives at his cabin door. He calls weakly for his steward to bring his dressing gown so that he can leave his bed, but Escolástica has lived too long on a rancho to brook such conventional modesty.

"You shall do no such thing, Commodore. You have been ordered not to move from your pillow, and move you shall not." She slips to his bedside and places a cool, experienced hand on his forehead. "You are still feverish, Commodore. I have brought willow root, which you must chew, and my *Costeña's* nettle tea. You must be very cautious of these fevers. They can be dangerous."

Sloat sinks back against his pillows while the lovely young woman ministers to him, bathes his forehead, orders fresh pillow slips, cold water. He is indulging himself, he knows, but the soft shape of a gray silk taffeta dress in his Spartan cabin disarms him, makes him feel like a child again, as if he were drifting off to sleep in his mother's lap. He relishes the sound of taffeta as Escolástica moves about his bedside, and the feel of her cool hand on his forehead. His cabin, a stale cell of hardwood and cold brass seems overwhelmed by pearl gray ribbon silk.[*]

Tica serenely spoons Tal-ku's bitter tea to his lips. Each day she returns to feed him a Gonzalez broth, María Antonia's tonic, and to read to him from his favorite English poets. His cabin boy lurks at the door listening to her read, basking in the musical sound of her voice in the close cabin.

Two weeks after she begins her visits, he says as he watches her unpack her basket of delicacies, "I must give up my command, Doña Escolástica."

"Oh, Commodore. Must you go? California has need of you."

Sloat takes her hand and closes his eyes. Escolástica sees how ill he is. "Yes, your health is more important," she says. "You must have time to recuperate. It is only that California is so adrift, like one of your great ships with no one at the 'elm." She struggles with the word and makes him smile.

"Commodore Stockton has arrived to replace me," he says.

"He is a tactless man. He will not be a success in Monterey."

"I know." Sloat sighs, and turns his head toward his cabin porthole. "He has no horse sense," he turns back to her, "if you understand me." He feels a sudden desire to protect her, to keep the world at bay. It seems to him a worthy cause that all the Pacific Fleet be charged with protecting this high-spirited Californian who rides the wind-swept shores of Monterey Bay.

Escolástica laughs. "We have a similar phrase, but you must not worry, Commodore. He will not undo all the good you have done overnight. And soon you will be back with us."

"That I hope. I leave to Monterey my most cherished companion, my chaplain, Walter Colton, who admires you greatly, by the way. I have named him *alcalde*. At least I leave knowing that in Monterey justice will be dispensed with a kind and intelligent hand."

"But can you spare him?" Escolástica asks, because she knows the man before her is not out of danger.

"I give him up gladly. He is my legacy to Monterey in return for the happy hours I have spent here and the many kindnesses I have received."

---

[*] This dress also rests in the Costume Collection of the State Historic Museum of Monterey CA

He seems to drift into a light sleep. Escolástica knows Tal-ku's potion is taking hold. He stirs, adding, "I have a gift to ask of you in return." He breathes more easily now. "My first mate has a new daguerreotype apparatus that is not at all dangerous. May I take a portrait of you with me when I leave? Otherwise New York will think I exaggerate the beauty of the Californian women."

"You will have your little portrait," says Escolástica laughing. "But you will take with you another gift from me as well, a true California beauty." She winks at the steward. "You may not see it, however, until your fever is gone. Let it be your prize for a rapid recovery."

Two days later, when the flagship *Savannah* reaches around the point on its way out of Monterey Bay, on the slack tide, Escolástica's portrait is by Commodore Sloat's bedside. Below decks, pawing and tugging at his ropes, is Escolástica's gift, the stallion Ten Thousand Dollars, the horse that she won from the last Mexican governor of California.

With Commodore Sloat out of the way, the ambitions of Commodore Robert Stockton and John Frémont coincide. They are both interested in the American conquest of California. Official news arrives that Mexico and the United States are at war over Texas. The details are hazy, but the two men deem that sufficient justification for setting out for Southern California -- without orders -- to smash the final resistance of the *Californios* who remain loyal to Mexico. The citizens of Monterey are glad to see the scoundrels go. An uneasy tranquillity reigns in Monterey.

With Job's second departure and Rachel's refusal to return home, Thomas seems to abandon any hope of resisting Escolástica. He knows his neighbors are not fooled by his flimsy excuses to visit the Dye *casa*.

He and Escolástica spend a great deal of time in the company of the new *alcalde*, Walter Colton, who arrives on shore with a trunk full of books that he offers to lend to Escolástica. The avid reader is delighted. She has long since exhausted her grandfather's library. Walter Colton observes the relationship between his host and hostess with a keen, dispassionate eye. They take him on visits to neighboring ranchos and on *meriendas* down on the beach with Escolástica's children and various cousins. They cook abalone strips on hot rocks and sprinkle them with salty seaweed. They take him on excursions up along the Carmel River, where the *Costeños* spear salmon with their long, polished willowspears and grill them on manzanita spits. Colton becomes the focus, the excuse so that they can spend more time together. But they both like Walter Colton enormously. His inquiring mind engenders in Escolástica a renewed pride in her girlhood California.

Colton seems disinclined to Americanize California. Tica watches him dispense justice with the same fairmindedness shown by the best of the Mexican governors and a sensitivity and affection for the people that reminds her of the best of the Franciscan fathers. The liquid sounds of the language intrigue Colton, and he chats to her children by the hour, determined to improve his Spanish. He bribes them with *piloncitos*, the molded brown sugar cones from Mexico. Isabela and Jaime adore him, and they troop along the edge of the lagoon with him repeating the names of all the birds and plants, teasing him if he forgets a name, making him repeat it. The children teach him much of the Kalinta lore that Tal-ku has taught them. Jaime can track rabbits in the brush as well as any Kalinta-ruk child. Isabela tells him acorns were once the Spirit-people.

Often now Thomas invites Escolástica to go riding in the early evening. While Tal-ku feeds the children their supper, Thomas and Escolástica ride together along the bluff, surprising herds of elk that browse in the long summer twilight. They ramble through the little redwood canyons behind Monterey. They no longer fool themselves; they both know that sooner or later they will reach a secluded spot and dismount. It is for those moments beneath the redwoods that they ride. They can no more stop themselves than can the late summer seeds that float past them on paper wings.

When Job returns in mid-October Harker can hardly look at him, and Escolástica prefers not to. In the company of the American soldiers some of the rough edges of Job's rugged youth seem to have reappeared. He seems to Tica a mountain trapper again, tougher, cockier, more determined to wring his own success from California.

Job leans against the wall in the patio. He mends a horsehair rope, but she can feel him watching her as she slips a bread loaf into the round oven with her long-handled paddle. An appraising stare. Is there longing there? She wipes her paddle and looks over at him. She cannot read his face. His eyes speak unfamiliarly, as if they have slipped into some Kentucky dialect she does not know. Has he ever cried for her, she wonders, looking over at him against the wall? When did he last cry? Does he suspect the soft sensuality of her face, or is he simply responding to her vague dismissal of him, the way she shrinks back when he touches her? He grows colder and sterner with her. Only with the children does he relax. His shoulders give way when Isabela climbs into his arms. Flickers of contentment shine on his face. But he demands that the children speak only English at home now, a rule they find hilarious. They ape the guttural and nasal English accents of their father with malicious perfection.

"Horse," Isabela coughs up the word when they go to catch their beloved *caballos*.

"Hooorrrse," Jaime clears his throat on the word with a sound that is less like a noun; more like a symptom of bronchial congestion.

Many young *Californios* are still away fighting. The news of the American forces in Southern California is garbled, ominous. It is a tense, turbulent time. Harker determines that he must send for his family at once. But now it seems from Rachel's letters that the youngest child, his favorite Rebecca, is seriously ill and cannot travel. He has not been raised in New England for nothing. He at once recognizes his favorite child's sickness as God's punishment for his transgressions. He prays. He blames Escolástica. He suddenly resolves to ride up to San Francisco and stay with his family until they are all well enough to come home again. He prays his child will be spared, entering upon innumerable silent negotiations with God for the health of his little Rebecca.

Indeed, I would have you understand, Sancho, that there is no profession in this world more dangerous than that of an adventurer.

Op. Cit., Vol. 1, Chap. 21, pg. 111

MONTEREY
1846

Frémont's brigands are back in the Monterey area pillaging, stealing horses, and enlisting newly arrived Americans into their gang to fight the *Californios.* But Harker sets out for San Francisco in spite of the unrest. He will stop for the night with the Gómez family at *Rancho Los Vergeles* out of San Juan Bautista.

"Let me ride with you, for safety's sake," Job insists.

"No," Thomas says, "I have nothing to fear from Frémont."

"Then at least travel the coast route," Escolástica urges. "There you will be safe on the ranchos of my family."

"No," Thomas says, "thank you, but I have business with Don José. I will rest the night with his family."

Harker sets off alone, without even a *vaquero* to accompany him. He rides hard until he is well out on the inland road before he reins his horse into a loose trot. He feels like a schoolboy on holiday, a mild November day. The rains have not set in yet. The golden hills have burned brown, the tawny shade of the buck deer, the puma. The sloughs have dried up; the brush is dusty. It soothes him to ride through the brown hills. The distant sun has lost its heat, the grasses have withered; the gray chaparral has curled up its leaves. The land lies waiting for the November rains to awaken it from late summer dormancy. It is a progression of seasons quite backwards from his boyhood Massachusetts, but seasons, all the same. This dormant period, when all the world looks dead and ash brown, is followed by a burst of green in November or December and a wash of color in March and April when the golden poppies cover the hills.

This quiet season soothes him. He has rubbed himself raw with lust and envy and shame. The cloud of dust his horse kicks up obscures the world behind him, frees him from the vision of Escolástica and the passions she arouses in him, frees him from Job Dye's sullen face, hides him from the faces of his neighbors on which he sees reflected his own guilt.

He squints his eyes, concentrates on erasing Escolástica from his thoughts. This plain brown track leading to his wife and children seems to him a sermon written in the dust. Soon he will hold his sweet Rebecca in his arms, gather his sons around him. Good, kind Rachel will be waiting for him, timid and yielding. He sighs. It is as if he rides quietly back from a cliff.

He was infatuated like a silly youth. A man of thirty-eight should know better, a man of his responsibilities. The tie on the front of Escolástica's blouse is to blame, the tie that begs him to release it, to push her blouse down off her shoulders, to bury his head in her sweet bosom as they lie together under the redwoods. He shakes his head to clear it. Escolástica's marriage is an unfortunate match, he muses with a twinge of guilt, since he was the matchmaker.

Better not to think about Escolástica until he can remove himself further from the situation. Calling it a "situation" makes her bosom recede from his thoughts, makes the longing for her seem nearly conquerable, a "situation" that can be resolved. He concentrates on the dun hills and the sparse grasses and the pale gray clouds of mourning doves he flushes before him on the dirt road.

Don José Joaquín rides out to welcome Thomas to *Rancho Los Vergeles*. As they enter the walled patio of the rancho, Doña Gabriela bustles up to greet him, her belly swollen with an expected child. "*Mi casa es su casa*, Don Tomás." A dozen Gómez children romp about the courtyard, scuffling with a leather ball in the dust, playing in the mud by the well, chasing chickens.

"And this new child will make how many, Doña Gabriela?" asks Harker, smiling, taking her outstretched hands in his.

"Ay, I have stopped counting. God has been most generous. But my sister-in-law is well ahead of me. She has eighteen children already."

"There is plenty of room," says Don José Joaquin. "Two leagues. That is playground enough, even for a California family." The children cluster around Harker, the younger ones shoving in front. They are shy and polite, but they remember that Don Tomás brings licorice in his pockets. They will not be chased away until they have received their gifts. The boisterous domestic scene reminds him happily of his own children. He longs to leap back on his horse and ride through the night to them.

A fat leg of elk turns on the spit in the patio, baskets of sweet purple grapes cover the table, and fresh bread is just coming out of the ovens, round loaves shaped by patient, sturdy fingers. Escolástica would be at home here. Thomas has been too long in town. He has forgotten the leisurely confusion of a rancho courtyard: the laughing and teasing, the harness mending, the search for hens' eggs. As dusk falls, he sits amidst a happy, raucous family who want for nothing and bless God for their fecundity. He misses his children. Once again he feels rescued.

Thomas sleeps so peacefully that night that he hears nothing until his old friend's son, Manuel Castro, shakes him awake. His host, José Joaquin Gómez, is shouting in the courtyard.

"You insult a guest in.... How dare you? I die before you remove Don Tomás from my house," José Joaquin shouts.

Doña Gabriela runs in barefoot, clutching a blanket around her, "Get out! Get out of my house," she shrieks at Manuel Castro. "Sons of vultures, shameless ones. Worse than Frémont's brutes. Out!"

Harker sits up groggily, pulls on his pants and his boots. He has no idea what this is all about, but the young, heavily armed *Californios* are all sons and nephews of his old friends.

Young Manuel Castro looks frantic. "Please pardon this rude inconvenience, Don Tomás. I am afraid you must come with us. Temporarily, of course. It is Frémont. We have just fought with him at the pass. Very bloody. Four of our men were killed," Manuel says hoarsely and crosses himself. "My cousin Rafael..."

"Oh, *Dios*," gasps Gabriela.

"This is an outrage," shouts Don José Gómez. "I too am an *hijo del país*."

"Make haste, please, Don Tomás," whispers Manuel Castro. "We must leave quickly or someone will be killed. The men are in an ugly mood. We were badly defeated by the Americans."

So Thomas Harker grabs his cape and hat, calms Don José as best he can and rushes off with the grim band of *Californios*. A horse waits in the courtyard already saddled. They set off at a gallop headed south over the San Juan Grade. Wide awake now, Thomas tries to piece together what has happened, where they are bound, but the troop travels in grim silence. The moon has set. Thomas is aware only of the creaking of leather and the drum beat of hooves. It isn't until first light that he sees that the saddle on which he rides is stained with blood.

It is two or three days before he realizes that he is all the young *Californios* have salvaged from their bloody defeat. As American Consul in Monterey, his role as hostage might be a lengthy one. He is being transported south in rapid relays, and although he is treated with every courtesy at the ranchos where they stop, he is attended at all times by a well-armed guard. One of the fierce young men who guards him is Escolástica's brother Toño. Thomas dares not speak to him at all.

He worries about Rachel in San Francisco with a sick child. He knows that she will panic when she hears of his capture. San Francisco is as full of stories of Castro's atrocities as Monterey is of Frémont's. Thomas asks at every rancho for news of his wife and children. He entrusts several secret notes to the sympathetic *dueñas* of the ranchos, who promise to attempt to forward them somehow to Rachel, but the country has been torn asunder. About Escolástica he hears nothing, and he dares not mention her name, particularly in the presence of her brother. Harker travels south in relative comfort, offered the hospitality of the ranchos they pass (the best bed linen, the choicest wines, pomegranates and dates), a prisoner among friends, a prisoner in his own country, the country he has schemed to create. Again he wonders if he is being punished by a just God.

The rains begin and drum on Rachel Harker's frame house in San Francisco day after day, leaking in around the stove pipe, turning the streets into rivers of mud, confining the children indoors, where they catch their mother's apprehension and begin to squabble. To Rachel the damp, cold drafts seem to lurk like wily savages at the cloudy windows and around the narrow doorway, creeping in at night to make the lamps smoke and the curtains quake. She is dazed. Already worried about her daughter's pneumonia, she is paralyzed by the thought of being left alone in this raw land with four small children. How could she ever get back home? Where is home?

She keeps vigil at her daughter's bedside, as if at some Catholic shrine, praying for her recovery, praying for Thomas's return. She feels curiously close to him during these weeks, an intimacy she has not felt by his side, as if in capturing him and holding him prisoner the *Californios* have rendered him more manageable for her as well. Her thoughts are with him as she presses cool compresses to her daughter's forehead, urges her to drink a little water.

"When is Father coming?" whispers Rebecca. "Why doesn't he come?"

"He will come. There is trouble between here and Monterey. He's having trouble getting past the soldiers. He will come."

"I wish he would hurry," says Rebecca sadly, and her mother's heart nearly breaks.

A month passes, one of the wettest Novembers on record. Rebecca recovers from the pneumonia, but it seems that her lungs have been affected. She coughs incessantly and grows weaker. Rachel is gaunt. Brown circles shadow her eyes. She has had no word from Thomas since his capture. The rumors have been kept from her: that his dismembered body has been found near Santa Bárbara, that he has been thrown into a dungeon in Baja California, that he has been tried for treason in Mexico City and shot.

Rachel sees all the bleak world as dark and rain-soaked. Even in her sleep nightmares of torrential rains beat down on her, drenching her, soaking Thomas until water drips off his flattened curls and rain runs down his cheeks, streaking his face with tears and rain.

In fact, the rain is only intermittent in Southern California where Thomas is held captive. The winter storms carry to the north in California. He spends his days in the sunny patio of *Rancho Las Bolsas* sitting with the old widow Doña Catarina Ruiz, who plies him with *suspiros de monjas* and scolds his captors, many of whom are her sons and nephews. To pass the time, Thomas labors at Doña Catarina's copy of *Don Quixote*, but by the end of Part One the similarities between his own circumstances and the delusions of Cervante's hero hit too close to home. He puts the novel aside.

Monterey, midway up the coast, is rained upon, but mistily, a soft rain that falls lightly and then lifts, allowing pale, veiled vistas of the bay and of the hills behind the town. Escolástica, a book in her hand, paces her tiny adobe looking out the window into the luminous gray mists of the bay. She can just make out the shadowy customs house and the damp, bedraggled shape of a stray dog hurrying across the street. She sits in the windowsill and reads, stares out again. She has heard all the rumors about Thomas.

She carries his child; she is certain of this now. During the two months Job was off on his expedition, she conceived. She suspected it before Thomas left. Now he might never know. Her pregnancy pleases her. God has blessed their union. She cannot think of the child with shame. How could sin taint so happy a love? She sits quietly in her little *casa* waiting, reading to her children, attending to their lessons. She is determined that both Isabela and Jaime read and write in Spanish and in English.

For once, Job agrees with her. His own illiteracy rankles. He is pleased that Escolástica seems to have calmed down. After all, she isn't a child. Haven't they been married seven years now? She is twenty-three years old, for pity sakes. And he has some stature, now that California is American. She must see that. He's sometimes felt like an oaf around her and her family, no education, the manners of a valley Indian. But now he can hold his own. He's American.

But if she's calmer, she's also more aloof. "You're not listening to me," he complains one evening as they sit before a fire in their little *sala*.

Escolástica is threading her needle. She narrows her eyes and sticks her tongue between her teeth as she guides the thread through the eye of her needle. Sewing makes her mean.

"See, you're not listening."

"I listen, but I have heard what you say many times before: 'Your rancho, your rancho. Your forty mares for your rancho. Your one hundred head of cattle.'"

"Your rancho, too, and your children's."

"I begin to wonder, Job." Escolástica looks up, "I did not understand until the *alcalde* explained to me that married women cannot own property in America. What a primitive idea! I do not believe you think of this new rancho as mine or Isabela's. It is difficult to feel much enthusiasm. I begin to wonder if I will ever see it."

"There's no need for married women to own property," grumbles Job.

Escolástica laughs bitterly, "Do not tell that to my Tía María Martina. She might have you whipped."

"There's the trouble with California. The women have no respect."

"They are partners, not servants. You will see. A rancho cannot be run by a man alone. It is too much."

"Then help me," pleads Job. "I know I need you. Help me. We could build the best darn rancho."

"Do you mean that, Job? I have not even seen this grant on the Upper Sacramento." She puts her sewing aside and looks at him narrowly, searching his face. "Could we leave Monterey behind us," she asks, "and begin again on this grand rancho?" A window seems to open up, breathing fresh air into the cramped little *casa*. She glimpses a way out.

He avoids her eyes. "Soon, Tica, soon. But I've got to get capital. With these Americans streaming in, I'll have enough to stock that rancho proper in six months. I'd be a fool not to cash in on this new migration."

"My grandfather began with only a few cattle. Even my father's first herd was modest. You need only have patience, Job. You do not need capital on a rancho."

"I don't have time, Tica. I don't have time to be patient."

"But we are young. I will help you." She kneels beside him and takes his hand. "Isabela and Jaime will help you," she says desperately. "It will be as it was when I was a child, all of us working together. We have six leagues, Job. We don't need capital." She still clings to his hand.

He looks down at her, her eyes shining. Those blind shining eyes. He loves her so much it shoots like pain through his breast. "But can't you see, Tica?" he says gently, caressing her hand with his. "Those days are over. Every year your uncles and aunts get themselves further in debt. They're risking their land, Tica. I won't do that."

"They would never risk their land. Those lands were <u>granted</u> to them," Escolástica says. "Even Frémont and his outlaws cannot…" She hesitates, pulls her hand away. "Can they?"

Job gives up. She will never understand that times are changing.

Escolástica knows that leaving Monterey behind them is their only hope. Escolástica, for her own reasons, gives up, too.

Christmas comes, a sad, wet Christmas of 1846 that Rachel is nearly too distracted to notice. Her San Francisco friends provide a meager celebration for the other Harker children while she tends to Rebecca. Christmas passes. The rains continue relentlessly.

Christmas seems unusually dreary in Monterey as well. The chill of wartime has struck many families. The men are still away fighting futile battles to the south. The boom economy causes inflation and shortages. It is a scanty Christmas. Flour and sugar are frightfully expensive. Currants and candies are unavailable at any price. For Padre Suárez del Real, it is the inevitable Christmas when the Mission San Carlos in Carmel is finally decreed too dilapidated and dangerous for holding services. The padre has already moved out of the mission and bought the *Casa* Bonifacio up the street from the Harker house. He succeeded Padre Sarría ten years ago. Now he himself is an old man.

The relinquishing of the mission, first as a home and then as a place of worship, might have broken a more worldly soul. But Padre Suárez has the sharp light of the Holy Spirit in his black eyes. Ideally suited as a missionary, he does not seem to notice that the age of the California missions is over; and his wayward flock, both *Californio* and *Costeño*, has not the heart to tell the old man. He shuffles along the crooked streets of Monterey just as he did at the mission, dispensing charity, administering to the *Costeños,* saving souls. His vast experience with sin and stupidity and greed render him nearly clairvoyant. His olive pit eyes peer out of his small wrinkled face, recognizing sins before they are committed, suffering before it has begun. He preaches now from the pulpit of the decrepit Presidio Chapel in Monterey, heedless of the falling plaster and the damp.

At Christmas time, Padre Suárez indulges his one worldly excess, the creation of a living nativity. On this traditional tableau the simple padre lavishes all his ambitions for earthly glory, his hunger for opulence, his childish delight in glitter. No angel's wings can be too large. No wise man's headdress can be too gaudy. The citizens never refuse the old man his one foible, although fabric for costumes is particularly difficult this year, and the weather is foul, and Christmas is a busy time.

Escolástica prays the padre will not ask her to play the Virgin Mary this year. He, of course, knows better. Isabela is chosen to be an angel, and Jaime is the littlest shepherd. Escolástica and Tal-ku are kept busy sewing until the last minute. The wings flop; the halo teeters. Jaime's sheep (the padre has insisted on live sheep, which everyone tells him is a mistake) are put in a makeshift pen behind the house. Job has borrowed them from the Estradas, muttering that borrowing sheep is a damn fool idea.

The sky clears on Christmas Eve in Monterey, and the populace troops off to the Presidio Chapel under bright winter constellations. The Christmas bonfire blazes on the hill, lighting their way, making the sheep nervous. Escolástica and Isabela ride, but Jaime and Job have to drive the sheep over to the chapel, and the sheep plunge into every mud puddle and gully, causing all the dogs in town to bark. They arrive at the chapel mud-spattered, with their unruly flock in open revolt, and the dogs yapping at their heels.

Jaime and Job drive the sheep down the main aisle of the Presidio Chapel and corral them before the main altar, where Padre Suárez is arranging the tableau. The Virgin Mary, a young Malarín girl in a deep blue *rebozo*, good-naturedly kneels before the altar with her sleeping infant. They are the picture of maternal love, and the circumstances surrounding the baby's birth are apt. But that is no one's business except God's.

The Three Kings look very grand this year. Balthazar wears a towering turban wound from Doña María Carrasco's mother's embroidered shawl. The padre has augmented their costumes with worn out vestments. The second king's robe drags on the floor tripping him. The third king's crown, cut from tin by Juan Amesti, sits unhappily upon his son Cornelio's head. Cornelio does not want to be a king. They bear brass basins borrowed from the sacristy, filled with seashells. As the church fills for Midnight Mass, Padre Suárez del Real, may God forgive him, is consumed with pride.

The entire town rejoices in the scene. Walter Colton can't believe his eyes. Nothing in his New England background has prepared him for this. He delights in the wackiness and the devotion. The padre has placed extra candlesticks on the altar, and they cast a flickering light on the tableau. As the padre reads the Christmas story, the Three Kings arrive from afar, tripping on their magnificent robes. The more athletic angels perch in the niches behind the altar. Only the sheep remain restless.

Suddenly one of the sheep, in the dumb, hysterical way of sheep, bolts and runs straight into the communion rail, where it manages to get its head wedged in the railing. It bleats loudly, worrying the other sheep, while the embarrassed shepherds try to dislodge the silly creature. Padre Suárez raises his voice above the sheep's complaints. The commotion wakes the baby Jesus, who begins to wail, and one of the angels falls off his niche and skins his knee.

In desperation Jaime gives the sheep a whack with his shepherd's crook, which sends the sheep crashing through the railing, knocks King Cornelio Amesti flat, and scatters his basin of seashells. The sheep careens down the center aisle and out the main door, and the rest of the sheep stampede after it. Jaime stands in the foreground of the tableau clutching his broken staff and sobbing inconsolably. *Alcalde* Colton suffers a coughing attack.

The violins and guitars begin to play. One of the kings puts the fallen angel back up in its niche. The Virgin Mary calms the baby, and the celebrants sing the Christmas hymn *Noche de paz, noche de amor....* But there is a sense of catastrophe about this Christmas.

"That also brings us to what certain cold-blooded people say," said Sancho. "'Don't ask nicely for what you can take for yourself.'"

Op. Cit., Vol. 1, Chap. 21, pg. 118

MONTEREY
1847

Early in January 1847, armed resistance to the American forces ends. The *Californio* soldiers begin to straggle home. The *Californios* release Thomas Harker, and he rushes to San Francisco to find that his beloved Rebecca has died just a week before. His prayers have been in vain.

"She called for you just before she.... She couldn't understand what kept you." A small, smooth stone of bitterness lodges under Rachel's tongue. "Men who deny a dying child her own father. Not so much as a letter.... Inhuman. They are heathens." Her resentment of the *Californios* has been ground down with waiting and uncertainty, polished by grief. A bright hatred shines in her eyes. She will not think of returning to Monterey.

In Monterey, Escolástica's brother Toño appears suddenly at her door on his way home from the south, where the final battles have been fought and lost. He obviously has waited for Job to leave the house. Tica scarcely recognizes him. His jacket is torn at the shoulder giving him a lopsided look. His hand is bandaged with a filthy cloth. His breeches are caked with mud. He has always been tall, but now, at twenty-two, after a tough four-month campaign, he has muscled out like a young stallion. He holds his dark head high, as if sniffing for danger. His restless eyes are black with distrust of the Americans.

"They are thieves, Tica. They are here to loot California. Even Harker, even your husband has made secret pacts to steal our ranchos." He wolfs down the soup and bread she sets before him.

"Calm yourself, dear Toño," Tica says. "They cannot do that. Commodore Sloat himself told me that the land grants will be protected. The American law is very clear on property rights. He told me this. He was an honorable man."

"And where is he now, this honorable man?" Toño paces the *sala*, unable to sit down. "I will tell you. He is on the Eastern Coast, where the American law is also, where we will have to go to fight for our land. Three thousand miles we must travel to plead our case in English, in American courts, where no other language is permitted. I tell you, it is an ingenious plot to steal our land from us. Already the Americans flap like vultures around *Rancho Arroyo del Rodeo*."

Around Job, Toño makes no attempt to conceal his hatred for Americans. After two tense, awkward days, he embraces his sister. "I must go," he says. "Beware of these Americans. They will steal everything you hold dear, Tica. You were right to have fear of them."

He races up the coast road as if pursued. Tica watches him until he disappears over the dunes beyond the lagoon. She had hoped to talk to him about Thomas Harker. Toño was the one man she could have confided in. But Toño is no longer the loyal little brother she once knew. His sullen hatred of the Americans has hardened him even to her. She has lost him.

Harker returns to Monterey in February to pick up the pieces of his trading company and to attend to his official consular duties. His business has prospered, but his partner Job Dye's woeful bookkeeping has left the records jumbled. Since most of his business is transacted on credit, Thomas has no idea of the state of his finances. Questioned on the matter, Job becomes defensive, dour.

Harker's consular duties are even more onerous. The new American government proves as disorganized as the old Mexican one. An imperious American general arrives with orders from the Secretary of War to govern California. General Kearny sets up residence in Harker's house uninvited, which gives Rachel another excuse not to return, and proceeds to administer California in a high-handed way, refusing any suggestions for a representative form of government. In the meantime

Commodore Stockton, under who knows what authority, has appointed his crony Frémont to be governor. Frémont and his rascals stalk around California issuing orders, defying General Kearny.

Thomas is thin, grief-stricken and guilt-ridden over the death of his daughter, angry about his business, frustrated by the Americans in power. He is also tormented by a guilty desire to see Escolástica. He spent two months determining to give her up. He prayed that if God saved his daughter Rebecca, he would never see Escolástica again.

At first he cannot imagine what has come over Escolástica. She has grown softer, more delectable. She walks into the store the first day he returns home, smiles, then looks around the crowded store and leaves again, walking serenely away, her hands clasped over her round belly.

Her belly. A week later, as he watches her walking down the street, it comes to him. She is pregnant, the sensuous, voluptuous body of a woman in early pregnancy. Is it his child? Their nights in her bed, their afternoons in fern-lined redwood canyons seem years ago. He becomes desperate to know if he is the father. Is this pregnancy what lies behind Job's brusqueness? Does he suspect that Harker is the father?

For a week Thomas has avoided Escolástica, an easy subterfuge since he is entertaining the new American governor in his house. Now he attempts to waylay her. He watches out his store window for her. He looks along the beach every morning. He rides out along the bluffs where they rode together in September and October. One afternoon he sees her there along the highlands. He lopes toward her, but she sees him and spins her horse southward, dashes off through fields of wild iris, across damp swales of shooting stars.

He rides after her for the sheer pleasure of pursuing her. He knows he cannot catch her. She is a better horseman than he. He lopes along the sea bluff watching her fleeting figure recede in the distance. It is a sunny, blustery day that lifts little clouds, white as sea foam, and sends them skittering across a china blue sky. The wind scoops up the tops of the waves, and the ocean froths. Sea birds sweep sideways along the bluff below them. He looks south across the short green grasses to find that Escolástica has stopped. She sits her horse, facing out to sea. Her turquoise *rebozo* has slipped from her head, and her hair flags out behind her in the wind. She does not look at him as he approaches her. She continues to stare out to sea.

"They return. The first whales, bringing spring with them. Look, they have their calves with them already." She turns, her eyes the color of the full spring sky, and he knows that she carries his child. He thinks he might die of joy.

"...When?" he stammers.

"Sometime in May, God willing."

"Does Job...?"

"I have not told him."

"I...."

"I, too, treasure this child, Tomás."

They ride silently together back up the coast, watching the whales cavort along the shore, breaking the surface with great lumbering bounds, rolling, flipping their tails. They spout, high white pillars of air that catch the wind and turn to spray, living fountains, Thomas thinks. The fountains of the missions are meager replicas of this splashing and spouting in a great blue bay.

Thomas thinks he could ride forever on such a day, with Escolástica by his side. Why is it that spring seems so fragile, so brief? Winter drags on interminably. Summer rages for months until it scorches the earth of every herb and grass.

Why does spring seem anchored by such a slender string, like the children's Chinese paper kites that flash and soar and blow away?

"So what I say, señor," responded Sancho, "is that I've been thinking, for days now, how little your grace actually earns from all this hunting for adventures, traipsing through these wildernesses and crossroads..."

Op. Cit., Vol. 1, Chap. 21, pg. 115

MONTEREY
1847

The next day Escolástica's elder cousin Antonia appears at her door. Escolástica rushes out to embrace her and her new baby. While she and Tal-ku settle them into their little *casa*, Escolástica studies her cousin's creased, careworn face. Antonia looks much older than her thirty-five years. Something is terribly wrong. Escolástica hasn't seen her since last July, at Commodore Sloat's ball, where she was honored as Governor Alvarado's wife. Since then Antonia has remained at *El Alisal* running the rancho, while her husband Juan Alvarado went off to fight again with the *Californios* against the Americans. She gave birth to her fifth child in December, alone on the rancho. Her husband did not return from the war until late January.

"What will become of us, Tica? War is a greedier mistress than a woman. I wish he would give up this ridiculous campaign and go back to his whore. Juan Bautista is a good soldier, but he is a bad manager. He gives too generously. He digs us deeper into debt. I fear we must sell *El Alisal*. Many of the horses and supplies for the campaign against Frémont he financed out of his own pocket. His creditors swarm like deer flies. Whenever we begin to be solvent, he gambles everything on another campaign. First he fought the Mexicans. Now he fights the Americans. He draws men to him with his brilliant smile and his silver tongue. Then I am left to feed them. We are desperate, Tica. I pray he does not gallop off on another campaign while I am here."

"Dearest cousin, calm yourself. We will find a way. But first you must take some chocolate while we sort this out. Perhaps my husband can help. Who are Don Juan Bautista's creditors?"

"They are legion, up and down the coast. He probably owes Harker the most. I dread facing that man."

"We will face him together, Antonia. You will not lose your family rancho."

That afternoon, the two women meet with Thomas Harker at the store. Job is also present. The room seems much too small. Thomas takes down two chairs from the wall, but one is too close to Job; the other next to Harker. Escolástica feels faint. The smells of spices and spirits that usually intoxicate her make her head reel. She goes to the door for a breath of fresh air. Antonia is so preoccupied by her own troubles that she perceives the tension in the room to be directed at her. She nervously takes the chair by Harker.

Thomas is relieved to be able to address Antonia's financial matters. It keeps his eyes off Escolástica. "Doña Antonia, we will solve this crisis. We must. There is other land, is there not, in the foothills?"

"*Rancho Mariposas*. I have not seen it. I do not believe it is fertile."

"That is no matter. These new Americans are interested in quantity, not quality. Could you convince Don Juan Bautista to sell it if I could obtain a price that would satisfy his creditors?"

"But Don Tomás, we are talking about a debt of three thousand American dollars."

"I know Doña Antonia, I know." And indeed Thomas Harker did know. He himself carries two thousand dollars of the debt on his own books, much of which was incurred while he was imprisoned by Don Juan Bautista's *Californio* forces. "Doña Antonia, if you can convince your husband to part with *Rancho Las Mariposas*, bring the *diseño* to me and the grant. I have a buyer, I think, and I can complete the transaction swiftly. But Don Juan Bautista must stay home, if only to keep the squatters off his land. It is said the Peraltas have over fifty squatters on the east shore of San Francisco Bay. They will soon be troublesome here as well."

Thomas does not mention that his potential buyer is General Frémont, Juan Bautista Alvarado's enemy. Thomas has in his safe a draft for three thousand dollars from Frémont to buy land near Mission San José. He is playing both sides against the middle, and he knows it. He must not antagonize the *Californios*, who trust him. He must steer a careful course. But buying *Las Mariposas* for Frémont would retire a worrisome debt on his own books, give him two thousand American dollars in capital and keep Frémont a few miles farther away from the *Californios* who despise him.

Antonia revives at this practical solution to their problems. She rides with Escolástica along the beach that afternoon, nearly her jolly self again. "And who, little cousin, has fallen in love with you lately?"

"Antonia, don't say that."

"Tica, you are as white as a phantom. What has happened? Is your husband being difficult? In my own troubles I forget that being married to a *Californio* is not the worst trial. These Americans hold their hearts clenched in their fists. Their faces are stone. Even Thomas Harker seems impenetrable. He was not telling all today. I felt that."

Escolástica sobs and turns away.

"Tica, little dove, do not cry. This is not like you. You must come and stay with us, get away from Job Dye for a little. You need a relief from all these Americans and their rigid ways."

It is hopeless. Antonia could understand anything except falling in love with another American. Tica cannot confide in her. Her tears dry in the spring breeze, and she begins to talk about the children.

"Mamá, we must make for the *Alcalde* Colton a *merienda*. Imagine, he has never tasted the beach strawberries." Seven-year-old Isabela is the instigator. Jaime is right behind her, as usual. April of 1847 is unseasonably warm, and the wildflowers are knee deep. It takes little persuasion for the children to organize their cousins for a Sunday picnic on the high meadows overlooking the sea. Walter Colton is delighted. He never tires of learning the Spanish names for the myriad wildflowers, *copa de oro, castilleja, gallita*. He twangs the names over and over in his high nasal voice, sending the children into fits of giggles. "*Copa de oro,*" they sing in their thin, lilting cadence, and the awkward syllables turn to music on their tongues.

The children persuade their father to come along, and a great procession rides up the bluffs to a green, grassy meadow that has been mown short for the occasion. Tal-ku lays out the picnic on rush mats: dried beef, cold quail, beans with dried tomatoes, wild onions, wild asparagus gathered near the mouth of the Carmel River. Escolástica kneels on the mats composing the cold meal, shifts the platters, moves the slender green onions next to the fat little quail. She dares not light a fire for fear of attracting bears. The sows feed cubs now, and they are ravenous.

Job watches Escolástica arrange armfuls of blue lupine and golden poppies in pitchers and bowls among the platters of food. He turns to Walter Colton, who stands beside him. "She looks like she's painting a picture. She cares more that the food is pretty than that it fills us. A strange place this is, Colton."

"Perhaps it is because all of nature conspires to such fertility in this land." Colton replies. "One need never want. Even the wild animals are sleek and fat." He gazes at a herd of deer browsing farther up the meadow, but he is thinking of Escolástica, quite obviously pregnant now, moving gracefully, naturally, obviously delighted with her expected child. In Boston pregnancy is considered an embarrassing, sexually transmitted illness. Here in California, where families of twelve or fourteen are common, pregnancy is an event as natural as spring itself.

Colton watches the children run up carrying flower crowns they've woven from the buttercups and poppies. They hold them out as if they were jewels, and Jaime places one on his mother's black hair as she kneels by the picnic. Then he throws himself laughing into her arms, nearly tipping her over while she kisses his neck, his cheek, his nose. Isabela presents her father and Walter Colton with crowns that look fairy wrought, of buttercups with broken stems and scrunched clover and brilliant, wilting tiger lilies. She curtsies shyly and scoots away; a little chickadee, Colton thinks, dainty and dark, scurrying off to join her brother.

"How fortunate you are, Job, to be a part of this California."

"Am I part of it? My children are, as native as those fawns in the grass. I sometimes wonder if you've got to be born here to be part of this place. After all this time, it still seems like some kind of dream. Not real. At times I'm afraid I'll wake up." This craggy man wears a wreath of golden buttercups on his brow and speaks in a near whisper, staring at Escolástica with such longing that she feels his eyes and looks up at him startled. Walter Colton fears that he intrudes and turns to ask Jaime the name of the little hummingbirds busy in the flowers.

Escolástica gives birth to a daughter on May 28, 1847. The birth is a long one. Tal-ku and one of Escolástica's aunts, Ignacia Bonifacio, are in attendance, scolding each other and arguing until Escolástica wishes they would take their prayers and potions and eagle claws and leave her to her labor. She lies with her eyes closed and her fists clenched, inhaling the flat, clean smell of the newly whitewashed walls, willing the child to come, pushing through the pain. When it is over, Tía Margarita bathes the infant in warm water, to Tal-ku's disgust, and delivers it with great ceremony into Job's arms as he stands in the *sala*. He has heard the infant's cries and then nothing, nothing but the rasping chatter of the two attending women. No sound from Escolástica. He receives the babe without even seeing it.

"*Y la madre*? The mother?" he manages hoarsely.

"Ay," says Tía Margarita, withered virgin, "it was nothing. She is still young." And she disappears into the bedroom, slamming the door and leaving Job alone with the infant an amazing wet little creature. She might have been plucked from some cloud, so pink is she, so perfect, right down to her little pearl fingernails and her damp eyelashes.

He returns her to her mother's arms a few minutes later. Escolástica lies pale, exhausted against the pillows. She looks to him like a flickering candle, as if giving birth to this tiny ounce of a babe has used up all the life within her. He balks at the sight of her, so weak, so nearly extinguished. The thought of losing her makes him frantic. He longs to breathe life back into her, to somehow rekindle her. He kneels beside her, stroking her hair, brushing it away from her face.

"You," Job says, "you all right?"

"Yes."

"It wasn't too much for you?"

"I am fine, Job."

From the day the baby is born, she is held in somebody's arms. Her mother nurses her, holds her on her hip as she cooks. Tal-ku carries her on her back, tied tightly on a willow board padded with moss as she gardens and sweeps. Isabela carries her proudly, as if she were a doll. Job holds her often as they sit in their patio in the long summer evenings. He seems more at ease with this baby, more gentle with her.

He and Isabela carry her to Harker's house when she is just two days old to show her off.

Thomas reaches out for the little bundle, takes her in his arms. His eyes brim with happiness. He cannot speak. He stands looking down at the babe he holds, and his tears fall on her.

Job and Isabela think that he is mourning his daughter Rebecca, and Isabela puts her hand on his arm. "Her name is also Rebecca, Don Tomás. That was my father's idea." Wise little Isabela looks up at him. "To take the place of your Rebecca, who has gone to live with God."

"Perhaps," Thomas says, looking down at Isabela's delicate little face, a slender miniature of her mother's. She lacks her mother's ferocity, but she has her dark beauty and intelligent green eyes. She is a gentle, affectionate child. She fusses over the old aunts and uncles of the town, takes them little treats from Tal-ku's ovens and grubby handfuls of blue lupine. Isabela gives names to all the chickens, and cries when Tal-ku kills one. She protects Jaime from the older boys and the dogs that roam the streets. She and Rebecca Harker were inseparable friends, chattering in a musical mix of Spanish and English and Kalinta that no one else could fathom. Isabela still lights candles and prays for her as she kneels in the chapel.

Thomas takes Isabela's hand in his and touches it to his lips. "Perhaps," he repeats. He hands the baby back to Job and looks up into his friend's face, this friend he loves and hates. He cannot risk saying more.

All these storms we've been caught in are signs that soon the weather will turn bright and calm and good things will happen to us, for it's not possible for either good or bad to endure, and from now on, having endured a great deal of bad, the good is already drawing near.

Op. Cit., Vol. 1, Chap. 19, pg. 96

RANCHO ARROYO DEL RODEO
1847

As soon as she can ride again, Escolástica decides to take her new daughter to her father's rancho for a visit. Her father has been begging her to come.

"Will you not join us, Job?" she asks.

Job swallows his pride. As usual, Escolástica has not asked his permission to go. She has invited him to come along. He smiles at his own tolerance. Is she breaking him to lead as she has so many strong stallions?

"We're too busy here," he says. "I can't stay," he takes her hand, "but I'll ride up with you. I'd like to see your father again."

Escolástica looks at Job appreciatively. He seems to have grown. He seems more generous in nature now. He is reaching out to her. Strangely, baby Rebecca seems to have formed a bridge between them.

The children shriek with delight when they hear of the expedition. For one thing, it means no lessons with old Tía Bonifacio. They will ride their favorite horses and have *meriendas* along the beach.

They set off up the coast road in mid-August, and the trip takes five leisurely days. The first day Juan Bautista Cooper accompanies them, so they stop for the night at *Rancho Familia Sagrada*, his family place along the Salinas River. The old man is a favorite of the children's. He has a deformed hand (the children call him *Don Juan el Manco*), and an old seaman's affinity for tall tales. He took a liking to Job when he first arrived in Monterey, and Job is very fond of the old man. It is Job's idea to stop one night with him.

"It'll be a short day for you and the baby. It would please old man Cooper."

Escolástica is tired when they arrive at the rancho. Doña Encarnacion Cooper remains in residence in Monterey, so Escolástica retires to a bedroom in the empty house. Doña Encarnacion's lace is famous. When Tica pulls the hand-tatted white coverlet over herself in the cool room, after the heat of the day, she feels covered by the mythical snow flakes Job talks about to the children, the delicate flower petal shapes that fall from the sky and blanket the world. She has never seen a snowflake, but the children often beg their father for stories of snow, snow so deep he sank to his waist in it, snow falling so fast it covered him from head to toe in white, and his footprints disappeared behind him.

While Escolástica rests, Tal-ku takes the children to the river, low now in late summer, to bathe and hunt for frogs. She insists that cleanliness gives strength. She hangs their clothes carefully on a willow, and she scrubs the children with the brushy end of the amole bulb while they writhe in her grasp.

Tal-ku's family village is farther inland, but she knows every stretch of the meandering waterway. She shows them which reeds to gather for baskets and where the quicksand is likely to be. They make pipes from the horsetail, then duck under the water and breathe through them. Jaime discovers a huge turtle that nearly snaps his finger off, and Isabela chases bright blue dragonflies through the shallows, singing the song Tal-ku taught her:

Beautiful dragonfly,
Soo-koo,
Come dance with me.
Beautiful Soo-koo,
Come dance on the water.
Come dance to the brink of the world.

Tal-ku wades along the stream gathering blackberries in her woven willow basket, and Jaime sneaks along behind her with his horsetail fern pipe, stealing berries as quickly as she picks them.

As they walk dripping and barefoot back toward the house with their baskets of berries and frogs, giggling and singing, Tal-ku suddenly jerks Jaime off his feet. Inches away in the dirt lies a four-foot rattlesnake coiled and shaking its dry hollow warning. In the late afternoon, the snake seems a pattern of dry brush and pebbles, one moment a snake, one moment a long shadow in the dust.

"You do not listen, Jaime. You must listen. The snake was warning you." With a cottonwood branch, Tal-ku flips the snake, balances it on the end of the stick with both hands so that it hangs full length helplessly.

"Kill it, kill it," shouts Jaime.

"No," cries Isabela.

Tal-ku flings the snake off into the brush.

"Why did you not smash it with a rock, Tal-ku?" Jaime demands.

"He did not kill you, Jaime. With one bite he could have poisoned you. He was an old one, full of venom. One rattle for every creature he has killed. You saw. He has killed many. He took pity on you because you were so small and a traveler in his land. It is <u>his</u> land, Jaime. Do not be so proud when you walk in the land of the snake. Walk lightly and listen."

Job and Juan Cooper watch the children trudge back up to the adobe behind Tal-ku.

"They are fine children, Job. You are blessed."

Job's face colors with pride.

"Also your wife is an exceptional woman, Job. Yes, you have been fortunate in this land."

Job shifts uncomfortably. He knows that whatever gossip surrounds Escolástica's escapades on horseback and on the dance floors of Monterey has made its way to Cooper's ears.

"It ain't easy ... a California wife," Job stammers. "I sometimes think Harker was right marrying one of his own kind."

Cooper stares straight ahead, squinting into the low sun. "*Hijas del país*," he says and sighs. "Daughters of the land." He himself is married to Encarnacion Vallejo. "Nothing worth having is easy," he says at last. "They are worth the trouble."

As soon as they ford the Pájaro River, Escolástica feels she is home. Her cousins' brands mark the cattle they pass, first the Rodríguez brands as they cross the fertile Pájaro plains of her Tío Sargento. But they do not linger. She urges them on, farther north, until they begin to see the familiar brand on the sleek flanks of the cattle. It is her grandfather's brand, modified slightly by her bachelor uncle, Guadalupe Castro, who now runs the rancho.

They climb from the marshes where the redwing blackbirds bugle from the cattails and the eagles build fortress nests in the cottonwoods. Up onto the hilltops they ride until they see the pepper tree that marks the rancho. And there on the hill, just as she remembers it, stands *Casa San Andrés*, its cool porches and verandas shaded by lush grape arbors hanging with fat purple grapes that make the children's mouths pucker.[*]

They ride into the walled courtyard, and Escolástica feels as if she has come back from an arduous journey in another world. Ancient Iss-ma works at a loom in the courtyard. The regular click of the shuttle, the low warble of the bluebirds in the lilac bushes, the swish of the breeze in the pepper tree all seem to her the sounds of peace. Tica is suddenly so sleepy she can hardly greet her cousins and Iss-ma. Es-ken had died two winters before. Tica apologizes as she is led off to rest.

She lies in her grandfather's four-poster bed listening to the healing sounds -- the shuttle's clack, the rustle of the hilltop breeze. She loves the fresh ocean wind that sweeps through her in Monterey. But this is a gentle meandering breeze from her childhood, a small stirring, like the chatter of children, that creeps up from the canyons in the morning, brushes the hilltops, then slips unhurriedly back down into the deepest gullies for the night.

Isabela tiptoes in and climbs into the bed with her mother.

"When I was your age, I stayed here with my grandfather. Two Mus-tak princesses lived here. One of them was Iss-ma, the old woman."

"Did you love this place very much, Mamá?"

Escolástica kisses her daughter's hair. "I still do."

---

[*] The house still stands today on that hilltop just south of the city of Santa Cruz.

Every day they ride out together while she tells the children tales of their great-grandfather, his adventures coming to California with Anza in 1776. "...and only six years old, Jaime, just a little older than you, and much of the way he had to walk on foot because the Indians had stolen the horses, through Apache country, over the mountains where snow lay so thick on Christmas Eve that his father, the soldier, built a roaring bonfire out of twelve tall trees. In the light of that bonfire a baby was born, just like baby Jesus, and they laid the babe in blankets stuffed with dry grasses to keep him warm."

Job tells of seeing his first rodeo on this rancho. And their mother was the head *vaquera*, "...rode the wildest horse and chased grizzly bears with her *reata*, although her mother, your grandmother, forbade it."

"Job, you exaggerate," says Escolástica laughing. "Your great-grandfather was the head *ranchero* until the day he died," she tells the children. "And when he died no one could touch his bay mare. They eventually released her with a wild herd in the valley. They say she still follows the herd, although this was nine years ago."

"What was her name, Mamá?"

"*La Bandera*. She had a thick black mane and a tail that billowed out like a banner when she ran."

"I would like to meet her someday," says Isabela.

Grandfather Castro's rancho is bounded on the north by Tío Rafael Castro's *Rancho Aptos*, which in turn is bordered by the enormous *Rancho Soquel*, owned by Escolástica's favorite Tía María Martina Castro. Like pearls strung along the white beaches of the bay, Escolástica's aunts' and uncles' holdings occupy a quarter million acres of California coastline.[*] At every rancho, as they ride northward, they are greeted by a fiesta. The *vaqueros* pass the word before them. The famous Rodríguez violins are tuned. The Castro cousins light the manzanita charcoal. The *matanza* is about to begin. In the little lull before the frenetic harvest of the cattle, the cousins rejoice in Escolástica's return with her three beautiful children.

The party grows until they arrive a week later at her father's *Rancho Arroyo del Rodeo* with four *carretas* full of food and a *cuadrilla* of horsemen, all hungry. Francisco Rodríguez lopes out to meet them.

---

[*] The beautiful *diseños*, the maps of the land grants, can still be found in The Bancroft Library at the University of California, Berkeley.

He is utterly unchanged, Escolástica thinks, his long hair still black as a crow's wing. He greets his daughter tenderly and delights in his grandchildren, especially the infant Rebecca, whom he is seeing for the first time. Escolástica misses the sight of her mother in the courtyard chopping onions, laughing, pulling bread from the oven. Escolástica's brother Toño is nowhere to be seen.

The household has been preparing for days, and a great *barbacoa* is planned in the arroyo under the redwoods. Francisco leads the way, with tiny Rebecca crooked in one arm.

"Tía Martina, my father is amazing. He appears younger than my husband." The two women sit under the redwoods on a carpet of wild ginger.

Tía Martina laughs. "These *Californio* men are undisturbed by the seasons. But give me a man who worries, Tica, a foreigner. They grow old quickly, but they know the value of the land. They make excellent watchdogs of our ranchos. I know," she says, laughing. "I have tried them all."

Escolástica chuckles. After the death of her *Californio* husband, handsome Tía Martina married an Irishman named Michael Lodge. He is her grand passion, she admits. She is so jealous of him that she will allow only old *Costeñas* to work on her rancho. When Michael Lodge sings love ballads in a clear tenor, he sings only to her. Martina still blushes to hear them.

"He has so much love for you, Tía Martina. He is irresistible," says Escolástica sadly.

Martina looks at her niece. In the flowing way of California families, she is not too many years older than Escolástica, daughter of her older sister. "Every man must love in his own key, Tica. They cannot all be tenors."

"No," says Escolástica. She picks up a little redwood cone from the deep duff.

"Does your husband love you, Tica?"

"Yes." She idly crushes the dainty redwood cone in her hand. "But he has a hard core where love cannot penetrate. It is as if his heart froze solid in the snowy mountains years ago. I cannot melt it. Perhaps no one can."

Martina knows she should give solace, offer advice. Her dear sister María would wish it. A cold, clear melancholy bubbles up in Escolástica, trickling out of her, like the secret springs on the hill, a small sadness welling up from so deep within her that the source is hidden. Martina wants to say, "Love your husband. All will be well. Go to Padre Suárez. He will help you." But Escolástica's sadness, a sadness as chilling as Job's impenetrability, silences her. Martina shivers and turns the talk to cattle.

Escolástica's father loans Job two hundred head of cattle for breeding purposes, as is the custom, and Job buys some horses from the cousins to add to the stock on his new rancho. He and Escolástica design a *fierro*, a cursive D̲, which they ride over to register with the *juez de campo* in the pueblo of Branciforte. It seems to both of them the dawn of their new rancho. The cousins help them brand the small herd that will roam the *Rancho Arroyo del Rodeo* until next spring. During the fiesta held in honor of the new brand, Job burns the *fierro* onto the gate post of the rancho, where all the family brands are burned, now twelve in all.

"Like the apostles," says Francisco proudly. "I wish our fathers were here to see this. The twelve apostles of the Santa Cruz. I ask God's blessing on us all. Now we must adjourn to the last supper."

Indeed, Job is to leave the next day for Monterey, although Escolástica and the children linger another fortnight. It is to be the last time all twelve brands are represented around the table at *Rancho Arroyo del Rodeo*.

The *butanos,* the polished cowhorn cups, are brought out and generously filled with the finest wines of the Santa Clara Mission. Much advice is offered to Job around that table on how to start his rancho.

Martina is curious about the Upper Sacramento. None of the family has been so far inland. The tales of Maidu massacres are legion. Exaggerated rumors of a Swiss who is founding an empire fortified with great cannons have reached the Santa Cruz.

Job has only seen the area once on his scouting expedition with General Fauntleroy, but he speaks excitedly of the vast herds of elk that roam the rich grasslands along the Upper Sacramento River and the shadowy antelope that race across the dry bluffs, almost invisible against the dust. He tells of the colored bluffs that bank the river along one stretch of his land grant. Even in his uneven Spanish, he grows eloquent when he tells of coming upon the bluffs at sunset, a flaming red reflected on the calm surface of the river.

"Six leagues," Job says, and raises his cup to Escolástica's father but looks at Escolástica: "I offer six more leagues to the family Castro-Rodríguez." His face shines with pride.

"Job," says Tica, raising her cup, "I would like to name the rancho *Río de los Berrendos* after the flaming bluffs. How I dream to see them."

"Soon, my wife, soon."

Perhaps the flaming red bluffs, *los berrendos,* will kindle his heart.

...the proper thing would be to turn around and go right back home, because it's harvest time, now, and we ought to worry about our own affairs and stop traveling from here to there and letting everything go from bad to worse, as they say.

Op. Cit., Vol. 1, Chap. 18, pg. 91

MONTEREY
1848

At first during the winter of 1847, it seems to be just another rumor. The only things more numerous than fleas in Monterey are rumors. Oddly, this rumor does not emanate from Washerwoman Creek. This rumor comes from the Americans, the trappers and traders and sailors. Thomas Harker is the first to think there might be some substance in it. Early in 1848 he buys a cupful of gold nuggets from an American and sends some of them off to Washington for analysis. The silversmith in Monterey pronounces the rest of the sample to be pure gold, and Harker commissions him to fashion a brooch from the nuggets. Thomas sketches a simple shape, composes an inscription:[*]

> *"No dejes a un antiguo amigo."*
> (Don't give up an old friend.)

Like a tidal wave that, indistinguishable at sea, flows in upon the shore, swelling farther and farther up the beach until the town is wading in its foam, news of gold floods the town of Monterey and the imaginations of its inhabitants. Job comes home one day early in 1848

---

[*] Today the brooch is locked in the Monterey History Association vault.

and announces that he is leaving to check his land grant on the Upper Sacramento. Escolástica knows this is a ruse. The hundred cattle and the two hundred horses he sent up initially have been roaming the rancho for a year now.

"Job, why do we not go up together?"

"First I've got to take a look. If this gold strike turns out to be as rich as some claim, that rancho will be worth real money now. I've got to see for myself how the stock is doing and what these gold rumors amount to."

As the spring winds buffet a half-deserted Monterey, Escolástica watches Job set out for the Upper Sacramento with four other American landowners and two Kalintas to take care of their camp. They look like boys on a holiday. Job rides the big cinnamon brown stallion her father gave him, branded with his own brand. For Escolástica this is the time of rodeo, the roundup, the branding, a busy season of the year. She chafes at being left in an empty pueblo while the men ride out, full of adventure.

Of course, the pueblo is not entirely empty. Walter Colton, the *alcalde*, remains, although all his servants have run off to the gold fields. "I am reduced to grinding my own coffee, Doña Escolástica, and fishing for my own dinner. I toast herrings over my stove. It is a desperate situation."

Thomas and the new governor are also left to their own housekeeping. Food is scarce. Dozens of empty ships lie at anchor in the bay, with no crews to sail them. The sailors desert for the gold country as soon as the ships reach port.

Escolástica welcomes the crisis. She and Tal-ku hunt the Laguna Seca and bring home fresh venison and quail. They gather abalone and mussels along the coast. Tal-ku digs wild onions and greens in the marshes, and the children pick Indian lettuce and wild strawberries.

Every week, news of the gold fields arrives in more fantastic form. Common sailors return with enough gold to buy the ships they slaved on. Prices soar. Harker's business is staggering when he can acquire goods to sell.

Rachel Harker seems determined never to return to Monterey. Thomas still seeks to avoid Escolástica, but now that the town has shrunk, it seems that he meets her on every street corner and that all the eyes of Monterey take notice of their meetings.

Escolástica has pulled back, too. The promise of a future on her own rancho, her idyll with Job up the coast to the Castro-Rodríguez land grants, seem to have reconciled her to her husband. Harker urged Job to go off to inspect his land grant and the gold fields. Now he wonders why. He himself should go to San Francisco to conclude some business, to visit Rachel and the children. He begins writing more frequently to Rachel and the boys, then realizes there are no ships to carry the letters. He lingers in Monterey into July, a cold, foggy July that begins to seep into his skin.

One morning he strides down to the beach in search of a sea captain. The sand swirls around him, and he is forced to pull his cloak closer as he walks the shore. He nearly runs into Escolástica before he sees her. She walks towards him, her *rebozo* whipping in the wind, her hair blown across her face. She looks like a shore bird in flight, dampened by the spray, buffeted by the wind. They both stop. Escolástica looks up at him, brushes her hair back. Her eyes soften; her lips part. Suddenly Thomas longs to sweep her into his arms, kiss her damp cheeks, her salty lips. But Escolástica lowers her head and plunges past him.

"Dear God," Thomas thinks, "bring Job Dye back soon."

Job does return in August bursting with news, but not about the rancho. Escolástica is horrified to hear him rant about the gold fields: "Monterey Bar on the American River -- richer than sin." He is speaking English again after his two months in the company of Americans, a coarse guttural language that renders his description of the gold camps even cruder. "We didn't know what we were about, Escolástica, a bunch of sons of mules out there with just farm tools. Seventy thousand we took out, Escolástica, clear of expenses. That's ten thousand dollars apiece, for six weeks' work." And he pulls out one of his sacks and pours a little pile of drab gravel onto the table, scratching it, fingering it, holding it up to the light in the palm of his hand.

"And the rancho, Job? The cattle?"

"Oh, it's all fine, fine," says Job with a wave of his hand. "We rounded 'em up, marked 'em -- a good many new calves. Nearly got me a grizzly bear, or a griz near got me, on the way up there, at Sycamore

Slough. Old griz came out of the tules, and I took a shot at him with my pistol like a damned fool. Then I caught him by the hind foot with my lariat, and Toomes managed a shot at him with his rifle. But he gut-shot him, and the bear caught Toomes' horse on the flank, an awful gash, then took off into the tules. Got clean away."

"Did you not follow him, Job?"

"No, we didn't have time."

"But, Job, it is not honorable to wound an animal and not put him out of his misery. It is not *caballeroso.*"

Job laughs. "Toomes wasn't feeling real *caballeroso* about that grizzly, I can tell you. He was scared spitless."

"And the rancho? Have the Indians started on the adobe, Job? When can we go?"

"Escolástica, don't you understand? There's a fortune to be made up there. Americans are swarming into California now. I sold the goods I shipped up to Sacramento for over twelve thousand dollars. They wanted clothes, shovels, mules. We'll turn our twelve thousand into hundreds of thousands of dollars. This is my chance, Escolástica. This is no time to worry about cows. I'm gonna talk Harker into chartering a schooner with me. I'll run it down to Mazatlán, load up with supplies and be back in time to make a killing in the mines before the rains."

"But the rancho, Job. It needs attending. A good rancho wants careful tending."

"The cows'll take care of themselves 'til I get back, Tica."

Job sails out of the harbor on the schooner *Mary* within the week. Escolástica and the children wave until the *Mary* rounds Point Pinos. It is a blustery summer morning that tangles their skirts, catches their curls, and tosses waves at them as they stand on the beach. They have to shout to one another to be heard as they turn and trudge up the sand toward the pueblo. Escolástica sees Thomas Harker standing at the verge of the beach watching the departure, too. She feels as if the tide is shifting under her feet, following her up the sand.

"I am tired of hearing that my relatives are lazy, Tía." Escolástica's aunt, Tía Ignacia Bonifacio, has come to tutor the children, but Escolástica needs someone to talk to. She is lonesome, restless. "That my uncles, who speak three languages, read the classics, play the violin and raise vast herds of cattle, are lazy because they will not become shopkeepers. These Americans are a nation of shopkeepers. They think of nothing but money. They have no concept of cattle-raising, of the skill involved." Escolástica pours chocolate with a brutal clanking of the cups. "These Americans would not survive one rodeo. They would sag in their saddles within a week." She closes her eyes to erase the image of Job at her father's rodeo -- sweating, sunburned, in love. "They would never have the stamina to endure the *matanza*. They must dole out their energies in meager portions, the same drop each day, no more, no less, as if they were invalids. Yet they call our *Californios* lazy."

"They lack a sense of the gracious," says Tía Ignacia, shaking her head. "They have no aptitude for hospitality."

"You are right, Tía. Hospitality they see as sloppy accounting. Generosity to them means extending credit."

"They are a peculiar people, untranquil. I cannot see that they will advance civilization to any degree. Having no wish to come in contact with them, I have abstained from learning their language. I hope they move on. Your esteemed husband excepted," Tía Ignacia adds politely. She sits very still in her stiff black silk, straight black hair parted in the middle, pulled into a knot, wrought iron features in her angular face. She might be an ornament on an old iron gate, so still she sits.

"My husband is sometimes as bad, Tía. He sails off like the west wind, distracted by the first shiny pebble. Who knows when he will return?"

"You must have patience, child," says the old aunt darkly. "You must devote yourself to your children and your religion."

Escolástica understands what her aunt is telling her. Nothing happens in Monterey that the Tías Bonifacio do not hear about.

"Why can we not go to our rancho? There we would have no need of money. Tía, sometimes I despair."

"Patience, Child, patience."

As if in protest to Tía Bonifacio's admonition, there is a knock at the door. Thomas Harker steps into the room.

"Ladies, good afternoon."

"I go now to the children."

"No, Tía," says Escolástica. "You have not finished your chocolate."

"It is I who must go," says Thomas. "I only call to alert you that three chests full of books have just arrived for you at the customs house."

"Books?" Escolástica gasps.

"Hundreds. They appear to be from Commodore Sloat," Harker says, mystified. "They came by naval ship."

Escolástica's mouth opens with delighted surprise, "Books." Then she shakes her head and laughs. "You see, Tía, always the Americans must pay or be paid. I gave the Commodore a good horse. Now he thinks he must repay me in my favorite coin: books."

Thomas, confused by Escolástica's explanation and by her harsh laughter, mumbles his compliments and leaves, promising to bring the books that afternoon.

"Thank you, Señor Harker. Do not trouble yourself. Just send them over."

As he leaves, he hears the old Señorita Bonifacio say, "Three chests full of books, Escolástica. That is a great gift indeed. And from an American." Tía Bonifacio is shocked.

"It is a generous gift, Tía, but do not be alarmed. I earned them in shrewd Yankee fashion. I traded an excellent horse."

Harker spends the rest of the day throwing things. He tells himself he is unpacking a shipment. There is no one around to hear the commotion, anyway. His clerks have deserted to the gold fields. That idiot Dye is off treasure hunting -- and with Harker's money at that. Thomas breaks good barrels, hurls crates of expensive watered silks.

Was Escolástica mocking him? In God's name, what had he done to deserve such treatment? If she had not dismissed him, he might have withstood the temptation to see her again. He might have gone up to San Francisco, visited his family and returned resolved to avoid her until her stupid husband returned. Why he persists in calling Job stupid, when he himself strongly supported the expedition, is a question he ignores in his rage at Escolástica. She has a cruel streak. She is vain, proud. How dare she be proud with him?

He beats his fist against a wine barrel, slumps down on a bale with his head in his hands. He sees it now. She is toying with him, tempting him back, taunting him until he burns to see her. No, not merely to see her. "Dear God," and Thomas weeps with rage.

Tica relishes Thomas's discomfort in her *sala*. She is in a thoroughly dangerous mood. Calling for her horse, she sets off at a gallop, heading up the Cañón Aguajito, a quiet valley behind Monterey. She rides her horse so hard that he begins to lather, and she reins him into a walk. But the gait does not suit her mood. In a few miles she kicks him into a lope again. She rides farther inland until the baked hills fold around her. The gold grasses shimmer on the hillsides. Even the patchy shade beneath the gray oaks looks hot. She reins her horse in when they reach the first creek and walks him along the stream for a mile or so before she lets him drink. She feels as restless as *Las Hermanas*, the black butterflies that flit along the riverbank. She dismounts and walks upstream, where she drinks from the cold water. This creek is spring-fed, and the cool water soothes her. She lies on the bank listening to her horse wade downstream. She feels as if she were recovering from a severe fever. She is calm at last, but weak, spent.

She must have dozed. She awakens to hear the liquid sound of children's giggles. Upstream, two naked Kalinta girls are gathering willow for baskets. They are perhaps eight or nine years old, sun-tanned, round and smooth as manzanita berries, oblivious of her presence. They walk in the creek, stooping, snipping the willow off with their teeth, splashing one another with quick flicks of their bare heels, so perfectly formed, so natural in their nakedness, as if they have stepped out of another era. Behind them in the shadow of the oaks stand three rush huts. Tal-ku has spoken of hidden villages, villages with no trail leading in or out. Tica has seen Tal-ku weave rabbit snares from little wisps of grass, pluck abalone from the slipperiest rocks. Tal-ku is superbly equipped to live in California. So are these little girls, perhaps better prepared than Isabela? Yet, unless they have hidden like outlaws they have been wrenched from their families and their villages, infected with smallpox and dysentery, "Christianized" to work as slaves. Have the *Californios* done to the *Costeños* what the Americans are now doing to the *Californios*? Is she being "Americanized"? Will Isabela be American? Escolástica is definitely in a dangerous frame of mind. She creeps back downstream to her horse, leaving the children to their play.

Thomas Harker returns that evening with a box of books. Both Thomas and Escolástica knew he would. He sits silently in the *sala* while she reads to the children from one of the new books. He listens to her liquid Spanish accent as she pronounces the English vowels, smoothes them with her lips, caresses them with her tongue. He wants to chase the children off to bed.

But she selects another book, begins another poem. Isabela and Jaime drape around her like baby seals on a rock, sunning themselves in the warmth of her body. The baby lies asleep in her cradle beside them. Thomas sits across the room willing the poem to end. By God, this Longfellow believes in length.

Finally she reads the last lines. Jaime yawns. Tal-ku appears and is gathering the two children when a knock at the door interrupts her. The two Bonifacio aunts have come to call, and they have brought their embroidery. Escolástica guesses it is no accident that their visit coincides with Harker's. The old aunts have eyes like the spider, as Tal-ku would say. They creep in, two skinny old ladies surrounded by six yards of stiff black silk, like two ancient tarantulas out for a stroll, and when they sit, they sit with such weighty permanence that Harker suspects they may stay a week. They deploy their skirts and shawls and petticoats around them, bring out needles and scissors and thread from their black lacquer Chinese sewing boxes, and they lay siege. After twenty minutes, Thomas gives up and excuses himself politely.

So it's true, after all, that it takes a long time to get to know someone, and you can't count on anything, in this life of ours.

Op. Cit., Vol. 1, Chap. 15, pg. 76

MONTEREY
1848

Job returns from an extremely successful sea voyage. His lean suntanned cheeks have colored in the salt sea air, and his blonde hair has lightened. His capital has increased substantially, he tells Tica. He is a rich man. He is tall and handsome, and he is desperate. Just when he should have the world by the tail, he is losing his wife. He has heard rumors as far away as Mazatlán. Escolástica refuses to deny them. She has become, in fact, quite insolent.

"It is difficult to appreciate your wealth when I am left home alone with none of it, forced to beg for credit from the local merchants until your return."

"You could have gone to Harker."

Escolástica laughs bitterly.

"Unfaithful?" she scoffs when he nags at her. "I have not had a husband for months. You have been off making money, an occupation you seem to prefer to being a husband and a father."

"At least my children have remained faithful..."

"Do not be so sure. They have become very attached to the *alcalde*. He reads to them when he comes for dinner."

"Him, too? I should be jealous of him, too?"

"You need not be jealous of anybody. It is as you please."

"Tica," he grabs her roughly by the shoulder, hurts her, "What's come over you?"

She looks him straight in the eye. She does not even wince at the pain in her shoulder. "What has become of you, Job? Of our plans, our rancho? Our dreams? You are turning back into an American," a word she pronounces with such loathing that it sounds filthy, somehow.

"Please, Tica," he says and releases her, watching her lower lip quiver, a full, moist lip, the color of ripe plums. He turns away. "I would be a fool not to take advantage of this rush. We'll get to our rancho. I need a little more time. This gold fever'll die soon. I beg you, Tica. Oh God, I love you."

Escolástica touches his hand. "Job," she says quietly, "Monterey is not good for us, for me. I am like a filly kept too long in a small corral. Soon she becomes nervous, mean, unpredictable. Let me go, Job, with the children. We will build the rancho for you."

He gazes into her huge green eyes so filled with hope, so blind to the new realities of California. He pats her hand patiently. "Escolástica, don't be daft. The Upper Sacramento is wilderness. There are Indians, all kinds of desperate men who've failed in the gold fields, criminals... You would have no family, no neighbors. It is a wild, dangerous place..."

"I know danger when I see it, Job. I, too, have faced the grizzly."

He is losing her. Job can feel it. Every time he reaches out for wealth and security, a place in California, his grasp on Tica slips. He is being pulled apart. Doesn't she understand that his California future hinges upon her?

The next day he climbs a ladder at the back of the store to sort some rope and harness leather. He stares down at Harker bent over the ledger. The gossip in Mazatlán named Harker as his rival. Job has had his own suspicions, but he hasn't wanted to believe the talk. He watches the hunched figure below him scratching numbers into his ledger. His friend. He hates him.

Job knows that Thomas has one great weakness: his ambition, his desire for respectability. Job doesn't give a damn about respectability. Job just wants Escolástica. If Thomas is his rival, he must foil him, and to foil him Job must threaten him with scandal. He begins to make inquiries. He calls on Walter Colton, the *alcalde*, later that afternoon.

"What do you mean, 'complicated'?" Job demands. "Infidelity isn't complicated. My wife has been unfaithful, so I'm thinking about divorce."

The *alcalde* does not ask for details. He has lived in Monterey for the past two years. Instead, he holds up a cross. "Can you swear on this cross that you have been faithful to your wife since you left Monterey so many months ago?"

"Is this the law of the United States of America?" demands Job Dye.

"No," replies the *alcalde*, "It is not the law of the United States. It is <u>my</u> law: 'Let him without sin cast the first stone.' It is not original."

Job stalks the *alcalde's* cramped quarters. "I'm made a fool of in my own pueblo. She won't deny it. She's not sorry. She won't give a name, though I've got my suspicions."

Colton could have supplied the name, but pride does not interest him. He is concerned with justice. "If you cannot swear that you have been faithful in your absence, go live with your three children and with your beautiful wife. She is every bit as good as you are."

The *alcalde* might have added, "She has fed me generously in these last months. Without her hospitality, I might have starved to death."

Colton is a Presbyterian, a preacher, an American plucked by Commodore Sloat from his ship and set down unexpectedly in Monterey to maintain law. He does not pretend to understand the Californians or the Indians or the Catholic Church, but he is an expert on human nature, and he recognizes a good woman when he sees one. Escolástica Rodríguez de Dye is a good woman. It would probably kill Job to lose her.

Job's negotiations with Harker are strained. Harker can't look him in the eye, and Job's suspicions fester. The rumors in Mazatlán haunt him. He must get rid of Harker.

"I'm thinking of divorcing my wife," Job says coldly, casually one day when they are alone in the store, his eyes on Thomas's round face. Thomas blanches white as whale blubber.

"Why?" The word forms on Harker's lips, but he emits no sound. "But," he tries again, "that's impossible. There is no divorce in California. The Catholic Church...."

"This is the United States of America now. Grounds of adultery." Job watches Harker's face. He makes no mention of his conversation with Walter Colton, and walks out of the store.

That night, Thomas Harker sits alone in his own *sala* with the lamps unlit. He has no desire for company. He leans on his desk, his head in his hands, his black curls falling forward. Divorce. Scandal. Political suicide. He will be ruined. Escolástica will be destroyed. A divorced woman in Monterey would be a pariah, even to her family. She would be disgraced, and he could not save her. She is a devout Catholic. She would never remarry. What is he thinking? He is in no position to marry her -- a respectable man with a wife and three children? Respectable? He would be throwing away his political future. He would only succeed in turning them both into outlaws. He closes his eyes, and a fleeting picture of them lying together on the beach, living on scallops and mussels distracts him. Dear God, they cannot wander the beaches for the rest of their lives. Escolástica's grandfather's voice sounds in his head like a bell across a steep ravine, "If you *Americanos* inherit California, you will not forget Escolástica Rodríguez."

He stands suddenly, as if to escape Grandfather Castro's words. He stares out the window into the night. Why has Job told him? To warn him off? Or is it too late? Job is a proud, hard man. Hard? Harker's love affair with Escolástica is common knowledge. How would he feel if he returned to San Francisco to find Rachel's name on every tongue, linked to some prominent San Franciscan? He would be outraged, he realizes, even though... he pounds his fist on the wall and turns away... even though he does not love her. Dear God, I have sinned. Thomas kneels on the bare wood floor, a Protestant, and all night he prays for forgiveness, for guidance. At dawn he still prays. His legs are stiff, his back aches, and his head is stuffed with appalling thoughts. There is no Protestant God in California. He must leave Monterey. It is Escolástica's only hope. It is a cowardly act. It is <u>his</u> only hope. He must never see her again.

He watches for Job that morning out his office window, and catches up with him as he walks toward the wharf. "Job, last night I made a decision," he says. "I must leave Monterey. My family is in San Francisco. There are new business opportunities opening up there. Would you consider running the Monterey business on a full partner's share?"

Job watches Thomas fidget nervously with his collar. He is careless in his dress this morning, as if he had slept in his clothes. "How long will you be gone?" Job asks.

"For good." And Thomas's tired eyes are so hunted, so beaten, that Job knows instantly that all the rumors he has tortured himself with are true. He realizes that before this moment he has not allowed himself to believe them. Thomas Harker has lain with his wife. Rage chokes him. He longs to throw his *reata* around Harker's neck, strangle him, drag him until there is nothing left of him but a shapeless lump, hack at him as he has seen the Apache do in the desert until his body is mutilated to bloody shreds. He hates Thomas Harker more than he has ever hated anyone in his life.

"Get out of my sight," Job growls.

"Do not..." but the hatred in Job's voice warns him off. He must not speak Escolástica's name. As if he were backing away from a mountain lion, Thomas moves quietly and speaks carefully. "I will leave all the necessary papers on my desk. I must leave early tomorrow for San Francisco, but I will keep in touch by letter. My compliments to your..." and again he sees the rage well up in Job's eyes,"...to your family. I regret that the suddenness of my decision will not permit me to say goodbye to them in person."

The following day a package arrives for Escolástica while Job is out of the house. It is the brooch, fashioned from some of the first gold nuggets brought to Monterey. A local silversmith has worked them into a graceful circle so that the golden folds look as smooth and rich as the summer hills. Escolástica rubs its gleaming, greasy surface, holds it to her cheek, turns it over. On the back is a daguerreotype of Thomas Harker and an inscription in Spanish:

"No dejes a un antigue amigo."
(Do not forsake an old friend.)

Her initials and his, cut so deeply she wonders if the soft gold bled. Their molten passion seems to turn cold in her hand. No note. He has left her.

My lord, brave hearts must learn to bear their suffering, in times of misfortune, just as they deal with happiness, when things go well....I've heard it said that this creature we call Fortune is a drunken, fickle female and, worst of all, a blind one, to boot, so she doesn't see what she's done, or who she's knocked down and who she's raised up.

Op. Cit., Vol. 2, Chap. 66, pg. 697

MONTEREY
1849

Another stunning loss: Toño sends word that her father, deeply in debt, has been forced to sell *Rancho Arroyo del Rodeo* to an American who is said to be building a sawmill on Soquel Creek. There is much money to be made in redwood lumber. He will cut down the redwoods from the family grove where the washday barbecues were held, their mother's grave site.

"I have applied for land south of here," Toño says, "inland, on the Pleito, where the Americans are not so thick. Who knows? They may not find us there."

More loss: news reaches Monterey that her favorite Tía Martina Castro's Irish husband, Michael Lodge, has been murdered for his gold on his way home from the mines.

Escolástica hears from a cousin that Job has sold their adobe in Santa Cruz, their first home, across the plaza from the mission. Job does not even mention it to her.

She stands proudly. She lavishes attention on her children. She never makes the mistake of admitting her love for Thomas Harker, although Job badgers her night after night until she begins to invite the

Bonifacio aunts to call in the evenings. She holds her head high, but she feels her California ebb beneath her feet. She makes no move to stop it. How does one halt the ebbing of a tide?

"I will miss you, my dear *Alcalde*. Gold seems scant remuneration for all that we are losing in California."

Walter Colton has been relieved of his duties and is going back to Philadelphia, where he has a wife and a young son he has never seen. He has come to say goodbye.

"It is indeed a new era, Doña Escolástica. Change is uncomfortable," he sighs. His thin face softens at the sight of her. "The first days of summer heat are unbearable until we acclimatize ourselves."

She studies his long fine face and his pale, intelligent eyes. Her grandfather's words echo in her ears: "California is changing."

"This is more than change, I fear, *Alcalde*. This is destruction. The California I know is being conquered as surely as the *Costeños* were vanquished by the *Californios*. It is ironic, is it not?"

"But surely not as cruelly conquered."

"The Franciscan Fathers did not intend to be cruel either, *Alcalde*. They simply knew a better way, and they imposed it. Righteousness is a dreadful weapon, *Alcalde*."

To this Walter Colton has no reply. He takes her hands. Her long, elegant fingers clasp his. "Doña Escolástica, my dear friend," he musters in his best Spanish, "Be brave. I treasure my time in California. I shall never forget your graciousness or your goodness," he says. He kisses her hands and sails that evening with the tide.

"Isabela, Jaime, enough of your studies. Tomorrow we shall take a *merienda* to the Carmel Mission. What do you say? Perhaps we can bring a salmon back for your father's dinner."

"Will you come, too, Father?" Jaime asks.

"The mission is crumbling to nothing. Why go there?" Job asks.

"Oh, come along, Father. There are bats in the towers," says Isabela.

"It is their heritage," says Escolástica.

"It's nonsense," says Job.

"Perhaps if you read Latin, you would not think so," retorts Escolástica.

But Job is right, of course. The mission is caving in. The adobe outbuildings have already melted to mud hummocks in the tall grass.

Ground squirrels and lizards inhabit them. The chapel is stone, and its tile roof still holds, although it is patched with sky, probably unsafe. The children love to hear the story of Escolástica's first communion here, when Grandmother marched out leading her frightened children, brushed past the soldiers and never stopped until they reached the Boronda rancho that night.

The next day Escolástica and the children wander in the dim chapel of the decrepit mission, whispering, examining birds' nests in the niches, newts in the damp corners, peering up at the hand-painted *reredos* behind the altar, dragging their feet on the cracked tile floor.

"This was Padre Serra's favorite mission," Escolástica says. "He is buried right under our feet."

"Ugh," says Jaime. He looks down. "Where?"

They brush away the dirt and rubble and try to read the plaques in the floor before the altar. Escolástica strays into the side chapel, wipes off the rotting wood altar with a corner of her *rebozo*. "It is hard to imagine what a majestic church this was," she muses. "When Our Lady of Bethlehem stood above this altar, what a sunny peaceful place this mission was in your grandmother's time."

She kneels and picks up shards of plaster. "This chapel ceiling was filled with fat gold stars on a field of blue. See, here is part of the blue. And the Fathers were gentle and kind. They had sweets tucked in their robes for the children. I have brought you some in their memory."

The children grab for the pieces of *panocha* she holds out to them.

"But you may not have them until you say a prayer and light a candle for your grandmother."

The children carefully light the candles they have brought and stick them with candle wax on the niche in the side chapel. They cross themselves hurriedly, "Let us go, Madre. There may still be fruit in the old orchard," says Isabela, for her mother has tears in her eyes, which confuses the children. They grab their sugar treats and their mother's hands and tease her away from the musty old chapel.

It was a civilization made of mud, thinks Escolástica, as they run across the ruined courtyard, tripping on the abalone shells that once lined the neophytes' graves. For all the gold leaf and white lime and blue plaster that adorned it, it was a civilization built of mud. It was not made to last.

After months of being nearly deserted, a city of old women and anchored boats and quarreling children, Monterey springs back to life. A constitutional convention convenes in September of 1849. The delegates ride in from all over California. Escolástica's cousin, Jacinto Rodríguez, arrives first, representing the nearby Pájaro. The distinguished Mariano Guadalupe Vallejo lopes into town, sitting so still in his saddle that he seems a part of his famous stallion. Behind him ride the tall, tattooed Indians that form Vallejo's personal bodyguard. Vallejo's heavy-lidded eyes seek out his old friends; his deep voice booms up the street as he hails them. Here is an *hidalgo* in Escolástica's grandfather's style. His dark blue velvet suit is embroidered with silver. Escolástica is overjoyed to see him. Vallejo and Rodríguez are two of only eight *Californio* delegates. The rest are American.

But the pueblo is gay again, full of parties and dances and hunting expeditions. It is a festive, impromptu, silly time. The delegates dance at the balls in their best clothes, then stumble off to their blanket rolls in the woods. There are no hotels, no restaurants. They pay *Costeñas* to do their washing in the creeks and spread their underclothes on rocks along the creeks to dry. They are the fathers of California.

The new *Casa* Jimeno, with its graceful balcony, and the *Casa* Ábrego, with its wide, welcoming porches, are hospitably thrown open to feed and entertain the forty-eight delegates. Escolástica plunges into the preparation of the many dinners and fiestas. Help is scarce, and much of the labor falls to Monterey's matrons, who aid one another and scrounge from each other's larders. The sailing trade has been so disrupted by the gold rush that imported goods are in short supply. One month there is no sugar; the next, no cinnamon.

"It is like being back on the rancho," says Escolástica, laughing, as she bastes the roasting side of elk with a fistful of wild sage. "We must resort to living off the land. Thank heavens the tomatoes and the peppers are ripe." Job's business thrives as the delegates pour in for supplies and food for their makeshift camps.

Old friends and cousins Escolástica has not seen since her childhood are reunited in Monterey. Their violins serenade her with tunes she has not heard since her father played them at *Rancho Arroyo del Rodeo*. They talk of *matanza* and calving and trouble with grizzlies as if nothing has changed.

Job's new American acquaintances are appealing, too, most of them young, eager men with strong faces, hearty laughs and a diffident manner in front of her. They seem so grateful to be invited into a home with "American" children. Isabela and Jaime and Rebecca play their parts, speaking to them in English, entertaining the men with Kentucky folk songs their father has taught them. The young men remind Escolástica of Job when she first met him, rough and red on the edges, clumsy in speech, quick to succumb to the charm of the *Californio* women and the hospitality of the *Californio* men. They take her hand shyly, as if afraid they might soil it. Nearly every evening eight or ten men occupy her table, set with her bone-handled knives and her grandmother's silver spoons. Job sits proudly at the head.

Tal-ku has recruited a young Kalinta girl, from where Escolástica cannot imagine.

Tal-ku herself acquires quail, venison, fresh corn and hot, wild onions. She returns home in the late morning, staggering under the weight of her baskets, never revealing her sources. The children, who go with her when they can sneak off from their lessons, whisper of wild *Costeñas* who share sweet blackberries and pine nuts fat as ticks. The old grandmothers' breasts swing back and forth like clock pendulums, Isabela says. The old men are naked as newts.

Thomas Harker has been elected a delegate. He is apparently too busy to visit the store. Escolástica ignores him. In fact, she cannot bear to look at him. He has humiliated her, left Monterey without even saying goodbye. Imagine Harker, good friend of her family, trusted confidante to her grandfather, slinking off like a cowardly lizard, sending her a brooch with an odd, ambiguous inscription and no letter! During the entire convention he never once calls upon her. He dishonors her, treats her like a whore. Obviously, the entire town notices his change of heart. Underneath his polished exterior, is he as uncouth a man as Job Dye? Her stomach churns at the mention of his name.

After months of hospitality and six weeks of hard negotiation, the delegates conclude their labors. A California constitution has been hammered out. The land grants are declared safe. A gala ball is held on October 12 to thank the citizens of Monterey for their generosity. The delegates themselves clear the tables and chairs, the rostrum, the impedimenta of the convention, from Colton Hall. They cut armloads of fresh pine boughs that the women weave into garlands. They light tall candles in the three slender wrought iron chandeliers.

Escolástica and Job arrive with Jacinto Rodríguez and the Bonifacio aunts, hummocks of black brocade, their famous family diamonds drooping from their earlobes and wrinkled necks like dew drops on withered seed pods. The young Estradas and Malaríns gather in tight, adorable clumps of lavender satin and pink taffeta.

Escolástica has donned the white lace dress she wore to lead the grand march with Commodore Sloat three years before. At twenty-six, she glows with the sheen of a well-tended woman. A comb studded with pearls catches her black hair atop her head. She enters the ballroom and stops, feeling that rare instant of silence, that inaudible intake of breath, that imperceptible turning of heads that mark the entrance of a beautiful woman.

For six agonizing weeks Thomas Harker has gritted his teeth and stayed away. Just when he thought he could escape Monterey without meeting her, without touching her, she taunts him with that dress. It is the dress she wore at Commodore Sloat's ball. The white lace dress. She has a cruel streak in her. He bows his head and closes his eyes. He is sweating.

Escolástica's cousins and old family friends jostle one another to dance with her, their lovely little cousin, their favorite. She swirls lightly, laughing, from one arm to another, as bright and bubbly as the sparkling wines the delegates have uncorked to celebrate the occasion. Job's young American friends line up shyly, begging for a dance with the gorgeous Mrs. Dye. She glides gaily from hand to hand until suddenly she stands facing Thomas Harker.

He finds himself standing before her, unaware that his feet have taken him across the room, that he has cut into the line of young Americans waiting to dance with her. Speechless, he reaches out his arms to her. He is waltzing with her. He is not exactly sure how it happened, but she is in his arms, and he thinks that he might faint from the roar of happiness in his ears. The temptation to kiss her is deafening. He can scarcely hear her words:

"So, after humiliating me for months, you decide to toss me this crumb, Don Tomás. You are too kind."

He is dazed. He has not understood her. He waltzes on. "Forgive me, Escolástica, I do not take your meaning."

"You treat me like a whore. You use me selfishly, then discard me without a backward glance. That is bad manners in my country."

A look of sheer horror comes over his face.

"Continue dancing, Don Tomás, I beg you. You draw attention."

"Tica, you cannot mean that. You must know what it has cost me... And then to see you every day for six weeks without daring to speak. Surely you cannot mean..." He bows his head. "It is hopeless, Tica." The waltz is over.

"Please return me to my husband, Don Tomás."

The Bonifacio aunts ask pointedly after Mrs. Harker, but Thomas is too entangled in his own conflicting desires to answer coherently. He must see Escolástica again. He must explain. Another meeting will be fatal, but he must see her. The rest of the ball is torture for them both.

Escolástica has seen in Harker's face the love he feels for her. What is wrong with him? Is he so weak? So afraid of Job?

How can his eyes shine with love for her at the very moment he turns his back on her? Harker stumbles and mumbles his way through several quadrilles and waltzes, avoiding another encounter with Escolástica, but they both know they will meet.

...because it is as fitting and natural for them to be in love as it is for the sky to have stars...

Op. Cit., Vol.1,Chap.13, pg. 63

MONTEREY
1849

At dawn the next day as soon as she has sung the morning hymn Escolástica calls for her horse to be saddled and brought around. She begins to dress. Job sits up sleepily in bed.

"Where are you going?"

"Riding."

"So early?"

"It is the time I often go, Job." She stands in her chemise, and as she bends over to step into her petticoat, the curve of her breasts above the batiste stirs his gut. He reaches out to her, "Come back to bed. The fog is in. Dear God, you are the prettiest woman I ever saw." Escolástica turns and looks at him from behind a lock of raven hair. Rumpled and unshaven in their bed, he looks younger, almost bashful, gazing up at her with such ardor.

"Do you think so, Job?"

"You are my wife."

She pauses as she buttons her boot, "But do you love me, Job? Would you still chase after me on horseback?"

"Escolástica, you are my wife!"

"Yes," she studies him lying in the sheets, his blond hair tousled, his skinny legs sticking out beneath his nightshirt, "but do you love me as passionately as you once did?"

"Christ, what kind of question it that to ask your lawful wedded husband?"

She finishes dressing hurriedly, grabs her *látigo,* and strides out the door.

Job lies angry and impotent in his bed. His wife rides out to meet Thomas Harker in all probability. His wife. He bangs his head hard against the headboard.

Thomas is far down the beach waiting for her. He has been there for an hour shivering in the fog, pacing back and forth with the shore crabs, straining his eyes for her horse.

He catches her as she leaps from her saddle, pulls her down into his arms, smelling her hair, her skin, kissing her neck, holding her to him. "My God, how could you ever think I did not love you?"

She pushes away from him, "Why did you leave me, without even saying goodbye, Tomás?"

"Because I realized I could only bring ruin to you, darling Tica. I cannot marry you. Job would not allow it. And Rachel and the children..."

"Tomás, you cannot marry me because God would not allow it. We can never marry. Must you cease loving me?"

"But Escolástica, it is immoral. It is dishonest."

"Ah, and it is more 'moral' to forsake me? It is more 'honest' to deny your love for me? By the saints, you Americans have a peculiar morality."

"Escolástica, Job threatened to divorce you."

"Divorce? Nonsense, there is no divorce here. We don't do that in California."

"California is a part of the United States now. It was the threat of divorce that drove me away."

"He has not threatened <u>me</u>. He would not dare. No man would be so vindictive."

"Job Dye would."

"But why? He does not love me. I am simply one of the possessions he has amassed."

"He does love you. In his own tight-fisted way. He is not a generous man, Tica."

"But the *alcalde* would not permit it. The Church would not allow it."

"Tica, Colton is gone. Now we live under American law. The rules have changed. Adultery is a crime."

Divorce. Tica feels as if the ground under her must be heaving. Surely a shock as devastating as this must be coupled with some natural disaster. She is dizzy. She stares helplessly out at the glassy bay. Two gulls bob on the swells, a seasick rhythm, up and down. Little waves roll unsteadily and collapse on the beach. Her world is toppling around her. She feels poised at a precarious angle, ready to fall. She grabs Thomas's sleeve to steady herself, then turns away. "What does that mean 'divorce'? Tomás, what is to become of us?"

"I do not know, dearest one. I do not know."

They walk together along the beach staring at the small gray waves that stagger toward the shore.

"I cannot live without you, Tomás." Escolástica stands quietly, her head bowed.

Thomas raises her chin. His hand rests against her burnished cheek. His finger traces her full lower lip. "I can never marry you, but I will never forsake you again, my dearest Tica. This I swear."

Job charters another ship and leaves to buy mules in Mazatlán. The hurricane season should be over by now. His last trip, he says. Thomas will look after the business while he is gone, and then he and Escolástica and the children will retire to the rancho on the Upper Sacramento. Thomas is delighted to see him leave. He stands on the wharf until the sails fill and the ship disappears around the point. Escolástica and the children ride up onto the point so that the children can keep their father in view much longer, but for Thomas, Job is gone, and he sighs with relief.

Rachel Harker returns from San Francisco, an American woman on American soil. She has sacrificed a child to this heathen country, and she will see it tamed. She is ferociously bitter that Escolástica's brother Toño and the *Californios* captured Thomas and held him prisoner while his daughter sickened and died. No longer ill at ease in Monterey, she dismisses the *Californios* and their queer customs as primitive and un-American. Changes will have to be made. She sets to work at once renovating and painting the house. She is polite but cold when Escolástica calls on her, as if she barely remembers her. There are too many pauses in the conversation, too many subjects that can't be broached.

An equilibrium has been reached. Harker devotes himself to Rachel and to his children with earnest diligence. He still rides in the morning. And his wife thinks it does him a world of good. His complexion is better for it, Rachel says. Monterey politely agrees.

Escolástica rides, too, sometimes with Tal-ku. Tal-ku's niece has taken over the baby Rebecca. Escolástica and Tal-ku ride as they did when Escolástica was a child. Tal-ku must have been little more than a child herself then, but Escolástica cannot be sure how old she is, and Tal-ku shrugs at the question. The Kalinta do not reckon in years. Still, her face is round and firm as the acorns in her basket, her eyes as black as berries. She wears the same shapeless sacking she has always worn, summer and winter. She goes barefoot except in the coldest months.

They ride together in the hills. The flatlands are inhabited by American squatters, who seem to have washed down from the gold fields, having failed at mining, and have no other place to go. The ranchos crawl with them. Every streamside meadow contains a tent or shanty with ragged, yellow-haired children scuffling in the dirt. The *rancheros* view them with a mixture of dismay and pity, these homeless tramps who have no sense that they are trespassing.

So Escolástica and Tal-ku take to the chaparral covered hillsides. Tal-ku leads the way along game trails, sometimes passing within ten feet of the American squatters, who never see them. Escolástica is conscious that a part of her has become as secretive as the foxes that bark at them in the brush. First with Thomas she learned concealment. Then, as the American settlers began to pour into Monterey, she learned to eclipse herself so that they rush by without ever seeing her. Now she learns to prowl the underbrush on horseback, as invisible as the deer in the chaparral, a stunning turnabout for a beautiful woman who has lived her whole life under the admiring eyes of the world. It fascinates her to be able to efface herself so totally, and it comforts her.

She studies Tal-ku's movements, watches her disappear against a wall or in a field at the sight of strangers. Like the wild rabbits who freeze in the open meadow, Tal-ku stands motionless, eyes extinguished, hands hidden, until even Escolástica forgets that she is there. She is amused to hear one soiled, scrawny American woman describe the *Californio* women as "not altogether white." The *Californianas* are cast in a new light.

And according to what I have heard, true love is not divisible, and must be voluntary, not forced.

Op. Cit., Vol. 1, Chap. 14, pg. 70

MONTEREY
1850

The Pacific Ocean is misnamed. It is not a peaceful ocean. As Job's ship, the *Mary*, rounds Cabo San Lucas on the way north in calm seas, the sky clouds over suddenly, and a blinding squall engulfs them. A late season hurricane sweeps in from the southwest, churns the ocean into mountainous waves. Gale force winds rip the sails before they can be lowered. With little room to maneuver, wind and waves batter the ship onto the rocks off the point. She wallows in the pounding surf, wrecking herself against the rocks, while the crew scrambles to salvage a lifeboat and get to shore. The merchandise sinks, the mules drown. Then, as suddenly as it appeared, the storm veers east, and Job and the crew find themselves marooned on a wide empty beach with a barrel of water and a sack of waterlogged beans washed ashore from the wreckage to sustain them. A passing ship finds them eight days later.

Once back in Monterey, Job contracts a fever that lingers, leaving him gaunt and weak. A messenger arrives with news that his Sacramento River rancho is overrun with squatters. He gnaws on rumors about Thomas and Escolástica. All his fortunes are ebbing away. He is losing everything.

The first rains of the autumn have swept in, and Escolástica has shut the house up tight to protect him from drafts. In spite of the pitcher of fresh bay leaves she has placed on the deep windowsill, the room smells close and damp.

When the children are at last in bed, Escolástica comes in to him, sits on the edge of his bed, places a cool cloth on his burning brow, sponges his neck and arms, lifts his head and offers him willow root tea she has made for him. She spoons the tea into his mouth, but he spits it out and turns away from her, shaking with bitterness and fever.

"Escolástica, you make a fool of me. You mock our marriage."

Escolástica gets up and moves to the window, inhales the heady fragrance of the bay leaves in the pitcher. Rain streaks the windowpanes. The roof leaks, just as Job's neighbors promised it would if he insisted on using iron nails instead of rawhide. A monotonous drip comes from the corner of the room, where Tal-ku has placed a clay pot to catch the water. Scalloped rosettes of bayberries cluster in the tips of the bay branches smelling of deep, deer-filled canyons. She closes her eyes and breathes in.

"Our marriage was one of convenience, Job," she says gently. "You wanted land, you wanted permanence in California, you wanted heirs. I have given you all that."

Job struggles out of bed, dizzy from fever and misfortune, "Escolástica, what's got into you? You didn't used to loathe me."

She sighs and turns to him, "Job you are unwell. Get back into bed."

"Tica, you loved me once."

She says nothing. Her eyes fill with pity.

Job sits down on the edge of the bed, bitter, afflicted. He grabs the bedpost for support, leans his forehead against it. This is the redwood bed he had carved for her in Santa Cruz, their wedding bed. He rubs the cool, dark wood of the bedpost, remembers her stepping out of her nightdress into the bright cloud of dust stirred up by the earthquake. He shivers, coughs, grips the bedpost. "I think of divorcing you, Escolástica."

Escolástica stiffens. "Even you would not be so uncivilized, Job." And she turns abruptly away from him and leaves the room. He hears the rustle of her skirt, the tap, tap of her boots as she goes into Isabela's bedroom, murmurs little reassurances to her daughter, sings her a lullaby. Escolástica has moved into Rebecca's bed during his illness. Except for the drip, drip from the leak in the roof, the house is as silent as a robbed tomb.

A second storm gallops in off the Pacific on the heels of the first, carrying more rain. The streets turn to rivers. The patio floods.

Wet chickens crowd under the eaves looking disheveled and miserable. Cooped inside, the children quarrel. Job's cough grows deeper and more persistent. At times he seems nearly delirious with fever and fury; at times he is nearly comatose with fear.

Job's bedclothes smell stale, but Escolástica is afraid to wash them; nothing dries in this weather. She brings fresh pillowcases into his room, lifts his head from his pillows and changes the linens.

"I'm ruined," he raves. "Lost everything. Damn this California!"

"Try to sleep, Job." She lowers his head back onto the freshened pillows, straightens the rank, rumpled bedclothes, tucks them in. She shakes the cream-colored blanket her mother wove for their bed.

"And damn you, Escolástica. I'll start divorce proceedings against you. I'll take your children from you. I'll take your land. I'll keep it up til you've got nothing, too."

Escolástica stops, hugs the blanket to her breast. "What a monstrous idea," she says. "They are infants. Isabela is only nine. Rebecca is but two years old. No law would allow that. Why would you even think of doing this cruel thing to your own children?"

"Are they mine? I've come to doubt they are even mine. You see?" His eyes glitter crazily, "You take everything from me, but you'll be left with nothing, too. I'll see you punished. We've got American law here now. You'll never set eyes on your children again."

"You call this justice, Job, or vengeance?"

"You deserve no better, Escolástica."

"You will fail, Job Dye, if you attempt this sinful thing. You will fail. Even American law cannot be so cruel, so unnatural, so uncivilized."

"Then come back to me, Escolástica," he says desperately. "Come with me to *Rancho Berrendo*. We'll take the children and make ourselves a life on our own rancho...."

"Oh, no, Job," she whispers savagely. She throws the blanket to the floor. Her green eyes flash. She advances toward him as if she held a *látigo* in her hand, "You do not buy love, Job, with threats and promises. You do not use your own children as barter for love. Not even an American shopkeeper would do something so loathsome, hold a woman's children hostage for her love!" She grabs her *rebozo* and rushes out the door. She is already late to meet Thomas.

"Obviously," replied Don Quijote, "you don't know much about adventures. Those are giants – and if you're frightened, take yourself away from here and say your prayers, while I go charging into savage and unequal combat with them."

Op. Cit., Vol. 1, Chap. 8, pg. 38

MONTEREY
1850

Thomas stares at her, incredulous. "Escolástica, reconsider." Their horses climb the hill behind the Presidio. The cool morning air smells of seaweed and pine. "Go with Job to the new rancho. Make him stop these divorce proceedings. Remember your grandfather's advice. Bend a little, 'like the silver spoons of your grandmother.' You stand to lose your children, your land. Dear God, you must reconsider. I beg you, for your children's sake. For my sake."

Escolástica laughs. "For your sake? My account with you is settled, Thomas Harker. I have given you much love. For my children's sake? God gave me my children. No man can take them from me."

"American laws are different, Tica. You don't understand."

"We will return to my California, Tomás. My California, not yours. This American California has nothing to do with me. My father's rancho is gone, but there are still many in my family. The children and I will return to the ranchos to the south, the San Antonio or the Pleito. Tal-ku will come with us."

"But the ranchos are disappearing," says Harker with despair. "One by one, they face extinction."

They reach the top of the hill and rein their horses around so that they look out over Monterey Bay and the little pueblo littering its shore like bleached seashells left by the tide. "You put too much faith in this new California, Tomás. More will remain of the old than you think. Remember, we *Californios* thought the *Costeños* were disappearing, yet still they hunt and fish in the Carmel Valley."

They watch the sea birds wheel off the point. A flock of sanderlings flares up and away, scattered to the wind. Escolástica shakes her head to loosen her *rebozo*. She feels the wind freeing her hair from the combs that hold it. Turning in her saddle, she studies the face of the man beside her, a face her lips have explored so often in the dark, his thick salty lashes, his full sweet-tasting mouth, his neck. In the glare of the morning light off the water, she sees for the first time a slackness in his chin, a waver in his eyes. It is a passionate face, full of warmth and weakness. She loves him, but she cannot rely on him. "I may not see you again, Tomás."

"Tica, do not say that."

"Dear Tomás, I think your courage begins to fail you. I hope your ambitions for California do not disappoint you, too. I hope you are still as much an American as you think you are."

"But Tica, I cannot leave you. I love you. I have sworn to your grandfather to take care of you."

Escolástica laughs, a bitter little laugh. "Perhaps you have taken care of me too well, Tomás. Some things are better left wild."

Escolástica's cousin, Antonia Alvarado, rides in from *El Alisal*. She goes directly to Job's office and confronts him from her horse's back. She refuses to dismount, although Job courteously invites her to. "I come to beg for your mercy, Don Job Francisco. There are rumors that you plan to divorce Escolástica. I urge you to reconsider. For the honor of my family. In the church there can be no divorce. The children need her..."

"I don't mean any disrespect, Doña Antonia." Job cuts in, "I know she's your cousin, but she's disgraced me, she's disgraced my children. She leaves me no way out. She keeps right on sinning against me."

"I, too, have been sinned against, as you well remember. It is the humiliation that hurts the most, I know. But do not be so small a man, Job Dye, that it crushes you. Take them all up to the rancho, and Escolástica will be yours again. You leave her too long alone. We *Californio* women need tending. Up on the Sacramento she will be yours."

"With respect, it's too late for tending, Doña Antonia," Job replies grimly.

"It is too late for many things," Antonia says. "The sun has already set on our California, Job Dye, and you have helped to drag it down. May God curse you."

She wheels her horse and spurs it away. Job steps back as if she has struck him with her *reata*. He clenches his fists. His rigid face pales with outrage and hurt.

November drags on. Job's health continues to fail. His finances deteriorate. His warehouse full of goods catches fire and burns in Sacramento. He has debts. Several times he resolves to stop this divorce nonsense. He was rash. He filed this divorce petition in a rage. But he is too proud, too sick. The machinery has been set in motion. He moves into the back room of the store, where he broods, cold and lonely.

Thomas and Rachel Harker disappear inside their house. No one sees them for days at a time.

And suddenly, in disbelief, in early December Monterey witnesses the first of many examples of American civil justice: a divorce proceeding. Escolástica's cousin, Jacinto, represents her. Job hires a lawyer just arrived from New York. The proceedings take place in the courthouse of which Walter Colton was so proud, and they are in English. They last less than an hour. The outcome is incomprehensible.

"How can justice perpetrate a sin?" Tía María Bonifacio shakes with rage. "How can the law separate children from their own mother?"

Tía Ignacia Bonifacio assaults the young lawyer from New York, "What is this barbaric culture of yours that should have such laws?"

"That should be such an enemy to the Catholic Church," chimes in her sister.

But they speak in Spanish, only succeeding in backing the stiff-collared New York lawyer into a corner of the courtroom where he huffs and blusters, unnerved by these old ladies who swing their rosaries at their waists as if they were chain and mace and rivet him with their black eyes.

Escolástica does not attend the proceedings. She refuses to answer the charge that her child Rebecca is illegitimate. "That is a matter between God and me."

When the new American judge gives his decision, Job comes to the house to tell her the verdict. No one else has the courage. He stands in the doorway of their *casa* gripping the lapel of his baggy black

233

American style suit. "It's done," he says, twisting his neck in his tight, uncomfortable collar.

She looks up at him from her missal. The sun has come out at last, and the pale wintry sunlight through the door behind him makes him look like a black cardboard silhouette, unreal. She can scarcely make out his face.

"I'm to give the children a Christian schooling."

"You?" she scoffs. "You, who can hardly read or write?"

"Divorce," he lashes back at her. "Grounds of adultery."

She thinks he's bluffing, standing just inside the doorway nearly throttled by his long black American necktie. "No," she says. Then out of the corner of her eye she sees Tal-ku's dark, terrible face as she slips into the *sala*. Tal-ku has heard something from the other *Costeños*. Finally his blow strikes home.

She stands, drops her missal, reels toward him so that she can see into his steel gray eyes. "Not my children, Job. No. This is too evil a thing you do."

Job lowers his eyes before her fury. "You sin against me, Escolástica," he says miserably. "You must pay."

"Pay or be paid," Escolástica hisses. "The American way. Shopkeepers!" she screams.

She stands tall before him, her long elegant neck arched in anger, her wide green eyes ablaze, her mouth twisted with rage. Her black hair is parted in the middle and woven into thick braids on top of her head. They catch the sunlight from the doorway, black as raven's wings. He bows his head. She is heartbreakingly beautiful.

"You write yourself a death warrant in California if you do this deed. You know that, Job." She stares at his face, his eyes red with fever, his mouth crumpled in bitterness. "Would you cast yourself out of this country? You, the tough mountain man who fought the Apache, broke trail over frozen passes to reach this land? The man who galloped after me so recklessly?"

She stares at him, thin, shrunken, in his baggy, black American suit — a scrawny, carrion crow hunched in the doorway.

"Job Dye, what have I done to you?" she asks quietly.

I was born free, and I chose the solitude of the fields so I could live free... I am a remote fire, a sword seen from far off.

Op. Cit., Vol. 1 Chap. 14, pg. 71

MONTEREY
1850

Isabela does not understand. Her gay, beautiful mother seems to have frozen solid. Her mother hugs her to her waist, kisses her, but her hands are cold. When Isabela brings her a new chick she has found hiding in a geranium pot, placing it in her mother's lap, tears fill Escolástica's eyes. Even Jaime, little clown, hanging upside down by his knees in the apple tree fails to coax a smile from her. Escolástica sits on the bench in the patio holding little Rebecca, stroking her hair, rocking back and forth until the child squirms away to follow Jaime, who is chasing Cuidado, the fierce black rooster.

Isabela watches her mother wilt like a rose plucked at midday and then clutched too tightly. She tries to revive her Mamá with a song she is learning on her guitar, then with a story Tía Bonifacio told her of the man, who walked right off the end of the pier while telling Tio José Luis a story. But her mother sits so still. Nothing seems to rouse her.

When night comes Escolástica lies on her bed fully clothed. The children, assuming she is ill, come to her, kiss her hands, lay their heads lightly on her breast, and lightly she pats their fine hair, strokes their ripe cheeks -- like peach skin, she thinks, kissing their heads.

Then Escolástica lies in the dark trying to think, to decide what she must do. But the town has become too noisy. Harness jangles, dogs bark, a loud argument erupts in English, glass breaks -- sailors probably. There are ships in port.

The wind blows. Raucous laughter. Monterey has a saloon now. Thin wooden houses held together by spindly iron nails have been built around the fringes of the town. Nothing rises from the ground in Monterey any more. The town has a flimsy quality to it, foreign and offensive to her, no longer her Monterey, but a noisy American town wrapped in frilly curtains, confined in long woolen pants, tangled in American law and ugly American justice, its inhabitants blind to the broad bay and the empty coastline.

The next morning Job appears at the door with four horses, two pack animals and a *Costeñan* nursemaid for Rebecca. He instructs Tal-ku to pack the children's' clothes. Tal-ku doesn't move.

"We are going to the pueblo of San José," he says to the children. "You will be able to go to school with the nuns."

The children shriek with joy. No more lessons from the Tías Bonifacio.

"Where will we spend the night?" Isabela asks.

"Will we see Grandfather?" Jaime wants to know.

Only little Rebecca is quiet. She clings to her mother's skirt.

Stunned by this haste, Escolástica stands in the doorway. "No," she says softly to Job, so as not to alarm the children. "No, you must not do this, Job."

"Isabela and Rebecca will go to the Convent School of the Sisters of Notre Dame. You have always said they are the best educated of the nuns. They'll get good schooling there."

Escolástica shakes her head, frozen in the doorway. "No," she says again. Rebecca clings to her knees, begs to be lifted up.

"Jaime will go to the College of Santa Clara. Father Suárez says that is the best place for him. He has a friend there, one of the brothers." Job watches Escolástica's face darken. "Do not attempt to stop me, Tica," he says in a low voice. "If your relatives intervene, there will be bloodshed. I will be forced to send for the American authorities. That would frighten the children."

For the second time in her life Escolástica stands paralyzed by an evil she cannot control. Her mind clouds with a long ago image of the Yokut boy lying in the dirt while the American trapper whipped him until the skin on his back hung in shreds. She and Toño hid in the bushes that day and watched the cruel beating, powerless to stop it. That repulsive horror of helplessness washes over her once again.

"Hurry, Mamá." Isabela twirls up to her mother, grabs her hand. "We must get ready. May I take my new dress?"

Escolástica kneels and pulls Isabela to her, kisses her dark curls. "I will not be going with you, my love. Not now."

"But…" Isabela pulls away.

"You will go with your father. I will come to you as soon as I can." She forces herself to smile. "You may take your new dress."

An hour later, the children hug their mother and mount their horses, giddy with excitement over the trip.

"Come soon, Mamá."

"You must hurry, Mamá."

Only Rebecca refuses to leave her mother's arms. She shrieks when Job tears her out of her mother's grasp and mounts his horse, holding the child before him in his saddle. Rebecca twists around and reaches out to Escolástica. Her tiny, plump fingers stretch towards her mother. Tears pour down her round, rosy cheeks. Escolástica's heart shrivels in her breast as she stands at the doorway blowing kisses until they are out of sight. Then she collapses on the floor, and Rebecca's howls mingle with her own.

The pueblo of Monterey suddenly quiets. All morning the town hangs suspended in the pale sunshine of a mild midwinter day. The streets remain empty. The Tías Bonifacio come to Escolástica's door, but Tal-ku turns them away. In the later afternoon Padre Suárez spends an hour at the little *casa* and goes away mumbling, head down, fingering his rosary. It is the ominous calm before a fierce winter storm strikes the coast.

As night falls, a bank of black clouds masses to the west, and the wind picks up. Escolástica lies on her bed weeping, raving, her head stuffed with mad thoughts. She feels stifled in Monterey. She needs room to think. She grabs her *rebozo* and whistles quietly for her horse *El Chocolate*. She bridles him but doesn't bother with a saddle, so great is her hurry to leave this hateful, confusing, confining place.

She rides south over the hill, tears streaming down her face. She spurs her horse, pursued by the fear that the Americans are coming after her. She had thought she could handle Americans as she had handled the stubborn, hard-mouthed horses on the rancho. They have changed the rules, abandoned every value – honor, tradition, family, religion. They have kicked her civilization into the sea. Americans who were received with gracious hospitality on her father's rancho, who professed a love of this country, now seem bent on crushing her California under the heels of their clumsy boots, grinding it into the brown adobe.

As she rides, nearly blinded now with tears, a wild confusion grows within her. "You will pay." Job's threat reels in her head. "Bend like the spoons of your grandmother." Her grandfather's voice comes back to haunt her. Thomas's beguiling broken promise, "I will take care of you." She begins to see that all they offer in this vast, windblown wildness is imprisonment. She must outwit them. They use her own babies as bait, her own dear babies. Her heart trips in her breast. They have stolen her babies. She closes her streaming eyes against the tug of her children's faces.

El Chocolate's warm whithers begin to lather beneath her. She pulls him up into a walk. Still she rides on, feeling him respond to the pressure of her knees. She reins him toward the coast, where the white waves beckon to her in the moonlight, ghostly shapes that rise up in the night wind.

As she watches the moonstruck waves dash themselves against the black rocks, a new rage surges over her heartbreak, overruns it. Her heart begins to throb with fury. She smiles a wily, maddened smile. They have destroyed her California, they have stolen her babies, but they will not conquer her. They cannot catch her. She slides from *El Chocolate's* back, clinging for a moment to his mane, burying her face in it, inhaling his warm, sweaty, familiar scent. Then she throws off her *rebozo*. She will not be caught in their traps. She will slip through their ropes. This is her land. She is an *hija del país*. Let them try to catch her.

When Tica's horse returns at dawn the next morning, riderless, Tal-ku takes her coiled basket of charms off the high shelf in her room, slips out of the house and sets off at a trot around Point Pinos. In the silver half-light of early morning, Tal-ku runs up along the sea bluff searching the black rocks below her, peering down into the foamy pools. Sea lions sprawl on the wet rocks, splashed by the waves. Shy otters slip into the water as she approaches. Crabs skitter off sideways across the sand. The shore teems with life as the flood tide washes over it. Tal-ku's sunken eyes search every slippery ledge, every churning crevice. She lopes on around the point to where the land juts out furthest into the ocean, a fist of rock catching the first powerful waves as they roll into Monterey Bay. Just beyond the point she finds her, a dark shape floating in a tide pool filled with turquoise anemones, their tentacles opened out like flowers in a deep-sea garden. Escolástica's green eyes look straight into the sky.

Tal-ku makes her way down the treacherous rocks, walking on the limpets and mussels that offer a foothold, avoiding the slick kelps. She waits for the next big wave to break, foaming around Escolástica so that her skirt seems to sway to the drumming of the surf. Then as the wave retreats Tal-ku dashes forward, snatches Escolástica from the tidepool, drags her up the shore, out of reach of the ocean. She gathers up Escolástica's limp, sodden body and heaves it, struggles to carry her, slips, falls. Hugging Tica to her breast she pulls her slowly, arduously, over the rocks, up the crumbling bluff. Finally, she lays Escolástica gently on the sea grass and collapses beside her.

When she has caught her breath, Talku begins to sing softly in the eerie early light, As she sings she sprinkles shells and agates over Escolástica's body. She places the small breast feather of a sea gull in Tica's hand for her long journey and then kneels beside her chanting in a high thin wail, looking out to sea

> *Go to the land beyond the ocean*
> *Go to the land beyond the sunset.*
> *Go quietly. Go quietly.*
> *Follow the sea foam.*
> *That is the spirit trail.*
> *Do not walk where I am*
> *Listen to me: Go quietly.*

Tal-ku walks back into town.

Padre Suárez del Real decrees Escolástica's death accidental. The waves on Point Pinos are dangerous, the rocks notoriously slippery. Riding without a saddle is perilous, especially for a woman. Escolástica is buried quickly and with simple ceremony before her father or brothers can be sent for. Only Thomas Harker and the Tías Bonifacio attend the service. They stand silently at opposite sides of the grave on the hill above Point Pinos while the padre's words are swept away by the wind's howl and the crashing surf, vestiges of last night's storm. At last the padre closes his missal and makes the sign of the cross over the grave, and the old aunts scurry away down the hill. The padre stands for a moment head bowed in prayer. Then he raises his eyes to Thomas Harker, who still stands before the open grave.

"God save you, my son," he says, "and your California." Then the old priest turns and trudges off.

Tal-ku disappears the next day, and walks into the Convent of Notre Dame three days later, her hair singed short in mourning, her face smeared with pitch. Rebecca shrieks and runs to her, buries herself in Tal-ku's lap, and Isabela throws her arms around her, and begins to cry. The astonished nuns dare not interfere. The children are too fond of her. The sins of the father are too great. Tal-ku's eyes still blacken at the sight of a priest, but she remains at the Convent. Although the children beg her night after night, Tal-ku never speaks of Escolástica again. One must never speak of the dead.

"They are where they ought to be. They'll get a good moral education," Job Dye writes to Thomas Harker from St. Joseph's Infirmary in Louisville, Kentucky. "I'm the one who quits that land. I'm sick and weary of California. I'm gratified to hear news of my children. I'm obliged to you for keeping an eye on them. As to their mother, my wife, she must work out her own salvation."

Enclosed in Job's letter is the brooch Thomas Harker gave to Escolástica Rodríguez Dye, their initials encircled in soft, gleaming folds, the brooch made from the first gold found in California.

> For years, this Cervantes has been a great friend of mine, and he certainly knows a lot more about misfortune than he does about poetry. There are good touches in his book; he starts some things, but he finishes nothing.
>
> *Op. Cit.*, Vol. 1, Chap. 6, pg. 34

GLOSSARY

Abuelo – grandfather
Adelante – onward, get going
Aguardiente – liquor, brandy
Ahora -- now
Alcalde – mayor, magistrate
Año Nuevo – lit. "New Year," name of point on CA Coast
Aquí -- here
Asado – roast
Asamblea – assembly
Ayuntamiento – council, municipal government
Ballena – whale
Bandido – bandit
Barbacoa -- barbecue
Bienvenida – welcome
Buenos días – Good day
Butano – cup made of polished horn
Caballero – gentleman
Caballo -- horse
Caldo -- broth
Californiano (a) Californian
Camarada – comrade
Camisa – shirt
Cañon – canyon
Caponera – lit. "coop," group of horses led by a bell mare
Carne Asada – roasted or grilled meat
Carreta – two-wheeled cart
Casa – house
Castilleja – Indian paintbrush
Cocina – kitchen

Comal – flat iron pan for cooking tortillas
Comandante -- commander
Compadre – best friend
Copa de Oro -- poppy
Coraje – courage
Costeño (a) a general term for Coastal Indians, usually referred to by tribe
Cuadrilla – group, band
Cuartel – barracks, headquarters
Cuidado – be careful
Desesperado – desperate one
Díos -- God
Diseño – lit. "sketch," sketch (map) of land grant
Don, Doña – title of respect, Mr., Mrs.
Dueña – proprietress
Estimado -- esteemed
Estofado – stew
Fierro – lit." iron," cattle brand
Frijoles -- beans
Gallitas (little roosters) – wild yellow violets
Garrapata -- tick
Gavilán -- sparrow hawk
Hidalgo – nobleman
Hija – daughter
Hijo del País – lit. "son of the country," native
Infanta – infant (f.)
Juez de Campo – title used for headman of the rodeo
Las blancas flores – the white flowers
Las Hermanas – lit. "sisters," California Sister butterfly, adelpha californica
Látigo – whip
Manada – herd
Manteca – fine quality lard
Mariposa -- butterfly
Matanza – lit. "killing," round-up and slaughter time
Melcocha – word used for molasses colored horses
Menudo – tripe soup

Merienda – lunch, picnic
Mira -- look
Montaña – mountain
Morir – to die
Muchas gracias – thank you very much
Paciencia -- patience
Padre -- father
Panocha – brown sugar cane chunks
Panuelo – kerchief
Pasillo – hallway
Patio – inner courtyard
Patrona – boss (f.)
Penique – penny
Perdón -- pardon
Piloncitos – little cones of sugar
Poblano – kind of pepper
Por favor -- please
Pórtico – porch, hallway
Presidio Fortress, garrison
Pronto -- quick
Puchero – stew
Pueblo – town
Quadrilla – band, gang
Querida – dear one
Ramada – shelter made of branches
Rancho (ranchero, ranchera) – ranch (rancher)
Reata – lit. rope, also lasso, lariat
Rebozo – shawl
Reredos – altarpiece, screen behind the altar
Ristra – string (of onions, peppers, etc.)
Rosa -- rose
Sala – drawing room
Sangre azul – Blue blood
Sebo – coarser fat rendered from cattle
Señor (a) (ita) – Mr. (Mrs.) (Miss)
Sinverguenza – rascal, rogue
Sobre las olas – over the waves

Sombrero -- hat
Sudario – lit. "shroud," prayer said at graveside
Suspiros de monjas – lit. "nuns' sighs," pastry of fried dough dusted with sugar
Tapash – dried leaf potpourri used for scenting
Terneras – veal (steaks)
Tío (a) – Uncle (Aunt)
Tontito – Little fool
Vamos – Let's go
Vaquero(a) – cowboy (girl)
Vaya – Go!
Yanqui -- Yankee
Yerba buena – lit. "good herb," native medicinal herb
Yerba Santa – lit. "saint herb," native medicinal herb

CPSIA information can be obtained
at www.ICGtesting.com
Printed in the USA
FSOW02n2024171016
26269FS